JULIA UNLEASHED

The Steak and Bourbon Series

Book 1

LAURA PRESLAN

Published by Advoture, Inc.

Published by Advoture, Inc.
Cover design by Miladinka Milic of Mila Book Covers

ISBN: 979-8-9915747-1-6

Books by Laura Preslan

STEAK AND BOURBON SERIES

Julia Unleashed

Kate Released

Alex Unchained (March, 2025)

To Eric and the brunch divas.

That sounds like a band, but it's not.
Maybe it should be.

We would only play instruments
you don't have to blow into.

Otherwise, we'd miss our entrances
from laughing too hard to blow.

Truth.

———————————

Chapter 1

———————————

Julia opened the door to her office – the one that came along with her new job as Director of Pricing at Lamp-Light Corporation. The red couch made her smile and the stuffed fabric flowers with jaunty little faces grinned back at her as she plugged in her laptop.

She had been told she could be intimidating. That she had sharp elbows.

She counteracted that by decorating her office with a vibe that said "Yeah, I'm really smart and capable, but you have nothing to fear."

She took a moment to admire the view of Mount Baker out her window. The Seattle area couldn't be beat for scenery if you liked water, mountains, and trees.

She was four months into her new job, and she loved it. Opportunities for high impact were everywhere. Her team adored her and the feeling was mutual. She took this gig as a lateral move with the promise of a promotion after she had proven herself. *Proven herself.* Like she hadn't already done that. She had concrete proof from business metrics.

But, this was a new team for her, and that meant starting over.

Of course, she had found out *after* she signed the offer letter that her male peer had received a promotion with his new job. Another example of the way the company overlooked talented women. She pushed that thought away. She would get there.

She was not where she thought she should be at thirty-nine. Her goals were off track. She was supposed to be a vice president by now. She joined the company in 2006 and worked her ass off for six years. It was 2012, and she should have been higher on the pay scale at LampLight given her scope and responsibilities.

But Julia had a plan. She was the money-maker, and she would make it happen.

She tucked her curly brown hair behind her ear. She had a meeting with the team's top salesperson in five minutes. There was no hurry though. He'd be at least ten minutes late. Top salespeople didn't have to follow the same rules as everyone else —as long as they kept raking in the deals.

Ten minutes later, Joe Spencer walked in, preceded by a cloud of cologne. He looked pointedly at his watch as if to say that his time was vastly more important than hers. "I've got about fifteen minutes."

Julia restrained herself from grimacing as the pungent smell of his cologne assaulted her nostrils. She kept her polite expression firmly in place. It wasn't that Julia resented the entitled sales team. She just wanted the respect she deserved for her ideas and execution. The recommendations she and her team came up with would generate about thirty million dollars for LampLight. And they needed it. Results were not looking good.

She dove right in. "I want to make sure it's easy for

your team to position the value of our products while keeping prices competitive. Your input is important to me."

"Okay, then show me what you've got." He took a seat on her couch and looked her up and down. She gritted her teeth, taking an extra moment to pretend she was adjusting her monitor to steel her face into a placid expression. Her reportedly sharp elbows were kept firmly at her sides.

As she wrapped up, Joe leaned back and clasped his hands behind his head. "That's such a great plan. If I were a dog, you'd have to keep me away from your leg."

"Excuse me?" She felt the filter she typically kept on her inner monologue slip a bit. Exhaustion weakened her façade.

"It's just a joke." He shook his head at her and rolled his eyes. "Lighten up."

Eew. Julia swallowed her desire to kick him in the nuts and hoped her expression masked her disdain. "Are you on board with the plan, Joe?"

"Yeah. It's about time somebody fixed this. You've really thought this through. I like it." Joe flicked something off the sleeve of his blue dress shirt. Julia watched it land on the dreary brown office carpet. Keeping her elbows in had worked.

"Great. I'll give you ten minutes back since we got through the details so quickly. If you have any more questions, just let me know." Julia stood to signal the end of the meeting.

"I have to get across town for my next meeting anyway."

Probably at the golf course, Julia thought as his departure released a second cloud of cologne that made her headache worse.

She sat back at her computer and took the win. She rubbed her tired eyes behind her red metal glasses. Joe was onboard. It was a good practice run for this afternoon when she had her first big strategy presentation to her boss and peers. If she didn't solidify her strong brand for having big ideas and getting work done, she would never get her next promotion. Another failure. Another delay. *Positive thoughts!* Her plan would work. It had to.

Julia had been given a lot of advantages in her life, and she knew it. Her middle-class upbringing in Ohio imbued her with the values of hard work, fairness, and high integrity.

Her parents and grandparents taught her that strength of character and high moral ground were achieved through self-denial. Doing things for other people was encouraged. Doing things for yourself was selfish. If you didn't have to work hard for it, it wasn't worth having.

Too proud to apply for financial aid, her parents scraped together the money to send her to Brown University. She graduated debt-free, which in her eyes was about the best gift parents could give their kids.

She owed it to them to capitalize on her privileges and go as far as she could. Their voices in her head drove her to work harder and keep going in the face of adversity. They fueled her success. Always driven. Always striving for more.

Always feeling like she was behind.

Julia emerged from these early lessons as a hardworking and frugal perfectionist. To combat the guilt she felt at her advantages, she focused on helping others.

But Julia secretly wanted nice things.

She struggled with negative feelings when she treated herself well. Her sisters needed the new clothes more than she did. Or the new car. Or the vacation. She had the better college education and should pay back the good karma bestowed upon her by giving her money to them.

Sometimes, the little voice in her head would say she had worked harder than they did, studied more, applied herself more. But then the guilt overrode that. Maybe she had just gotten better DNA and it was easier for her.

Julia's answer to the conflicting drivers was to strive to make so much money she could do both – be generous AND create a luxury lifestyle for herself. But until she reached her financial goals, she had to continue to push off her own desires.

Money was her ticket to future happiness.

Julia had joined LampLight in a more senior role than others the same age. She had advanced quickly in the first few years. But she had hit a wall. The promotions and advancement stopped, and she had made a couple of lateral career moves to try to restart the promotion engine. At LampLight, promotions equaled more decision-making power and more money. The lateral moves put her even farther behind her financial schedule.

But this new job would be different. She would work harder than she ever had to make it happen.

Julia sighed and refocused her energy on her team. Her positive impact on them was starting to show. She thought of the low morale, under-skilled team she had inherited and contrasted it with the eager and motivated team she could see forming. She loved creating a vision, leading people through it, and helping them achieve goals they didn't think they could hit.

This team had the potential to be one of her best ones. She just had to keep showing the way and letting them run. They had all worked tirelessly to pull together a set of data-based recommendations to fix issues at LampLight. All she had to do was get her leadership team's support and her team could execute.

She made her way to the conference room where her

team was assembled for their all-hands meeting. Seeing their smiling faces reminded her of the importance of the leadership team meeting later that afternoon.

"You all know the reveal of our new monetization strategy happens this afternoon. All of my peers will be there, and my goal is to gain their support for our changes." Julia took a moment for dramatic effect before continuing. "I couldn't be prouder to be the one to represent your great work. I wish you could all be there."

"We know we can't attend with you, J-Money, but you'll represent us well." Kate's comment elicited nods from other team members. Julia appreciated Kate's energy and optimism. "And when the time is right, we'll all go kick some ass together!"

"Thanks everyone." Julia basked in the light of their support. *This is why I do the hard work*, she thought. She loved Kate's nickname for her. She sounded like a badass and it reflected her goal to make money for the company and herself. "Let's walk through our post-meeting game plan so we can hit the ground running after we get the nod to proceed. Nothing can stop us now."

Chapter 2

Julia slipped into the restroom for a quick check in the mirror. Yep, her lucky suit was crisp and unwrinkled. She tugged her suit jacket down and nodded at the image in the mirror. The new hair product had pretty effectively tamed her curly hair. As she peered a little closer, she could see a streak of gray above her left ear. It might be time to start coloring her hair, she thought. *No one cares what you look like. It's about your brain!*

She knew that plugging an almost thirty-million-dollar hole would definitely be enough to get her the promotion she deserved. Her vision was insightful. The strategy was sound. Her team was behind her.

The stakes were high. She had done everything she could to prepare. She was ready to nail it.

"I WAS JUST TALKING about our new head of the pricing team," her boss Blane said as she entered the conference room.

"Blane. Dave. Nice to see you. I hope you were saying

good things." Julia looked back and forth between her boss and his Chief of Staff, a joking, questioning look on her face.

"Of course, of course," Blane motioned her to the seat next to him. "Dave and I were just talking about adjusting the meeting agenda to talk through how we could get out of this pesky revenue gap for the quarter instead of our scheduled strategy discussion." Pesky was one of Blane's top words and he used it to describe problems both big and small. He ran a hand through his thinning hair as he spoke.

"I have some ideas on that." She didn't want to sound cocky. She adjusted to a more humorous tone, tilting her head like a newscaster. "Stay tuned for an important update."

Blane laughed turning to Dave. "What'd I tell you? She's a real firecracker."

"I know – Julia and I worked together a few years ago on the enterprise sales team. We share some battle scars."

Julia shifted her attention to Dave, taking in his full head of blond hair, Van Dyke beard, pale blue linen jacket, and patterned shirt that fit like they had been made for him. "Yeah, that team aged me, but somehow you manage to look exactly the same, Dave."

"I may have had a little work done." Dave pointed at his smooth forehead. "Luckily, I can still look surprised." He demonstrated by raising his eyebrows.

Blane interrupted their walk down memory lane. "Here comes trouble." Jeff, the vice president of sales entered the room. "Looks like we can get started now that Jeff's in the house." Blane laughed heartily and clapped the vice president of sales on the back.

Julia caught a whiff of Jeff's sharp cologne from across the table as he took his seat on the other side. *What was it with salespeople and cologne*, she wondered. He and Joe, the sales manager she had met with earlier, were cut from the same cloth – former frat boys with matching haircuts who spoke in sports analogies and sexist phrases.

Blane cleared his throat and started the meeting. "I got a sneak peek at the month-to-date December numbers people, and things aren't looking good." Julia saw several of her peers shift uncomfortably in their seats. "I propose we change the agenda to focus on how we can increase revenue in the short term. We have to act with urgency. Who'd like to go first?"

Julia had seen the same pattern and was ready for the topic. She would just skip her strategy slides and head right to the changes she wanted to make.

Jeff jumped in even before the sound of Blane's words had dissipated. "I need lower prices. We're losing deals all over the place because of high prices."

Here we go, Julia thought. The first thing sellers always blamed was high prices. Julia was not going to rise to the bait. "We've done the competitive analysis, Jeff, and our prices are in line if not a bit lower than the competition for similar inventory." Her professional façade stayed firmly in place.

"That's not what my people are telling me, Julia." His tone smacked her right in her integrity sensor.

Julia kept her tone neutral. "If you can share some concrete data on that, like bids we've lost or price sheets from competitors, we can lean in and see if we need changes."

Jeff's face showed he didn't like being countermanded. "Yeah, well what do you suggest then?"

"My team and I have a lot of ideas. Blane, okay if I go ahead and share? I don't want to jump the line."

"The floor is yours," he said with a flourish of his hand toward her.

Julia walked to the front of the room and plugged her laptop into the projector. *I got this,* she thought, psyching herself up for a great presentation. She tapped into her inner presentation diva and jumped right in.

"As you can see from this chart, it looks like we're going to miss our quarterly target by twenty-eight million dollars. My team and I have some ideas about how we can stop the revenue leaks and add profitability. There's a lot of math to support what I'm going to show you, but I've summarized it so you don't have to slog through the numbers."

"Thanks for that." Jeff's quip had everyone laughing.

Julia continued. "We noticed sellers built a lot more discounts into their deals this past quarter, over twice as much year over year." Julia stopped to let that sink in. "If we do a better job managing discounts, we can close the gap and end the fiscal year strongly. Let me walk you through what I mean. You'll see –"

Jeff interrupted her. "That makes no sense. We only give discounts to help win deals. My people need to do that so they can close business and meet their quotas."

Julia continued. "You'd think that Jeff, but when you look at the data by salesperson and percentage of quota closed, you can see most discounts are given out by salespeople who've already hit their quota." Julia was excited she had anticipated that question and had the data to prove it.

Jeff waved his hands back and forth like he could erase her point. "But you can't just look at it by salesperson. You don't know anything. You have to review it by account. They only give the discounts to the important customers who buy a lot from us."

Julia ignored the insult. Jeff's hand waving released

another wave of cologne. She clicked to the next slide. "I thought that might be the case, too. But here are the accounts that received the discounts along with their annual spend for the last two years. As you can see, we're granting discounts to every spend level, not just the high-volume buyers."

Julia's adrenaline pumped. She had anticipated that question, too. Again, she waited for Jeff to see the light and get on her side of the argument. The data was right in front of him on the slides.

Barry, the vice president of marketing who had previously been staring out the window, suddenly jumped in. "Julia, you'd have to look at this by product. While the amount of the discount might be large, I'm sure the discounts are being given on our low-value products just to unload the inventory."

It was like Julia had scripted the questions. *She was on fire!*

"I hoped so, too, Barry." She moved to the next slide and ignored the twinge of injustice that she had to educate someone who had been promoted before her. "This view shows the dollar value of the discounts by product. See how our most profitable, best products are being most highly discounted? This is exactly the opposite of what we should be doing. And it's costing us in lost revenue."

The questions stopped. Julia moved on to her proposed policy changes. "You can see why we need to take immediate action. My team and I have designed some new policies to stop these revenue leaks and generate additional profit for our team. With these changes, we can close the gap and be back on track to hit our numbers for the fiscal year!"

Julia had made her case, and it was lock tight. They had no choice but to agree. She inwardly patted herself on the back. Her promotion was in the bag. Her team would be proud of her.

"I'm not doing a thing to change sales behavior." Jeff flicked her recommendations away like annoying gnats at a picnic.

Wait, what?

Julia faced a table of uncomfortable stares. She didn't understand what was happening. The changes had to be made. It was obvious. It was all right there in the analysis.

Blane cut into the conversation. "Okay, let's move on for now. Other ideas?" Blane shook his head at her. *Was that disappointment on his face? This can't be happening.*

Julia flumped back down in her seat, deflated.

AS SHE SAT through the rest of the meeting, all of the talk was about how to support Jeff and the sales team better rather than holding them accountable for solid business practices. They would damage their brand in an unrecoverable way if they implemented the changes Jeff wanted. Where had she gone wrong? Why wasn't the data enough to convince them?

Blane concluded the meeting. "Thanks for coming, everyone. Great meeting. Let's finalize the plan by next week for how we'll close that revenue gap. Get your ideas going and we'll regroup." *Like she hadn't just shown them exactly what to do.* "Those pesky customers aren't going to take care of themselves. Let's get back to it!"

Chapter 3

Julia went over and over what happened in the meeting on her drive home. Her rumbling stomach distracted her. She called Cliff, her husband of fourteen years, to let him know she was on her way home.

"What would you like to do for dinner?"

"Dinner? It's Thursday. Band practice," Cliff reminded her.

"Oh right. See you in about a half hour. Love you. Bye."

Negative thoughts about the meeting swirled in her head as she drove down Lake Sammamish Parkway. What the heck was up with Barry? He had complained to her about Jeff's shitty business practices just last week when they talked about their holiday plans. But today, he sided with Jeff? And Blane, looking at her like *she* did something wrong. She'd done an amazing job showing them the way and they'd blocked her, shut her right down, like they didn't care about the business.

After fighting her way home through traffic in the dark

and rain, an exhausted Julia pulled into the cul-de-sac and saw Cliff's car in their driveway. It was almost always there.

He'd been effectively unemployed for nine years, picking up an occasional job or volunteer gig for a couple of months, but not making regular money and not sticking with any of them.

When she'd met him in her first job after college, he'd been a brilliant and confident executive moving up the ranks with ambition and zeal for corporate life. They were one hundred percent aligned on their goals of making money and changing the technology world.

Those were the days.

She was waiting for that previous version of Cliff to reappear. She knew it was in there somewhere. She just had to keep trying. *If you didn't have to work hard for it, it wasn't worth having.*

She heard Cliff in the music room practicing guitar riffs. Part of his typical wardrobe, a sweat suit, sat on top of the washing machine. Selah, her rescue dog, came to greet her, flopping onto her back for belly rubs. Julia always felt more centered after a few moments with Selah. Cliff continued to play the opening riff from *Heartbreaker* over and over.

She wondered what he did all day as she looked at the dirty dishes in the sink. *Certainly not take care of the house,* she thought. Julia went to work getting everything ready for the band at warp speed, doing the dishes, tidying the kitchen, making guacamole, and putting out a big bowl of chips. Just in time. The doorbell rang.

Rob, Stephen, and Lisa arrived and headed into the kitchen after dropping off their equipment in the music room.

"You always take such good care of us," Rob said around a mouthful of guacamole, wiping a bit out of his trim beard. His blue eyes twinkled behind his dark, blue-framed glasses. He played bass in the band, and since Julia had been a bass player since she was eleven, she had a soft spot for him. She loved when he came early to band so they could talk a bit. It didn't hurt that he was six feet tall and blond with an athletic build and a contagious smile. *Eye candy and good conversation.*

Julia smiled at his praise. He had a way of half-flirting/half-conversing that made her feel special and important even though she'd figured out pretty quickly he did that with everyone.

"Thanks, Rob." She felt like she smiled at him a little too long. He held her gaze and smiled back. Julia turned to Lisa, the rhythm guitarist in the band. "What're you drinking?"

"Any kind of beer is fine. I need to loosen up before practice. I'm starting to freak out I won't be ready for our gig."

"Nothing to worry about. You have weeks to prepare." Julia liked to be supportive. "You'll be ready."

"You think so? Thanks." Lisa hunched her shoulders as her freckled face blushed.

"Stephen?"

"Beer." He was a man of few words. Odd, because he was the lead singer. She guessed he saved it for the microphone.

"I think I just heard Frank pull up," Cliff called out from the music room. Seconds later, the front door opened.

"Sorry I'm late!" Frank bustled into the house.

"You're not late. For a drummer." Everyone laughed at Rob's joke as the band assembled in the music room.

Julia left them to it and headed upstairs to her home office. She could catch up on the work she hadn't gotten to during the day because of her steady stream of meetings. Soon, their rendition of *Crazy Little Thing Called Love* emerged from the music room.

She leaned back in her chair and studied the picture next to her monitor. She and Cliff wore leis and Hawaiian shirts while posing with a people-sized tiki statue on their way into a luau in Maui. She remembered bending her knees since both the statue and Julia were a bit taller than Cliff.

His rich brown eyes laughed into the camera. She hadn't seen that smile in a while, probably since that trip two years before. She was still refilling her credit card points balance since she had used them all to get a free hotel on that trip. She smiled at the memory of saving money while also having a nice vacation. She had paid for her younger sister's Spring Break vacation with the savings.

Her next memory from that trip created a flash of embarrassment. Julia had been in the mood and had put on some sexy lingerie to entice Cliff. After two nights, she hadn't even elicited a comment from him. She snuggled up to him in bed and put her hand in his boxers. He had politely asked her to leave him alone so he could go to sleep because he was tired. She wasn't attractive enough to turn him on anymore.

When was the last time they'd had sex? Julia couldn't remember. He refused to talk about it, like nothing was wrong. Maybe it was her fault since she didn't put much effort into her appearance. She reminded herself that sex was only part of a relationship. Julia enjoyed Cliff's company and friendship. That should be enough.

But it wasn't.

She would try harder with him, and they would end

this sex drought. All she had to do was get through one more week of work and she'd be off for the holidays. Then she'd have time to re-ignite their sexual spark. She wanted good sex. She deserved good sex.

After dealing with dozens of emails, Julia shut down her laptop so she could work through today's frustrations on the elliptical machine.

She increased the incline to sweat even more as she thought through what happened in the leadership team meeting. She had been on a good path with Blane. He seemed to value her skillset. She didn't love how chummy he was with some of the sales leaders, but that was par for the course. She was used to being unpopular since pricing was consistently blamed for all kinds of sales issues. It was never the salesperson who was at fault – it was the high prices, Julia snickered to herself.

Prior to Julia's arrival, her team had accepted the status quo and assumed they couldn't drive change. Julia boldly tackled long-entrenched problems with sellers who broke the rules, systems that let them, and incentives that didn't drive the right behavior. *Fairness and integrity.* Two of her most favorite words.

She showed her team how to fix these problems and morale was high. She couldn't let them down. She knew she had blown a big chance at making the case for change in today's meeting.

Her promotion seemed very far away even though she'd been able to taste it that morning.

JULIA CAME DOWNSTAIRS to say goodbye to the band after her post-workout shower. As usual, Selah inserted herself between Rob and the door. The two of them spoke a secret language that Julia found adorable. Selah blocked the door and flumped on her back so she could get belly rubs before Rob left.

Julia headed into the kitchen to clean up the detritus from the band's snack and heard Cliff and Rob discussing getting together for a beer the next night.

"Bye Julia!" Rob yelled to her in the kitchen.

She stepped out to say goodbye, but he was already out the door.

"He's so nice." She spoke to the back of Cliff's balding head as he climbed the stairs.

"His wife doesn't seem to think so," Cliff quipped over his shoulder, dismissing Julia's comment with a back-handed wave. "He's living in his mother's basement instead of at home." Cliff disappeared around the corner upstairs. *Why did he have to walk away when she was mid-conversation?*

With a heavy sigh, Julia encouraged Selah to go outside one more time before bed.

She heard the flap of the dog door and was about four seconds too late with the towel as Selah shook the Seattle rain all over the kitchen cabinets. "Oh puppy! I was almost there." Julia dried off her happy dog who turned it into a game, dashing back and forth and grabbing the towel. They indulged in some tug of war, her unhappiness with Cliff forgotten.

When Selah trotted off, Julia toyed with the idea of leaving the wet towel on the mudroom floor but instead put it in the washing machine. She found Cliff's dirty mountain biking clothes in the washer. Might as well start a load of laundry.

Cliff was already in bed with the television on when she and Selah made it to the bedroom. She recognized the scene from *The Bourne Identity* which he had watched approximately one thousand times.

Feeling the stress of her week pulling her down, Julia

washed her face and turned out the bathroom light before climbing into bed. "Are we still on for our date night on Saturday?" Julia needed something to look forward to.

"Hang on, this is the best part."

Julia watched the car chase scene for the hundredth time. Switching off her light, she lay awake thinking about what life would have been like if Cliff had stayed on his original career path.

When they'd met on Wall Street eighteen years before, they were both full of promise and motivation to do something amazing. He could program in twenty-two languages, and she was fresh from the Ivy League looking to put her stamp on management consulting in New York City. They had such fun in the early days.

Back then, Cliff would have talked to her about what happened at work. He would have given her some advice and then taken her mind off the problem with sex. Tonight, he just went to bed.

He had changed so much since he got laid off in 2003. Overnight, she had become the sole bread winner, and he retreated into himself.

It increased the pressure she felt to make more money as the years ticked by and he hadn't returned to work. They had planned for an early retirement, but with his lengthy unemployment, that was over ten years away.

Maybe, when he got a job again, he'd be more like he had been. She had clung to that hope for almost nine years now. She pushed him to get a job, begged almost. It always ended in a fight.

She just needed to invest more time in him and their relationship. She felt guilty that she had let things go so far without working to fix the issues. She would do better.

One more week of work and she could focus on him. He had just finished a training session and bought the equipment to be a voiceover artist. Maybe that would perk him up. A new endeavor usually did.

Her exhaustion was more powerful than her thoughts and she fell asleep as the sound of the television played in the background.

Chapter 4

"I just don't seem to have the energy I used to," Julia told Doctor Sweetman the next morning. He had a smile that looked more appropriate for a used car salesperson.

"Getting older does that to people." The doctor winked at the intern shadowing him.

Please stop winking.

"What else is wrong?" His tone turned more exasperated, his knee bouncing as he sat on his swivel stool.

The paper liner on the exam table crinkled as Julia shivered in the cold room. Doctor Sweetman, she thought, did not befit his name. She squared her shoulders. "No matter how much I sleep, I don't feel well-rested."

"Low concentration, low energy, poor sleeping habits, reduced mental capacity." He ticked her symptoms off on his fingers, then looked up and flashed her his toothy grin. "Well, I'm sure you don't have dementia. People with dementia don't know it – family members bring them in." This time, his smile was big enough to reveal a dimple on his right cheek.

"Okay, look," Julia adjusted her glasses, giving him a

penetrating stare. She didn't like how he added mental capacity to the list – she never said anything about that. "I came to see a doctor because I feel like crap, and I want to know if something's wrong with me. Is this just what thirty-nine feels like, or could I have a problem?"

"You're fine. Just take some Vitamin D." He patted her knee. "Everyone needs that in the Pacific Northwest."

"Please, just order some bloodwork." She shouldn't have to tell him how to do his job.

"You don't need bloodwork. Your symptoms suggest you might be depressed. Think that might be the case?"

"No. I have a great job, a long-term relationship, friends I enjoy, and a comfortable life. I am not depressed." Julia had nothing to be depressed about. Depression was triggered by real problems. She pulled her knee out of patting distance.

"If you say so." He swiveled around to his computer and entered a bunch of codes while speaking in low tones to the intern who continued to giggle. After what seemed like an eternity, he held out the order for blood tests. "Think about what I said. You may want to see a psychologist."

"Thanks." Julia snatched the order from his hand and waited for him to leave so she could get dressed. Now she was unhappy, feeling crappy, and had a healthy dose of embarrassment piled on top. She had her blood drawn and drove to work.

⬒

JULIA ARRIVED at the office with fifteen minutes to catch up on email before her meetings started. Not taking her eyes off the screen, she reached into her desk drawer for a granola bar to get some energy after her blood draw.

As usual, she didn't have a lunch break in her schedule. Another day of back-to-back meetings.

A big deal needed her input. She declined the discount, citing other similar deals that didn't require such large pricing concessions.

Blane's comments and Jeff's lack of understanding from the day before tempted her to just approve the deal, but she thought they could win it without so many concessions. She made an alternate recommendation, hit send on the email, and headed to her next meeting.

Yesterday's horror followed her like a cloud.

JULIA MADE it through the final meeting of the day and was packing up to head out when there was a knock on her office door. "Hey Dave! Great timing. I just finished my last meeting and have some time. What can I do for you?"

"Just stopping by before I head to the airport. What'd you think of the meeting yesterday?"

"Overall, it was good," she fibbed. "I'm bummed that we didn't push harder on improvements and that I didn't get more support for my team's ideas and policy changes. Want to have a seat?" Julia gestured toward her couch. A break with Dave would be good. She hadn't seen him much since he relocated to Los Angeles.

"No thanks, this is just a drive by." Dave shifted uncomfortably. "You were pretty tough on Jeff."

Julia was incredulous. "Tough? How? I was just outlining an issue and recommending a course of action. I was helping by showing everyone the data." *Bland face, bland face,* she told herself to combat the heat creeping up her neck.

"You definitely did that, but you also said Jeff is a bad corporate citizen." Dave walked to the window to check out her view of Mount Baker before the early afternoon sunset hid the mountain.

"No I didn't – I just explained how we could plug a gap. I brought cold hard facts to the table to drive change." Julia rubbed her eyes under her glasses, glad she hadn't bothered with make-up that morning – nothing to smear.

"Maybe that was what you *intended* to do." Dave turned back toward her, his face sympathetic. "But it certainly came across like you were attacking him, even though you did it in a nice, respectful tone. Given our current financial results, that was a pretty brutal thing to do in front of Blane."

"Brutal? How is it my fault that the data made Jeff look bad? The facts are the facts. If that made him look bad, that's his problem."

Julia did not enjoy the power dynamics of Dave standing and her sitting. "How about a soda?" she asked, getting up to reach into the mini fridge under her desk.

"I'll take a club soda."

Julia handed him the cold can before continuing. "I'm just doing my job. I can't be friends with everybody on the team. If Jeff thought I was doing a good job, it would mean I wasn't being tough enough."

"Now Julia, did it feel good to show all that data and be prepared to answer the questions?" Dave again demonstrated he could move his eyebrows as he gave her a questioning look.

"Of course it did." Being good at math was core to her job.

"Have you thought about the impact on Jeff's ego? The team gave you about twenty hints you were pushing too hard, but you just kept nailing him."

"I wasn't nailing him. I was pointing out the facts and

answering questions." Julia couldn't believe that's how Dave saw it.

"That may be, but you locked him in a four-sided box. The only way out was to admit that he and his team were making bad decisions and being irresponsible with the company's money. Look at it from his point of view. Like I said, you nailed him."

"That is totally unfair. Why would people side with him instead of the data?"

"Julia, be reasonable. You didn't have to throw his bad behavior in everyone's face and be such a bitch about it."

Julia took a breath to collect her thoughts so she didn't overreact to being asked to *be reasonable* followed by the b word. She had done her job. She was protecting shareholder value. Jeff's team was acting poorly and had gotten away with it for far too long. Everyone talked about it behind closed doors. She was the only one who had the courage to take him on.

She swallowed her anger, again. Dave mistook her silence as an opportunity to continue. "Face it, Jules. You showed up for a battle with a cannon and all Jeff had to defend himself was a pocketknife. You scared the shit out of him."

This again, Julia thought. *Oh Julia, you're so scary. Men with delicate egos don't like you because you point out their bad behavior.* "I get it. I shouldn't be scary, but he's tanking the business. Why does that make it okay for his team to give away millions of dollars of discounts without consequences?"

"It doesn't, but you've created a real problem now."

"No. He created the problem." Julia's tone was sharper than she intended.

"I hear you, but you bruised his ego and now he's on a rampage."

Julia pictured Jeff running through the hallways yelling obscenities about her. "Fuck."

"Yeah. Sorry to be the one to tell you. He told Blane to fire you."

An icy fist closed around Julia's heart. *Could she actually get fired over this?* "Fire me? For doing my job? Come on!"

"I know, and I certainly defended you as did Blane. As long as Blane is around, you're safe."

The stress of preparing for the meeting and then having it all blow up consumed her. Julia's shoulders dropped as her breath whooshed out of her lungs. She hung her head in defeat.

Dave gave her a look filled with sympathy. "I don't know how you can get out of this one, Julia. Maybe it's time to look for a new job. No one would blame you. It's a tough gig."

"Leave? Me? I just got my team in good enough shape for us to start doing the work we need to be doing. I can't give up now." *Especially just because some moron has an ego problem.* "I need to figure out a plan." She knew that at the end of the day, she was right.

"It was just a suggestion, Julia. I know a lot of teams who'd be happy to have you." Dave threw out his empty soda can. "How can I help?"

"You already did by telling me this was going on. Clearly, I didn't read the room properly. I thought we were in problem-solving mode and all topics were fair game. But lay off calling me a bitch, okay?"

"Sorry. I felt bad as soon as I said it. Trust me when I say Jeff called you worse things. That probably didn't help much," he added quickly at her baleful stare.

"I know you're trying to help." She let him off the hook. "Thanks for the insight, Dave. I'll figure something out."

"It'll be tough to fix, but I don't discount your capabilities, Jules. My money's on you."

"Wow. Pricing jokes. Well played."

"I have to dash. My plane leaves in two hours and I have to change into my flying clothes."

"Seriously Dave, thanks for the feedback."

"I'm in your corner. And remember, feedback is a gift." He made jazz hands as he left her office.

Julia's laugh sounded a bit hollow, even to her.

Chapter 5

"My next meeting is here. Thanks for your time." Julia ended the call Monday afternoon and waved Rachel in. Her bio break would have to wait. Again.

"I need some couch time." Rachel relaxed against the flower-shaped pillows on the famous red couch. Julia wasn't surprised she needed help. She worked for Joe Spencer, the cologne-dipped sales manager.

"That's what it's here for," Julia said, pushing her own problems to the back of her mind. "What's up?"

"Joe keeps asking me to bend the rules and overwrite the prices on quotes. I don't know what to do. If I do it, I'm breaking the rules, and if I don't, he'll give me a bad review. What should I do?" Rachel twirled her dark hair around her finger. Julia would wait until Rachel was in a better place to coach her not to do that because it made her look really junior.

Julia had been looking forward to an update on an action plan the two of them had crafted together. It looked like that would have to wait. The answer to Rachel's quandary was obvious, but she wanted to help Rachel work through the problem on her own. "What do you think you should do?"

"I think I should stand up to him, but I don't know how." Rachel pouted.

"What does that look like?"

"In my mind, it always ends with him screaming at me that I'm a goody two shoes."

Julia liked coaching rather than directing. "Any other approach you could take?"

Rachel looked pensive for a moment. "I could just not do it."

"Yeah, but he'd notice that. Is there another way to get to the lower price?"

"I guess I could change the product mix and add products that already have lower prices – that could get me the same result."

"That's a good idea, Rachel." They continued to discuss Rachel's course of action until their time was almost over.

"Thank you so much for the pep talk and help!" Rachel was like a different person from the one who had entered Julia's office.

"That's what I'm here for." Julia smiled. She loved helping others overcome obstacles and encouraging them to persevere. She also hoped they could get back to the actual agenda for the last few minutes of the meeting.

"You're such a good listener and you know so much about the business!" Rachel continued to gush. "Thanks for the great advice, as usual. "

"Ha! I literally got the exact opposite input last week." Julia shook her head at the memory.

"What? From whom?"

"It doesn't matter." Julia was embarrassed she had

brought it up. It wasn't Rachel's problem and Julia didn't want people to know she was upset about it.

"Okay well, I'm kind of stuck on a few of the recommendations we discussed last time we met. Mind if I get your guidance on how to work through it?"

"That sounds great, Rachel. Let's dig in."

JULIA WENT RIGHT into a one on one with Kate after her meeting with Rachel.

Kate started with a bang like she always did. "How'd it go on Thursday?" Julia sighed and looked at her from under raised eyebrows. "That good, huh?"

"It was a nightmare. I went over the data and recommendations, and they couldn't get around their own egos to see that the changes are necessary."

"Typical. Are you really that surprised though? I mean, sales has gotten away with terrible behavior for years. A lot of cultural change has to happen before anyone will embrace data-based instead of emotional decisions."

"You're right, Kate. As usual. I was hoping that this time would be different. Joe was onboard and I gave the same pitch in both meetings. I'm not going to give up."

"Nor should you. The team needs you and so does this company. You'll figure it out." Kate gave her a supportive smile.

"Damn straight." *At least she hoped so.* "What's next on your agenda?"

"Oh, so many things I need your help with, J-Money."

JULIA'S PHONE rang as she was packing up to leave for the day. "Hi, this is Natalie from Doctor Sweetman's office calling with your results. Everything's completely normal for your age. The STD and HIV tests came back negative as well. You could use some extra Vitamin D. I'll email you the details. Celebrate the good news!"

Julia thanked her and clicked off the call.

Damn. *And why had they tested for STDs and HIV? Did they think Cliff was cheating on her?* She couldn't think about that right now. Doctor Winkyface was right about it not being medical. Julia had wanted an easy explanation, but the results did not provide it. Something else had to be wrong.

She thought of the doctor's parting words about her being depressed. That couldn't be it. She didn't have anything to be depressed about. Well, she hadn't when she had the appointment. Now her promotion was even farther away. Her stomach grumbled. Had she eaten lunch?

She called Cliff. "The test results came back. I'm fine."

"That's great news, Boo," Cliff said, sounding a bit out of breath.

Julia cringed at the nickname but hid her annoyance. It was short for Boo Boo Bear. Cliff started calling her that as a joke. She asked him to stop but that egged him on and now he called her Boo all the time. "I guess, but it makes me wonder what else could be wrong. Are you working out or something? You sound winded."

"Working out? No. When are you going to be home?"

"About forty-five minutes. Can you make some dinner? I'm starving and could use a quiet evening in."

"Sure. And I want to talk to you about something when you get home."

"Okay. I'm heading out now."

Julia's anger came back with a vengeance as she started her commute home. She couldn't shake the cloud the meeting created. Her heart beat quickly and she knew without a mirror nearby that her face was bright red. Indignation gripped her. *Fairness and integrity.*

Jeff never pulled a punch when he yelled at her about prices. Or when he called her the Sales Prevention Team. No one defended her when she was attacked by her peers for holding the line on deal approvals. Yet, when she brought clear and accurate data to a conversation, she was labeled a bitch? She just couldn't win.

Was Dave following up with Jeff to tell him not to be such a bad corporate citizen or to be more respectful? Probably not. Her peers shouldn't hide behind the façade of Jeff's delicate ego. And to call her a bitch? Really? A guy would have been patted on the back and congratulated for being assertive. Textbook discrimination.

If she acquiesced, she would let down her team and LampLight shareholders. If she held the line, she would be hated by her peers. She might even get fired. And without Blane's support for her recommendations, she was sunk.

Taking a deep breath, Julia brainstormed ideas for how she could undo the damage. She could apologize to Jeff. No. Apologizing would diminish her power position and give him the upper hand in the relationship. It would also mean she'd have to back down from her recommendations. She had to stand her ground.

She could slow down her plans and make change gradually. She wouldn't get as much done, but her colleagues would like her more and she could execute smaller changes. Her life would be simpler, and it would be easier for her team.

That idea started to sound good. It was simple. True, she wouldn't achieve all of her goals, but she would still have positive impact. This scenario felt comfortable.

Except for one thing, she thought. She'd be doing the company a disservice. How could she see a problem and not fix it? She had to demonstrate strong leadership to her team and show them it's possible to effect change.

If she took the easy way out she wouldn't be able to sleep at night. She wouldn't fulfill her promise to herself to help the company and the team.

She could do what Dave said and just quit. Get another new job. With another lateral move. But she had just whipped this team into shape, and she loved pricing. She didn't want to give up because of a few jerks. She was stronger than that. She just had to work harder. *If you didn't have to work hard for it, it wasn't worth having.*

Julia came through the mudroom door and was met by Selah who looked very happy to see her. Julia stroked her behind the ears and let the calmness from being with her dog wash through her. She heard Cliff in the kitchen. "Hey, I'm home. What's for dinner?"

"I didn't feel like cooking. Let's just go out."

She didn't have the energy to go out. And she didn't want to spend the money.

"No. I said I wanted to stay in and I meant it. I'll see what I can pull together."

What could she make that was easy? A look in the pantry showed she had the makings for veggie chili. She started opening cans and chopping onions. With the chili simmering, she made some cornbread to go with it. The cooking and time with Selah put her in a better mood. Dinner was on the table in forty minutes.

She poured a glass of wine to go with her chili and offered one to Cliff. He joined her at the kitchen table as she served dinner and plunked down on the comfy cushion in the window seat. "You said you wanted to talk about something?" It required effort to pick up the spoon and eat.

"Yeah. Would you mind if I take a road trip with Rob

from the band? His cousin's moving across the country. She's flying with her pets and needs someone to drive the moving van. I'd keep him company."

"When are you thinking of going?"

"The day after Christmas."

"Oh, that soon. I thought we were planning some quality time together over the holidays." *For us to end our sex drought,* she added to herself.

"I know, but I want to go. I need a break."

You need a break? From what? Julia thought. Cliff sounded so happy. Julia chose to give him what he wanted. "Okay, go if you want to."

"Then I'm going."

Chapter 6

Julia had to figure out how to tell her team she had failed them. Her final team meeting of the calendar year was later that day. Kate had been so supportive and wasn't surprised, but Julia needed more than just understanding from her team. She needed a plan to fix the situation.

Julia reflected, for the forty-seventh time, on what happened in the leadership team meeting. Dave said she had scared Jeff. Jeff said she didn't listen and didn't know anything. But Rachel complimented her listening skills and knowledge of the business. How could she get exactly the opposite feedback within a few days?

It was different with Rachel because Rachel looked up to Julia as a mentor. It was a respect thing. Jeff hadn't ever bothered to get to know Julia or to figure out if she had a clue. He'd started attacking her from day one. She figured it was typical sales behavior, but maybe it was more.

Maybe she really did scare him. But what was scary about her? She knew her stuff, she always had data to back up her recommendations, and she held her ground. She anticipated questions because she had already worked through them as part of her strategy. That was her super-power – seeing the interconnections between people and processes. It shouldn't scare him, it should impress him.

Unless *he* didn't actually understand the business. No. He wouldn't have gotten to be a vice president if he was oblivious to the operational details of his sales practices. *Or could he?* Maybe he didn't know how the pieces fit together. Was he so busy golfing and glad-handing he had never learned how his team worked?

Joe Spencer knew. And things had gone well with Cologne Joe. *Why was that different?* Maybe it was because she had tailored the meeting and the presentation to him, knowing he had a short attention span. She showed what was in it for him. She hadn't done that at the leadership team meeting. The admission pained her.

She knew better than to go in guns blazing, but she got caught up in Blane's energy thinking he really wanted to dig in and solve the revenue problem. Coupled with her own desire to impress Blane, she had trampled on Jeff's ego. Maybe she had activated some fear in Blane, Barry, and the others as well. *Because she knew so much about the business.* That should be an asset, not a curse!

Maybe her ego had gotten the best of her. She was so focused on impressing the boss in her quest for a promotion that she didn't see their fear. That felt bad. Unfair, actually. She had been doing the right thing for the business and that should be enough.

But sadly, it wasn't. She had learned years ago that ego management was an important part of the job. And she missed it in her zeal to solve the problem and be a hero. Damn.

How could she fix this? How could she gain their respect and help them understand she had positive intentions? She couldn't come across as a know-it-all who was trying to tell them what to do again. She had to gain their respect so they would listen.

But she had been told she didn't listen. She listened. She also happened to understand quickly and didn't need things repeated. Maybe they didn't know she had heard them. She had to demonstrate she was listening more.

Listening more.

Insight struck like lightning.

She could go on a listening tour. She could visit each sales office to gather their feedback on what was happening rather than lecturing and convincing. She would invest in relationships and gain the respect of the sales teams in the field by listening to them.

After recruiting Jeff's direct reports and the people below them to her cause, there would be a groundswell of support for her team and their recommendations for change. It would be a lot of work, but it would be effective.

She got a lot of feedback that people didn't know her team. She would fix that. She would be the public face of her team and build up the recommendations together based on information from her Listening Tour. That was it. Now she was getting somewhere.

Julia's fingers flew over the keyboard as she crafted the presentation for her team meeting. She would explain what happened in the leadership team meeting and enroll them in her plan for a listening tour. She would pitch it to them as a good thing, allowing her to gather more feedback.

She would bring people along. It would be more scalable. She would get them excited about running additional analyses to find new pricing improvement opportunities. She had to keep momentum going with her team since she had failed to get the green light on their plans. She didn't want them to feel discouraged.

She quickly planned visits to all six US offices. If she

managed it just right, she would spend a bunch of time on the road right after the holidays, but she would be able to hit all of the US-based offices in about eight weeks. It would be a lot of traveling, but if her plan worked, it would be worth it.

That terrible meeting was just a setback. One that would take a while to come back from, but if she was successful, it would allow them to reap the benefits for years. And it just might fix her problem. Fix it. *Yeah, she would call it Operation Fix-It.*

JULIA WALKED through a sanitized version of the story with her team. "But sellers always get away with that shit," Susan said, her eyes flashing with anger. "How can you stay so rational about it and just keep going with a new plan?"

It was a great question. Julia dug deep for leadership energy because she knew this was a big moment. "Because there's no other choice. We're the ones who can fix this, so we have to persevere. If it were easy, it would already be done."

"I hear you, but I'm not surprised this happened." Susan continued to push. "Our last boss got eaten alive by the sellers. We hope you last."

Julia laughed even though the comment struck home. "I'm here for the long haul. We'll get there through a charm offensive and Operation Fix-It. Trust me."

"We do." Several team members spoke at the same time.

"When do we start?" Kate asked, always brightening the mood.

"Right after the holiday break," Julia answered. She

recharged her energy from their belief in her. "All the deals forecasted to close this quarter are signed, sealed, and delivered. I'll be on duty in case anything pops up, but you should all go and have a great week off. We'll jump back in after the break. Happy holidays everyone. See you in the new year."

Exhaustion filled every part of her body as she rolled her shoulders and felt her neck crack in three places. Yes, definitely time for a break. Starting with a nice celebratory dinner with Cliff to launch Operation Fix -It.

JULIA DROVE HOME in the dark even though it was only five. That's how Seattle was this time of year. Selah greeted her at the door when she got home. "Where's your daddy?" she asked the dog. "Cliff? Are you here?"

He breezed into the kitchen. He was actually wearing jeans. *Pants with a waistband, awesome!* "Hey, want to go out for dinner?" Julia asked. "I figured out what I'm going to do about what happened in that meeting last week and I want to celebrate."

"No can do, Boo. I'm having a beer with the band. We have to narrow down our playlist. I'm actually running a little late. See ya later."

Julia scratched her ever-faithful dog on the head. "Thanks for sticking with me, puppy. Looks like it's you, me, and a salad. We can celebrate Selah-style with play time and a nap." Selah thumped her tail.

Chapter 7

The rich scent of wine, garlic, and onions simmering in the oven filled the kitchen. Julia sat down at the table with a thud after cleaning up from the prep process for boeuf bourguignon.

She usually made elaborate feasts for friends on the holiday, but not this year. Dinner for Cliff was all she had the energy to execute.

She was glad she hadn't headed to her parent's house in the Midwest for the holiday. They lived in separate worlds, and it required a lot of energy to fit back into theirs. She just didn't have it this year. Their phone call earlier while they opened presents was plenty.

Julia perked up at the thought that she and Cliff might have a special evening together after dinner since it would just be the two of them.

She had a few hours of simmering time left on the meal and Cliff wouldn't be back from his mountain bike ride for a while. She could take some time to make herself pretty. She thought Cliff might come around and be more interested now that he had another new career opportunity brewing.

———

"TOO BAD NOBODY was taking a video. I came over the jump and landed so hard I popped my tire." Cliff was pumped up. Julia was happy to see a glimpse of his former personality. She knew he was still in there. "I didn't even realize it until I kept pedaling after the landing and almost wound up getting stuck in the mud and going over the handlebars. You should've seen it."

"Are you okay?"

"Oh yeah." Cliff paused to swallow a mouthful of savory stew. "Rob had a spare inner tube. He fixed up my bike and we were off to finish the ride. It was epic."

"Who would have thought when we lived in Boston that there was a place like Seattle where you could mountain bike year-round?"

"Yeah, as long as you don't mind getting soggy from the rain." Julia had a flash of Cliff's muddy mountain biking clothes on top of the washing machine. "Great dinner by the way."

"Thanks, I —"

"Time to watch the game." Cliff abruptly left the table. Julia heard the TV go on as he took his customary spot on the couch. Selah looked at Julia hopefully for some leftovers. Julia gave in before tackling the dishes.

JULIA CAREFULLY UNWRAPPED her black body stocking from the tissue paper. She looked fondly at the lace stockings with a swimsuit-shaped top and a little flap in the crotch. Very low cut.

It was a bridal shower gift fourteen years ago, but as she examined the intricate pattern of stretchy lace, she noted with slight embarrassment it still looked like new.

As she slipped the body stocking up her freshly shaved legs, she was surprised it fit so well. She had achieved her goal of losing twenty pounds by Christmas. She was still a thirty-nine-year-old woman with a doughy middle and cellulite on her thighs and butt, but she'd lost enough weight that she looked pretty good.

Julia joined Cliff on the sofa and waited for a commercial. She muted the television and cuddled up to him suggestively. "Hey, since you're leaving tomorrow, I thought you might want to have a little fun tonight." She nibbled on his ear.

"I am having fun. Dinner was great." He pulled away without taking his eyes off the television.

"I mean f-u-n fun as in fooling around." She leaned over so he could get a nice view of her cleavage.

"I don't know. I'd like to watch the rest of the game. It's tradition."

"But you know how it ends! You've watched the replay of the 2002 Super Bowl a million times!"

"I know, but it's so great to see The Patriots win again and again. It's the tenth anniversary of their first Super Bowl win, Jules." He looked at her like she was crazy to not join in his excitement. "And then we can open presents. You're going to love what I got you."

Julia grabbed the robe she had flung onto the other sofa, wrapped it around herself and retreated to her side of the couch. Cliff picked up the remote to unmute the sound.

She was furious that the game was more important than what she wanted. Then the embarrassment set in. What was she thinking parading around in lingerie while he was watching a game? She knew better than that. She checked her watch. It was only six thirty. Even if he watched the rest of the game, she could still try again later.

And she did want to give Cliff his present.

If she overreacted, she definitely wouldn't get what she wanted. She changed tactics.

"Want some dessert? I made the pie you like."

Cliff's face brightened even though he didn't look away from the TV. "That'd be great. Can I get some ice cream? Oh, and some coffee?"

Julia went into the kitchen to fix Cliff's dessert, sighing as she scooped the homemade ice cream onto the warmed slice of apple pie. She couldn't believe that rather than having sex, she was serving him pie and ice cream. While wearing an unnoticed black lace body stocking.

Julia had no appetite for dessert.

She sat through the game, glad she was wearing the robe to stay warm. How many other women were sitting around for hours in a body stocking waiting for an old game to end so they could have sex? Hopefully, for their sakes, not many.

The game finally ended. "Any interest in picking up where we left off earlier?" she asked.

"Earlier? You mean when you shoved your boobs in my face?"

Julia's face heated up like the apple pie.

"Think I'll head to bed." Cliff stood up and stretched. "I have a lot on my mind for the trip, and I have to do an audition first thing in the morning."

"It's only nine," Julia snapped. *And it's a three-minute audio clip for a voiceover audition.* "And didn't you say you wanted to open presents?"

"Yeah, but I'm flying to New Jersey with Rob tomorrow to start our trip. You know I don't sleep well when I travel. I'd like to get a good night's sleep tonight. But you're right." Julia felt a flicker of hope. "Let's open presents. Then I'll head to bed." The hope was extinguished.

Cliff retrieved a large box from under the tree. "Open it." He gave her a huge smile, oblivious to her anger.

She wanted to be the present he opened. Tearing the paper away, she found a food processor. She was speechless.

"I know how you love kitchen gadgets."

"A food processor." *So she could cook for him.* She had to wait a beat before she said more.

"I'll open mine." He misinterpreted her silence.

He quickly dispensed with the wrapping paper. "Oh wow! A Crunch Box pedal! This is the one that makes any amp sound like a Marshall amp. How did you find it? These are impossible to get!"

Without waiting for an answer, Cliff sprinted to the music room and pulled a guitar off the wall to play with his new toy.

Disgusted, Julia gave up. She made sure the dog went out one last time before bed. She stopped to look at her Christmas tree. It overflowed with ornaments and lights. *It looks silly and dressed up for no reason, like she was,* Julia thought. She set her new food processor under the tree, where it seemed to mock her.

The slap of Selah's dog door closing snapped her back to reality. She picked up Cliff's empty soda cans, snack bowls, and dessert plate and put them in the dishwasher before going upstairs.

Julia wasn't tired and didn't want to go to sleep. She retreated to her usual place, the bathtub, to think about what had just happened and what she could have done differently. Why didn't he want her? She felt ugly and unsexy. Unwanted. Unfulfilled.

Cliff came in to brush his teeth. "Thanks for the pedal. It'll sound great at the Showcase."

"You're welcome. Thanks for the food processor." She felt the sting of tears gathering behind her eyes. She was glad he didn't look at her. She couldn't disguise her hurt.

"I'll close the bathroom door so you won't disturb me. Take your time."

He thought he was being nice. How sad. She sighed and decided she had to accept that she was going to continue her life sex-free. Sex just wasn't part of her marriage anymore. She certainly wasn't going to cheat on Cliff.

She finished her bath, put her lovely unused bodysuit into the hamper and curled up in bed beside a snoring Cliff with her well-worn *Love at Christmas* romance novel. At least she could read about other people having sex.

Chapter 8

Julia woke up just after six. Her body didn't want to sleep any longer. *So much for sleeping in on vacation,* she thought. Cliff and Rob had left the previous day and were probably already in Ohio on their way back from New Jersey. As soon as the sun came up, Julia took Selah to the dog park where the yellow dog happily chased the ball and romped with some new doggie friends.

It was a beautiful sunny but cold day with a brilliant azure-blue sky. Julia traded her glasses for her prescription shades. The air tasted fresh and clean. Watching the bald eagles lazily circle overhead filled her with a sense of freedom and joy.

I've been waiting, for a girl like you, she belted out as she drove home. She loved the eighties station. It was a good thing no one was in the car with her. While Julia was an excellent musician, she knew she was not a good singer. Cliff often asked her to stop.

Time to tackle the Christmas tree, she thought when she got home. Selah would be nice and tired for a few hours. Julia could get to work taking it down. As much as she loved

Christmas, once it was over, she liked to put her house back in order quickly.

She had the lights, garland, and ornaments off the tree and put away in no time. As she did every year, she laughed at herself as she relabeled the sections of the fake tree and put them back in the bag. She lived in the land of evergreen trees, yet she didn't like the idea of chopping one down for her own enjoyment.

With the last box neatly stored in the attic, she put her hands on her hips and surveyed the orderly room. Everything back in its proper place, she enjoyed the cleanliness of a job well done.

Time to catch up on some reading.

The ringing phone jolted her out of a rather contrived plot twist involving not one, but two fake identities in her latest romance novel. She could see the ending a mile away, but it was still fun to read light novels because they didn't tax her brain.

"Hi Boo," Cliff said.

She winced at the nickname. "Hey! Are you having fun?"

"We're running late because his cousin wasn't packed and ready to go. We spent the day finishing the packing yesterday and loading today. So annoying. We'll head out early in the morning. I need to go to bed."

"Oh yeah, it's late there," Julia said remembering the time difference. "Good night. I love you."

"Good night, Boo." He ended the call. He usually ended by telling her he loved her. That was odd. But no big deal. *He was probably just tired.*

JULIA OPENED HER EYES. She felt rested. Worried it must be past ten for her to feel so good, she glanced cautiously at the clock ready to chastise herself for sleeping in late. The clock showed it was 6:17AM. She hadn't slept in at all. *How odd.* She felt better than she had in months but with less sleep than she thought she needed.

Starting day two of her holiday cleaning routine, Julia listened to one of her favorite jazz CDs and attacked boring kitchen cleaning duties. Cliff didn't care for the music. She hadn't listened to it for a long time. She felt like a rebel. Bopping along to the straight-ahead blues tunes, she got through her chores with time and energy to spare.

She snacked on a peanut butter sandwich. Cliff hated peanut butter. Julia was glad she wouldn't have to listen to his complaints about it.

Her phone beeped. It was her friend Melanie asking her to meet for a drink. It had been too long since she went out with her girls. She immediately texted back a hearty YES! and they made plans to meet the next day. She let her other bestie Lesley know about the plans. Girl time was much needed!

———

IT'S ONLY FIVE THIRTY? Day three of vacation and Julia woke up raring to go. *Why was she sleeping so little and feeling so great?* She chalked it up to the holidays, the post-Christmas cheer, and being on vacation.

"Come on, Selah, let's go to your favorite place." Selah followed Julia out of the bedroom after a full body stretch. They headed to the dog park before the sun rose over the Cascade foothills. It was a beautiful and crisp morning where everything seemed a bit more vivid, a bit brighter.

Julia chucked the ball and watched Selah speed away.

She hadn't checked in with Cliff this morning. She always did, so it was odd she hadn't thought to call him. And she hadn't been thinking about him.

She didn't miss him. She was enjoying herself without him. She felt free and alive and unbounded. She was listening to music he hated. Making food he didn't like. Hanging out with friends he didn't enjoy. And she felt great.

What did this mean?

She threw the ball again for Selah who happily chased it.

It was like a huge weight had been lifted with Cliff's departure. She loved him and believed that if she just kept supporting him, things would get better. But as time went on - had it really been nine years? – she had to face reality.

Reality hit her hard.

He was never going to get another job. He would play at it, making half-hearted attempts, but he wouldn't find something productive to do with his time.

And it was her fault. She was the problem. She was enabling him. While she blamed him for not taking action, she had created a protective shell, and he had no reason to go back to work.

She had to face the brutal fact that a lot of this situation was her fault. The cycle had to be broken. But how?

Maybe they could go to counseling. They'd tried it years before when Cliff's parents decided she wasn't good enough for their son. The counselor spent several minutes of the first session lecturing Cliff about supporting his fiancé rather than his mother.

He'd refused to go back. Clearly counseling was out.

What else could she do?

"Hey Selah-pie. Do you need a break?" She spoke to

her tired dog who walked rather than ran back with the ball for another throw.

A break. They could take a break.

Just for a while. Just until he got his life together with a decent job and some confidence.

Maybe separating would jolt him back to his old self and he could become a productive member of society again. While they were apart, she could work on breaking out of the pleaser pattern. And then they could get back together.

She felt a warmth on the cold day she knew wasn't coming from the weather. It stemmed from taking control of her relationship and not letting Cliff be the center of attention anymore.

She had to take action to help herself. She had to learn something from the emotional and physical shift caused by his absence. She deserved to be happy.

She tried to push away the guilt that her happiness might come at Cliff's expense.

Chapter 9

A blast of stale beer, smoke, and fried food hit Julia as she opened the door to her friend Melanie's favorite bar. Smoking in restaurants had been banned years before, but somehow the sillage of cigarette smoke managed to linger in this place.

Why did she and her friends come here? *Oh right, cheap drinks and decent food.*

She spotted Melanie at the bar playing electronic poker. Melanie pointed to a booth on the other side with her long, manicured fingernails and they met halfway there.

"Hey girl," Melanie yelled out with her typical exuberance. She dyed her hair multiple shades of blonde and spiked it in various directions. It suited her perfectly – fun, colorful, and a little crazy. "What're you drinking?" Melanie asked as a server walked over.

"I'll have a vodka and cranberry, but could I have it in a tall glass with double the cranberry and half the vodka?"

"Sure. But I've never heard it ordered that way before – only the other way around." The server cackled like someone who'd been smoking for forty-three years. Melanie pointed to her glass and got the nod that a refill of her customary Jack and Coke was on the way.

"So, how're you doing?" Melanie switched gears from bar gal pal to serious friend. "I know you've had a rough couple of months at work."

"Yeah, I hate that I let work interfere with Melanie time. I haven't seen Lesley in even longer. To say I was happy to hear from you is an understatement. We have to get our monthly happy hours back on the calendar!"

"Done! I get it. It's easy to get caught up in work drama. There's plenty to go around."

"Thanks for understanding. I've missed you." They shared a sympathetic nod.

"Things feel serious. Let's switch it up." Melanie clicked her manicured nails together. "You can only eat one dish for the rest of your life. What is it?" She always had a question at the ready to lighten a mood or change topics.

"Pasta with butter and parmesan cheese."

"Good one. For me, any kind of pizza." Melanie paused, then shook her head, her earrings dancing with the movement. "That's not true. None of that Hawaiian pizza crap with pineapple." She wrinkled her nose. "That's just rude."

"Hundred percent. Pineapple does not belong on pizza. Period."

Lesley sailed through the door wearing a flowy, gauzy shirt with zebra and leopard prints, her long brown locks rocking fresh blond highlights.

"Hello ladies." Lesley slipped into the booth next to Melanie. "Sorry I'm late."

"Julia and I were just discussing food. You didn't miss anything."

"I got tied up at work – before you say it, yes, I'm the one who works while everyone else is off – anyway, this guy on my team is resisting the direction I'm taking the team, and I made the mistake of spending extra time trying to convince him."

"As my boss at a big consulting company used to say, 'Julia, I will carry the wounded, but I will shoot the stragglers' and I agree with him."

"That's terrible." Melanie could barely get the words out around her laughter.

"He just means there are some people who won't come along for the journey. It's tough, but sometimes you have to cull the herd to help the others move faster."

"Ouch, but I get it." Lesley looked like she was pondering the wisdom of the advice. "So how about you two? How was your Christmas?"

"My sister and I had our regular get together with our husbands." Melanie sipped her Jack and Coke. "We ate too much and fell asleep early."

"Sounds like mine except with my mom and stepdad."

Julia took a long sip from her cranberry juice-heavy drink to avoid answering. Two pairs of eyes were on her when she looked up from the straw.

"Jules? You okay over there?"

"Christmas was not great." Julia sighed at the memory. "Cliff bought me a food processor."

Melanie made her wrinkle-nosed rude face. "Did you want a new food processor?"

Julia just looked at her.

"Hey, I was trying to be diplomatic!"

"He's gone this week, traveling across the country with Rob from the band, and I'm glad he's away."

"Sometimes you need a break." Lesley nodded her agreement.

"It's more than that. I'm going to ask him for a separa-tion. I want to see if he can get his shit together."

"What??" they said in unison.

"What happened?" Melanie asked, the first to recover.

"Well, it's been building for a while, but it all came to a head this week with him being away. You know how I've been dragging for the last several months?" It felt more like years.

Lesley spoke with sympathy in her voice. "I know you've been struggling. Do you think he has something to do with it?"

"How can he not? He's the one I see every day. I went to the doctor and all the bloodwork came back normal."

"That's good," Lesley said. "But there's more, isn't there?"

"Yeah. With him gone, I've been feeling great this week." Julia flinched at the admission. It sounded harsh out loud. "I think I want to live apart from him at least for a little while to see if it spurs him to get a job and stand on his own two feet."

Lesley and Melanie looked at each other, as if they were deciding who would talk first. Lesley gave Melanie the nod that she could start.

"Wow, this is big." Melanie leaned closer. "I understand how you got to this point. You're usually so sparkly and full of energy. Yet, Cliff seems so... withdrawn."

"You're being nice, Mel," Lesley said. "To be a bit more blunt, I don't see why you're with him at all. I mean, I figured he was a maniac in bed or something because I've never understood the connection."

"Thanks for the honesty. I love you guys." Julia took a quick break to clink glasses before continuing. "I wish you'd met Cliff back in the day. He was so different then."

"You're with who he is now, not who he was then," Lesley said.

"I'll print that up on a t-shirt for you," Melanie added, sipping the last of her drink.

Julia let that sink in. "I'll be forty in May. This isn't what I pictured for me or for us. If we don't make this change now, when will we?"

Lesley's face turned serious. "I agree with you. I've never seen you light up when you talk about him."

Julia nodded. "I came to the same conclusion. Somewhere along the line, my caretaking after he lost his executive position crossed the line into being unhealthy and taking his life away from him."

"Hang on," Lesley interrupted, her finger in the air. "Did you fire him?"

"No."

"Did you encourage him to stay home and not go back to work?" Melanie added.

"No, of course not. I hound him to get a job. Probably too much."

"And he chose not to go back to work. *He* gave up on his career. It wasn't you who did that." Melanie and Lesley looked at each other and nodded.

It was Lesley's turn. "You're a caretaker. It's great to be a caretaker, but you've just taken it too far with Cliff. Back to what your former boss said, maybe it's time to decide if Cliff is wounded or if he's a straggler."

They shared a moment of silence.

Melanie jumped in. "So, back to the sex. Is he awesome in bed? Is that why you've stayed with him so long?"

Julia laughed. It was good to laugh about it. She told them the story of her massive sex drought.

"Are you telling us you haven't had sex in a couple of years?"

"Honestly, he wouldn't touch me more than once a year, and pretty much only after a lot of cajoling on my part for… well, it's probably been the last five years of our marriage."

"What? That can't be!" Lesley said, spitting out a bit of her margarita in the process.

"Oh yeah," Julia continued. "I even made him read an article about the dirty thirties when women become more interested in sex after thirty because their eggs are starting to dry up. He was unmoved."

"What did you do?"

"Well, I told him since he was my husband, he was my only choice for sex. Then I basically begged him to have sex with me, but he refused. And I guess part of me was relieved, because he needed a lot of pointers and guidance when we did finally get around to it. It rarely worked, if you know what I mean."

"Yeah," Lesley said, "It's tough to be like 'a little to the left, no to the right, okay faster.' You just want them to know what to do!"

"Oh my gosh. My theory was totally wrong." Melanie signaled for one more Jack and Coke. "Are you going to try someone new while you're separated?"

"No! Absolutely not. It's just temporary so he can get his shit together. We won't get divorced. It'll probably be, like, two to three weeks. Just enough to show him I'm serious about changes."

Melanie cocked an eyebrow. "Okay. But, listen, one more thing. I'm on your side here. But… don't just move out. My first husband did that to me. He just announced one day he wanted a divorce."

"Ouch." Lesley winced.

"Yeah," Melanie said. "It was tough to be surprised by that. So have a care. You've been stewing about this for a few days. Give him some respect and let him catch up before you move out," Melanie concluded.

"And, if I may get personal," Lesley added, "have you invested in a good vibrator?" They all giggled.

"Actually, no," Julia said. "I've never tried one."

"No!?" they exclaimed together.

Lesley was the first to regain her voice. "You have no idea what you're missing."

"I guess not. I wouldn't even know where to start. There are so many." Julia shrugged.

"Well, you better do some shopping on the way home," Melanie stated with mock seriousness. "I'll give you some pointers."

"No pun intended," Lesley added with a snort.

Chapter 10

Don't jump right in, Julia reminded herself. She already knew she couldn't have the conversation she wanted to with Cliff the moment he walked in the door. Rob would be with him, and she didn't want to cause a scene.

Food always helps, she thought.

She was pulling jalapeño corn bread out of the oven when she heard the moving van pull into the cul-de-sac. She met Cliff outside as he slid out of the passenger seat, looking stiff and tired in the light snow starting to coat the ground.

"You made it!" she said as she gave Cliff a hug he barely returned.

"Hello!" Rob came around the front of the truck with a burst of energy. "Do I get one of those, too?"

Before she could answer, he enveloped her in a big bear hug. It lasted three seconds too long. She pulled away and turned back to Cliff, feeling a bit off-center.

"Welcome home. You guys hungry? I have food ready if you want some."

"That'd be great." Cliff said. "We got stuck behind a snowplow at Snoqualmie Pass. I'm starved. Thanks Boo."

Julia winced at the nickname, her face flushed. She glanced at Rob, hoping he hadn't noticed, or at least had the grace to pretend he hadn't.

"Thanks for knowing we'd show up hungry." Rob grabbed Cliff's bag. "I appreciate the sustenance."

They followed Julia inside where they would share a late dinner.

When Selah saw Rob come in behind Cliff, she went racing toward him. She brought her favorite toy for a quick game. "That's my girl." Rob crouched down to give Selah some tummy rubs.

"I changed my mind. I'm going to grab a quick shower." Cliff headed upstairs before she could say a word about dinner getting cold.

She sighed and turned to Rob, interrupting the latest bout of doggie love. "How was the trip?"

"It was good to have Cliff along for the ride." Rob sounded cheerful, as always. He got up and followed Julia into the kitchen. "It smells great in here – what is that heavenly scent?"

"Just some guac and chips, chili, corn bread, pickled veggies, Mexican-style coleslaw, and tortillas in case you want to turn it into burritos or tacos." It assuaged some of Julia's guilt to cook Cliff's favorite foods.

"Cooking is a mystery to me – I have no idea how people can get things done all at the same time, and you listed off the menu like it was no big deal. I'm impressed."

"Thanks," Julia said as she blushed a second time. "I cook to relieve stress. Over the years, I've gotten pretty good at it."

"I'm sorry for the stress that caused it, but I'll certainly benefit from it if the chili tastes half as good as it smells. Why don't we start with some guac and chips while we wait for Cliff? It'd be rude to eat without him."

"Good point. Anyone you need to alert you're back? Camille? Your cousin?" Julia set out plates while they talked.

"Yeah. Well. No. Uh. Definitely not Camille." He scratched the back of his head. "I wasn't going to tell people yet, but we've called it quits."

"Oh, Rob, I'm sorry to hear that. Are you okay?" She remembered when she'd met Rob's wife Camille. Julia had come right from work to one of the band's gigs wearing her favorite tweed skirt in purple and black and Camille had complimented her on it.

Julia, completely misreading her audience, blurted out she had got it on clearance. Camille had arched a sculpted brow. "Next time, just say it's Chanel," turned on her heel and strode away. Julia's hopes the four of them could be friends disappeared in that moment.

"Yeah, it's been building for a long time now. I've tried so hard to make her happy, but she's really negative. I can't seem to help her move toward a more positive path. We've been separated for a few months, and I've been living in my mother's basement. I had to go through the motions with her family for Christmas because she doesn't want to tell them yet."

"That was kind of you." Julia wished his situation could be different and have a happy ending. "Do you feel better now that you have some closure?" She wondered if she was asking for herself as she thought about her upcoming conversation with Cliff.

"Well, that's the problem," Rob continued. "I feel guilty for leaving her. She's so unhappy I don't think she'll ever find anyone else. She'll be alone. I hate that."

"It's not your problem to solve, Rob," Julia said gently. "She has to have the capacity to make herself happy before you can reach her."

As Julia turned to give the chili one last stir, she realized sometimes the advice she gave to others was exactly the advice she should take herself.

CLIFF JOINED them after his shower. Julia spooned up the chili and plated the tacos. Rob's phone buzzed with an incoming text.

"It's my cousin," he said reading it. "She says the roads are icy near her and I won't get up the hill to her new condo in the moving van."

Cliff rolled his eyes. "You have to love the way Seattleites protect the salmon and don't salt the roads. Want to stay here tonight? Julia, we don't have any plans, right?"

"Nope, just hanging out." Looks like the conversation would have to wait.

"That'd be great, if it's okay with both of you." He looked back and forth between them.

Julia made peace with the delay in her conversation with Cliff. It would be unfair to blast him with it right after he got home anyway. And it would be nice to get to know Rob better.

———

THE NEXT MORNING, Julia was up early starting on breakfast for the three of them. She heard footsteps coming downstairs in the morning and looked up from her breakfast preparations to greet Cliff. But it was Rob who smiled at her. "Good morning," he said with energy, but also quietly to not disturb Cliff. "What can I do to help?"

Julia stared into his bright blue eyes. She realized it was her turn to speak, but she had been appreciating the dress shirt with contrasting collar and cuffs that looked like it had been tailored for a perfect fit. She couldn't help comparing it to the sweatpants Cliff favored.

Snapping back to reality, Julia finally answered. "I have things under control here. I was just putting the pancakes in the oven with the bacon to stay warm until everyone is up. I won't make the scrambled eggs until Cliff is here, too. They're ready to go in the pan." Julia pointed to the bowl of whisked eggs. "Coffee is in the pot, juice is in the fridge, and mugs and glasses are on the table." She was babbling. She looked back down at the eggs to break the flow.

"Mind if I get myself some coffee?" he asked.

"No, not at all," Julia handed him a mug. Rob filled his cup halfway and went to the refrigerator to top it up with cold water.

He looked at Julia with a sheepish grin. "I like it baby temperature. I can't drink it when it's too hot."

"That's cool - pun intended," Julia laughed, forgetting to be quiet for Cliff. "I'm the opposite. I love it piping hot." He raised an eyebrow at her.

Rob took a seat at the table and so did Julia. She was determined to learn something about him since he always diverted the conversation away from himself. She thought it better to stay away from the topic of his dissolving marriage.

"How is it that you got stuck hauling your cousin's furniture across the country and she didn't drive with you?"

"I actually volunteered. I love driving. I find it very Zen. I've made the trip several times. With her pets, it was easier for everyone if I just did it. That's what families do."

She was amazed at how cheerful he was even though

his marriage was breaking up and he had to be tired from the trip. "What's your family like?" she asked.

"They're fun. We're pretty close. We all live in the area. You remember meeting them at that gig?"

"Oh yeah, we had a great time." Julia had met his mother Arlene, whom he had been calling Leenie since he was a child, and his sister Carla. They'd entertained each other throughout the evening.

"We used to hang out a lot. I've seen less of them since I've been with Camille. She doesn't feel the same way about them as I do. She calls them the out-laws instead of the in-laws." Rob laughed.

"I call mine the out-laws, too, but having met your mother, I can honestly say it's for very different reasons. Your mother and sister are fun and happy people. Cliff's parents are not shy about the fact that they don't like me at all. Not one bit."

"You must be exaggerating." Rob looked shocked. "You're like the perfect daughter-in-law."

"Are you kidding? They don't like that I have a job. They'd prefer I stay home and pop out babies. They don't respect that I don't want children. Never have."

"But they can't expect everyone to do that," Rob said. "Everyone has a choice."

"Yes, as long as it's the same as theirs. But enough about them. I think I hear Cliff." Julia heard him padding down the stairs. "I'll get the eggs going."

Cliff came into the kitchen wearing his customary uniform of sweatpants and a polar fleece sweatshirt. "What'd you have there?"

"Blueberry pancakes with bacon and eggs."

"My favorite breakfast. Thanks, Boo." Cliff sat down at the table. "Can I get a cup of coffee?" Julia was already pouring one for him.

Rob jumped up. "Are you sure I can't help?"

"Don't worry about it, Rob. Julia likes doing it all herself." Cliff settled deeper into the chair while Julia heated the syrup and stirred the eggs.

Rob caught her eye. Was that sympathy? Or something else?

Chapter 11

"Where's Cliff?" Rob asked as Julia did the dishes.

"I don't know. He disappears into his office a lot. He's probably checking on the status of his latest auditions."

"Oh right. He told me about his new concept for voice-over work. That's cool." Julia just looked at him. "Well, I should be heading out. It's about time I get over to West Seattle and start unpacking. And you need to get on with your holiday."

Holiday? Oh, right. It was New Year's Eve today.

Rob went upstairs to get his bag and came down carrying the dirty sheets and his damp towel. "Would you like me to put these in the washing machine? I should've put them in there first thing this morning. Sorry to leave you with a mess."

"Throw 'em on the floor in the laundry room. Thanks." Julia stared after him as he headed out. *A guy who cleans up after himself. Wow.*

"Thanks for dinner and breakfast and letting me stay here last night."

"You're welcome. Happy unloading." Julia opened the

door. The two of them stood there looking at each other. She was sorry to see him go.

She snapped back to reality and stepped away from the open door so he could leave. She stared at the closed door for a few extra seconds before squaring her shoulders and going in search of Cliff.

"WOULD you like a glass of wine? I just opened a bottle."

"Drinking in the middle of the day?" Julia ignored the judgy tone.

"I thought a glass of wine sounded good, and since you like to stay home and avoid the drunk drivers on New Year's Eve, what's the harm?"

He took the wine from her as she poured a second glass. "What do you want to do this afternoon before you make dinner and we watch the fireworks on TV?" he asked.

"Cliff, we have to talk." She chastised herself for starting the conversation with such a cliché, but it was too late now.

"What've I done this time?" He rolled his eyes.

"It's what you haven't done," Julia said, her voice soft and her tone as non-judgmental as she could manage. "I've asked you to get a job about a thousand times and you haven't done it."

"Don't start that again. You know I've been trying. Do we have to do this now? On New Year's Eve, when I just got back from a trip?"

"I'm afraid so," Julia continued. "It's weighing on me that you don't have a job. You're running through money and trying to build new skills, but nothing comes of it. I'm trying to be a supportive wife, but we're coming up on the ten-year anniversary of you being unemployed."

"I had a job for a few months!"

"Yes, I know, but you quit. Two years ago!" She gathered her courage for what came next. "I think we should take a break."

Cliff's face went white. He put his wine down. "What do you mean by a break? I was just gone for a week. I feel a lot better now."

"I mean a break, as in we separate. I've done you a disservice by making it easy to be unemployed. I keep thinking you'll go back to work on your own, but after almost ten years, I think you need a push to get back on your feet."

Cliff just looked at her like he was in shock. "Why is this happening so suddenly? Things seem fine to me."

"Of course they seem fine to you. I'm doing all the work." She gentled her tone. "I had a lot of time to think while you were gone, and I concluded that I'm enabling your lifestyle. If we go on like this, I'm afraid you'll never recover."

"Recover from what? You make it sound like I have a disease or something."

"Recover from this pattern of not working, staying at home. Spending money you didn't make. Wasting your brain and your time. I think it's eating away at your confidence."

"I don't have a confidence issue! I have an issue with idiots who won't hire me and pay me what I'm worth." Cliff drank more wine.

"Cliff, I don't see how quitting the contracting job I got you at LampLight, not finding another one, and spending money on starting multiple new careers that don't pan out lead to you having a fulfilling career." She took a sip of wine to calm her nerves. "I want to break that pattern. I've become your caretaker instead of your partner. You're too reliant on me."

"No, I'm not. My life is full of things. You know I've tried and tried to get a job. You want me to be a clerk at a bookstore making fourteen dollars an hour just so you can tell people I'm employed?"

Julia couldn't hold back her eye roll. "It's not for other people. It's for us."

"I've just started the voiceover work. Maybe it'll take off!"

"I'm tired of waiting. You aren't contributing financially. It's not fair to me. Our original goal of retiring at forty is now at least ten years away."

"Fair? We can talk about fair. You made me move out here in the first place for your dumb job. How was I supposed to know there weren't any jobs for me in Seattle?"

"You're being ridiculous. Hundreds of thousands of people have jobs here, Cliff, and if you recall, you'd already been out of work for three years before we moved."

"Ridiculous? I'm being ridiculous? You're the one threatening to end our relationship over a job!"

"It's not just about a job. It's about you contributing to this relationship financially, emotionally, and physically. I haven't exactly been feeling emotionally supported lately either. You won't even talk about our sexual issues."

Cliff just looked at her. "So now you're saying you're cutting me off because I don't bang you enough? That's just because we've been married so long. Everyone gets into the no-sex zone after a few years."

Julia paused to absorb his anger. She counted to five in her head. "I'm not suggesting anything permanent. Once you get a job and prove you can contribute more to our relationship, we would get back together."

Cliff got up and paced to the window, then turned to look back at her. "Maybe you just need a break from work."

"No, Cliff. I need a break from us. I'm also hoping that being apart will rekindle our sex life. I've tried to come to terms with your lack of a sex drive, but it's difficult."

Silence hung in the air for several seconds. Something she couldn't identify flashed across Cliff's face. He slumped back onto the couch. "There's something I should tell you."

Is he gay? She knew she shouldn't think that about her husband and was instantly ashamed it was her first thought.

"I have a sex drive," he said. "In fact, I have a really strong sex drive." Julia chose not to interrupt even though ten questions exploded in her head. "The truth is I have video sex every day." He fixed his gaze on his wine glass instead of her.

Julia felt relieved, happy to hear Cliff did still feel a spark. She was hopeful in a way she hadn't been all week that they could fix their sex issue. "I don't mind that you whack off to porn – I mean, porn isn't my thing, but if that works for you, we can watch it together. At least we could try it!"

"It's not porn." He sounded insulted. "It's video sex."

"Sorry." Julia tapped on her forehead. "Not computing."

"There's a group of people I met online. We like rough stuff, and I would never want you to see that."

Julia didn't know what "rough stuff" was. And she didn't understand why he'd lock her out of his sexual experiences. A knot formed in her chest as she tried to fit the pieces of the story together. "You mean like you're cheating on me with other people via video?"

"It's not cheating because there's no actual physical contact, but yeah, we all get off together."

Understanding blossomed in Julia's head. "Let me get this straight. For the last several years, you've refused to have sex with me – your wife – but you're whacking off with your online friends? Every day? Sounds like cheating to me. And even if it isn't, yuck."

"It's not like that. It's just that vanilla sex isn't a turn on for me anymore." He sounded nonchalant, like Julia should be able to understand because it was so simple. "It's not about you. To get turned on, I watch some pretty hard-core stuff."

"We stopped having sex years ago. How long has this been going on, Cliff?"

He rubbed his palms against his sweatpants. Julia watched him open and close his fingers a couple of times. "Actually, to be honest, since before we were together. I used to go into New York City and get porn in Times Square even before I knew you. And then it morphed into video play."

Julia reached for her wine glass. Her hand was shaking, a clear sign her brain was gearing up for a rare burst of anger. The conversation about jumpstarting Cliff's evolution had turned into exposing an eighteen-year-old secret.

She took a bracing breath. "After all the conversations we've had about sex that ended with you saying you just weren't interested anymore – years of making me feel unwanted, ugly, and unattractive – you were just lying to me?"

Cliff's wine glass made a tiny clink as he set it down on the table. He wouldn't meet her eyes.

Julia took another deep breath. "All this time, the real

reason you don't want to have sex doesn't have anything to do with me?" Her blood began to boil because she already knew the answer. She felt the flush starting in her stomach creep upward.

"It's not like that." He actually sounded exasperated! "It's like a reward. Like, I do it after I work out. You're glad I want to be in better shape, aren't you?"

She felt the tightness in her jaw as her teeth clenched. "Don't you dare try to turn this into something positive like being healthier. You sacrificed our sex life for videos and lying!"

"No. I didn't want to have sex with you long before I started working out." Cliff's face showed he knew he'd said the wrong thing. "I mean, um, er, we had problems before that…"

Everything made sense to Julia in that instant. Here was the explanation for why Cliff couldn't account for what he did all day, why he didn't have the drive to get a job.

The shock of realization replaced the sympathy she felt toward him.

It left no room in her brain for the guilt she carried and the story she'd told herself that she had created this situation.

Cliff looked panicked. "I knew if I told you about the porn, you'd be mad. That's why I never told you."

"You think I'm angry about the porn?" Julia's eyes flashed with heat. "I don't care about that. What I care about is trust." She rubbed her forehead with her fingertips.

"Trust? I don't understand what trust has to do with it." Cliff looked confused.

"I trusted you were being honest with me. But instead, it turns out that protecting yourself from embarrassment and not confronting the real problems are more important to you than having a healthy relationship with me. For years and years and years! That's what I mean by trust."

"I love you. I don't know why you're making such a big deal out of this."

Julia felt a crack in her head, like a shattering of their connection into pieces so small they couldn't be put back together. "You know what, Cliff? I want you to get out." She hardly recognized the low, calm voice that came out of her. "I thought I'd be the one to stay in a hotel for a couple of weeks, but this conversation took a very unexpected turn. You have to leave."

"But where will I go?" His incredulity was evident in his tone.

"A hotel? Back to your parents? A friend's house? I don't care. Just not here."

"I'm sorry. I'm so sorry! I've been keeping this to myself for so long. I didn't know what to do. I don't want to move out." Tears started to slide down his face.

"This is a complete break of trust. I've been carrying you in a relationship that feels a lot more like mother and son than a married relationship of equals. You just placed the last straw on the camel's back and now everything is broken." Julia's own tears trickled down her cheeks.

"No. I mean… I mean," he stammered.

"There's nothing you can say, Cliff. I want you out of here. Now."

He blinked. The reality of the situation seemed to be sinking in. "Boo, listen. I'll go to a hotel and let you have some space. But I want us to stay together. I want to work things out. I understand why you're angry. I want to fix this. Please don't give up on me."

"I'll try not to." Julia heard the lack of conviction in her tone and felt it in her heart. She wondered if she was capable of rebuilding such badly broken trust. But they had been friends for over eighteen years. "I'll try," she repeated with more certainty.

⊏═⊐

WHAT A WAY TO *spend New Year's Eve*, she thought. She went through the motions of cleaning up the kitchen and making sure Selah had gone outside to do her business. Everything was a blur. Her whole body was numb with betrayal. She heard Cliff puttering in other parts of the house and hated every noise. He had to leave. Period.

Julia moved to the guest room that night. She couldn't stand the idea of sleeping in the same bed as Cliff. She felt betrayed and angry. She was horrified he'd been lying to her while she had been punishing herself for not being attractive to him anymore, not doing enough to help him.

She hoped a night of sleep would help her get a better perspective on the situation. Perhaps she would see it differently in the morning.

Finally, she poured herself a glass of wine, went to the guest room, shut the door and turned on the TV. "New year, new life," she said out loud as she toasted the screen with her last sip and the ball dropped in Times Square.

Chapter 12

Julia's head ached, but it wasn't from over-indulging on New Year's Eve. Her restless night had not dulled any of the pain. It was only 4:30AM. After tossing and turning for almost an hour, she gave up.

The words "new year, new life" echoed in her head as she showered in the guest bathroom. She wanted to wash off all the negativity from the conversation the night before.

She looked down at the bathroom counter where she had set her engagement and wedding rings before going to bed. It was Cliff's grandmother's engagement ring, and Julia had always hated the huge two-carat diamond. She knew many women would kill for that ring, but she found it gaudy and attention-grabbing.

She left it where it was on the edge of the sink, the satisfaction of the small rebellion warming her.

Julia tiptoed into her home office and fired up her computer to write up a financial separation agreement. She thought about the romance novels she read where the women do stupid things when breaking up with their partners resulting in a lot of heartache and upset, particularly about money. She didn't want that to happen to her. She wanted financial separation and protection in case he went crazy.

They had fully combined finances. It had seemed logical to pool their resources when they had similar salaries years before.

Previously, she didn't think she could bear the conversation about separating their finances and giving him an allowance. It would have been degrading for him, and painful for her to treat him like an employee. But now she had to do it.

She tapped away on her laptop, keeping her emotions in check, and focusing on the task at hand. She offered him twenty thousand dollars to get him started. He had to open new bank accounts, and she would remove him from hers. She knew there would be a discussion about how to divide up the assets, but this would be enough to set him up in an apartment and pay for his first few months. She would take him off her bank accounts as soon as they opened after the holiday.

As she printed out the agreement for him to review and sign, she was struck by how quickly things had progressed. She was calm and orderly. She had done some research and laid out the steps in her mind. Protect the money, move him out, get a divorce, and move on.

She wondered if she was being overly harsh about the video sex. Why hadn't she seen the signs earlier? Why had he kept it from her for so long? Was she so hard to talk to about problems? People at work seemed to bring their issues to her all the time. Why wouldn't her husband?

She went around and around in her head examining her emotions and trying to find a different outcome. Eighteen years was a long time to just end in one night. But the break in trust was monumental. *Or, was she just using that as an excuse?* Was she looking for things she could be mad at so she could be the innocent party?

After a few minutes of circular thinking, she kept coming back to him preferring to stay home and jack-off rather than being a partner in their relationship. The video sex was just another example of his selfishness. And selfishness was bad.

Whatever the reason, and even if she was over-reacting, she was very sure her marriage was over.

▭

"MORNING," Cliff said.

She was eating a bowl of oatmeal when Cliff came into the kitchen.

"Morning," she replied, keeping her face purposefully bland.

"You made coffee?" he asked.

"Yep, there's some left if you'd like it." She resisted the urge to get up and get it for him like she usually did. Another small rebellion.

He poured himself a cup and joined her at the table. "What's that?" he asked, pointing to the folder in front of her.

"It's a financial separation agreement." She kept her tone civil.

"You were serious? We're really going to break up?"

"Yes. You profoundly hurt my feelings and broke my trust." Her tone was flat. She did not look at him.

"Why do we need to separate finances?" Cliff's panic-infused tone had returned.

"You need to stand on your own two feet and stop

spending money you didn't earn." Her patience for being nice was used up.

"That's a low blow, don't you think?" he shot back. "I've been trying to get back to work for years. And it was my money that paid the downpayment on our first house."

He had a point, but she had been paying the mortgage for almost ten years without contributions from him. She thought that evened things out. Julia was not going to repeat last night's argument, or the countless other times she had implored him to get a job. She bit back her retorts.

"I think this is fair. I'll give you twenty thousand to get started. That'll give you enough to get an apartment, pay first and last month's rent, and cover living expenses for a couple of months."

"Fair? What's fair about putting me on an allowance?" His face flushed red.

"Really? Come on, Cliff. What's fair about me carrying you for ten years? Even more than the sex stuff, that's the basic point of my decision to end this. You have to become a productive member of society, and as long as I'm footing the bill, I don't think you will."

"Fine. Let me know when you're calm enough to have a real conversation about this."

You passive aggressive fuck, Julia thought. "Oh, I'm very calm. The picture of calm. A veritable fountain of calm."

He slapped his hands on the kitchen table making Julia flinch. "I'm tired of arguing." He shoved his chair away from the table and stormed out.

You're tired? she thought. She couldn't stop the incredulous chuckle and shake of her head.

SINCE NEW YEAR'S Day was a Tuesday this year, Julia had a short week at work. Planning ahead, she had moved three days of work attire to the guest room closet. As she pulled the second outfit off the rack to get ready for work, a fresh wave of anger rolled through her. If he wasn't gone by Friday, she would have to transfer more clothes. Why couldn't he just leave?

Julia was delighted Selah had chosen to sleep in the guest room with her. Julia crouched to give her some love and scratched Selah behind the ears just like she liked.

As she left the guest room, Julia could hear Cliff snoring. *Lazy sack of shit.*

Whoa. Tone it down, girl, she told herself. They were not speaking except to grunt at each other in the hallways or kitchen when they passed one another. She should do a better job of controlling her anger. She had work to do.

Chapter 13

Julia juggled the post-holiday business planning season with execution of Operation Fix-It. Her trip to LA was scheduled and her slides were ready to go. She would mostly be listening, but liked to be extra prepared with slides just in case they asked her for details.

"Earth to Julia."

Julia's attention snapped to Kate who was standing at her door. "Oh hey, Kate. Do we have a meeting now?" Julia felt a tinge of panic.

"No, I just stopped by to ask a question. You were a million miles away. Is everything okay, J-Money?"

"Of course. Just getting back into the swing of things after the holidays. Did you have a good break?"

"Let's just say I won't be going back to Chicago for a while."

"That sounds tough. Are you okay?"

"Yeah. Thanks for asking. I have a work question. Remember that ad agency that said they would walk because we didn't give them what they wanted by the end of the calendar year? Well, they're back. Check out what they want now."

Julia and Kate put their heads together to review the deal.

HALF THE COMPANY was still on break. Her meetings ended early. Even with Cliff there, she was more productive in her home office because people couldn't just stop by and interrupt her. It was nice to commute home when it was still light out. Maybe Cliff would surprise her and be out apartment hunting instead of being at the house.

His car was in the driveway. She found Cliff on the sofa watching television. She braced herself for the coming confrontation as she hung her jacket in the closet.

"Hey there," Julia said. "Any news?"

"No. Why are you home so early?"

She ignored his question. "Have you looked at apartments?"

"No."

"Did you look into getting a job?"

"No."

"Cliff, I'm serious about this. You have to move out! I gave you your start-up money. Have you at least deposited the check?"

"Yes. I opened a new account." He had a little too much pride in his voice. He wanted praise for doing something small because it required effort on his part. Julia looked away so he wouldn't see her eye roll. She didn't ask him to congratulate her when she took him off her account.

"Thanks for getting that done," she managed to say calmly. "But you have to find a place. I can't wrap my head around what's next for us while you're still here. I feel betrayed. I need space to get over the hurt. And you need to get a job."

"I heard you the first twelve times. I don't know what to do or how to do it," Cliff lamented.

"Well, I would think the first step would be to give Lucas a call and see if you can get your old job back. If you recall, you quit. He didn't fire you."

"I don't want to go back there," Cliff yelled. "That work is beneath me."

"I'm so tired of that old line! You aren't a high-powered executive anymore. I don't think getting the perfect job is the best attitude right now versus getting any job. It'd be easy to get that one back, and it's easier to get a job when you have a job. Will you please call Lucas?"

Cliff shrugged. "I'll email him. I don't want to talk to him."

Julia tried to be glad about this little spark of hope and progress. She dropped the subject and went to change out of her work clothes.

CLIFF POKED his head into Julia's home office. "I just got my shitty job back. It turns out they need people, and they offered me more money. With overtime, I could rake in about eighty big ones a year."

"Great news. I know you don't love that job, but that's good money."

"I start Monday. I'm heading out to buy a new laptop."

She should have felt better. She should have been glad he was employed again.

Instead, she was angry. Angry because now she had even more proof he had wasted the last two years since he quit that job, making no money when all along he could have been bringing in over eighty thousand dollars a year. All it took was one email and he was back in.

Julia sighed, saddened to feel that even though he now had gainful employment, it wasn't enough to make her feel good about him again. At least it made it possible for Cliff to move out.

She tried to remain positive and nurture what was left of their relationship. Julia knew she didn't want to be with Cliff anymore, but she also believed they would stay friends. She couldn't picture her future without Cliff in it. So much history there.

CLIFF CAME HOME from the store with his new laptop in tow. She could hear him come up the stairs as she continued working in her office. He stopped by her door on his way to his home office across the hall, or what she now thought of as his masturbation station.

"Hey, the band will be here in a half hour," Cliff reminded her. "Can you get the food and drinks ready? I would, but I'll be busy setting up my new computer."

Julia gritted her teeth. "Sure."

"Oh, and Boo, could we not tell them about our situation yet? I don't want to upset them or answer a lot of questions or make them think we wouldn't be able to rehearse here."

Julia was enraged he was asking her to wait on his band and assumed they could keep practicing at the house. "Okay," she stammered. "Shame to make *them* uncomfortable."

"Thanks."

He appeared to have missed her sarcasm.

Chapter 14

Operation Fix-It was getting positive attention. Even Jeff mentioned he had heard about her listening tour and thought it was a good idea. Of course, he had smirked at her when he said it, but she would take the small successes. It would be a good update for Blane in their upcoming one on one.

Julia headed to her boss' office for their monthly meeting. "Hey Julia, come on in." He motioned to her to take a seat. His office was about three times the size of hers, but the decorating left a bit to be desired. Two framed pictures, one of his wife and one of his two teenaged children. "How's January treating you so far?" he asked.

"Good." She lied. No reason to involve him in her personal drama. She didn't want his sympathy or worse, have him think her brain wasn't dedicated to her job because of personal distractions. "I'm looking forward to my trip to Los Angeles next week as the start of my listening tour to gather feedback from sales. Jeff and his team are onboard." Okay, that was a slight fib, but Jeff had told her he was supportive.

"That's great." Blane leaned back in his chair, his white shirt straining over his belly. "That was a rough meeting before the holidays. I get what you're trying to do. We need changes. But Jeff's in a tough spot. He's under a ton of pressure to make his revenue goal, so go easy on him."

"Of course." It hurt to suppress her rage at the unfairness. They all had difficult, high- pressure jobs. Why did Jeff get all the sympathy? "I leaned into the feedback and have changed my approach."

He nodded at her. "You're being so polished. I know you must be pissed. I would be."

She was shocked, in a good way. Maybe he saw more than he let on. "I'm good, Blane. Trying hard to make a big, positive impact and get that promotion we discussed when I took the role."

"That interaction with Jeff was definitely a setback. You need his endorsement to get that promo. I'm interested to see how much damage control you can do by our quarterly leadership team meeting in New York in March." He smiled warmly, like he was trying to be encouraging. "I'm rooting for you."

Rooting for her? Blane was her boss, for fuck's sake. He had the power to promote her. He could overrule Jeff. "Working on it." She hoped her smile hid the dagger behind it.

"Let me know if I can help in any way."

Several ways Blane could help flashed through her mind. Tell Jeff to back off. Give her that promotion. Give her a raise. Support her in a meeting instead of shutting her down. Help her implement her changes. Give her more people so she could get more done. "Thanks Blane. Appreciate it." Julia remembered Dave's words. *As long as Blane is around, you're safe.* She couldn't afford to alienate Blane, too. And honesty would certainly do that.

Julia dragged herself back to her office to finish her meetings for the day. She was drained. Did she have the energy to keep fighting the good fight at work and resolve her relationship issues with Cliff? How much could she take before she cracked? Was it worth the pain and work to get the promotion, or should she give up now? What if Cliff put up a fight?

She was drowning.

Stop with the self-pity, Julia commanded herself. *Get back in there.* She squared her shoulders and held her head up high. *If you don't have to work hard for it, it isn't worth having.*

SHE FOUND Cliff in the kitchen when she got home.

"I got an apartment."

"Oh, that's great, Cliff." A wave of relief washed through her. "Thanks for taking care of that."

"It's right at the bottom of the hill, just five minutes from here. I figured I should stay close since this is temporary. I got a six-month lease which is the shortest amount of time they allow."

"When are you moving in?" She didn't care if she sounded callous. She wanted him out. And he wasn't coming back.

"It's available now. The only problem is I'm going mountain biking tomorrow with Rob, and I have a voice over skills class on Sunday, so I don't have a lot of time to move my stuff."

"Oh, I can take care of a lot of the set-up for you." It was a knee jerk reaction. She could have slapped herself. *Idiot.*

Cliff put his hands on his hips and looked around the room. "I guess I need to buy new furniture."

"Or, you could rent furniture until you know where you'll be permanently. You'd get it immediately." She didn't want anything stopping him from moving out.

"Oh right. I might be back here and then we'd have extra furniture." *Well that backfired.* She was just trying to save money and time. "But where do I rent furniture?"

"Why don't you try Rent-A-Room? Rachel used them when she had to wait for her stuff to arrive from London."

"Good idea. I'm going to check out their website now." He headed upstairs.

Julia just sighed. How had he been reduced to a child who couldn't figure things out for himself? Where had that up-and-coming executive gone? And why had she agreed to help him? She had to break the pattern!

▭

WHILE CLIFF WAS off on his mountain bike ride with Rob and a few other riding buddies, Julia outfitted his place. *Anything to get him out of my house,* she thought. *This is actually helping me more than him.*

She was wadding up the packaging from the new bedding she purchased, washed, and put on the bed when it hit her. She was fooling herself.

She knew her behavior was self-destructive. Lesley's words echoed in her head. *I am with who he is now, not who he was.*

What if she put the work in to break out of the pattern and still didn't like who he was now? She didn't miss him. She didn't crave his company. *I just don't like him anymore,* she finally admitted. Her next feeling was guilt. Guilt for kicking him out. Guilt for not doing more to help him.

Just stop it! She chided herself for the eightieth time.

She promised herself this was the end. She would not

let guilt motivate her to help him in the future. She would leave him no choice but to help himself. Her grand gesture of setting up his apartment was her way of saying goodbye to her old life. And to him. "New year, new life," she said to his perfectly appointed apartment.

JULIA WENT HOME to accomplish a few of her own chores. She opened her online bill paying system and began paying her bills. She came across a few large charges on her credit card and some checks she didn't write – an apartment security deposit, two months of rent and a six-month payment for the rental furniture.

She double checked that he was no longer on her accounts and noted he had snuck the charges in during the processing window before the changes took effect.

It added insult to injury that her muscles ached from setting up his apartment only to find out he used her money rather than making a dent in the twenty thousand dollars she had given to him for that purpose.

She gave herself a second lecture of the day. Enough with the enabling! Would she never learn?

She got a call from Cliff around five saying he was on his way to the apartment and he was going to stay there that night.

Good, she thought. He had started his new life. She needed to start hers.

Chapter 15

On Monday evening, Julia rang the doorbell at Cliff's apartment and waited for him to answer the door. He had agreed to watch Selah the following day and then take her to Doggie Day Care on Wednesday. If her flight home from LA was on time, Julia would be able to pick Selah up at Cliff's Wednesday evening.

She couldn't remember the last time she had knocked on a locked door when Cliff was on the other side – probably eighteen years!

While she waited, she looked around the apartment complex. Units were arranged in four apartments per two story building, and she counted five buildings within sight. Her bar for apartments was low given her time in New York City, but this one was pretty nice. It was freshly painted, and updates were being made to the pool house.

She heard the locks click as he opened the dead bolt and the doorknob. "Hi," he said, looking awkward.

"Hi. Did you order a dog?"

"Want to come in?" No acknowledgement of her attempt at humor.

"Sure." Selah held back outside the door like she didn't want to go into the apartment. Cliff tried to entice her by opening the door wider.

"Hello Selah." Cliff knelt down to give her a scratch behind the ears.

That was all the encouragement Selah needed, and she was through the door and flopped on her new bed. Julia was glad she had prepped Cliff's apartment for her dog.

"Would you like to stay for a drink?"

"No, thanks. I have to wake up way before sunrise tomorrow to head to the airport. I should get home." She could have kicked herself for mentioning home, as it had been his home, too, until a couple of days before.

"Okay, well, have a good trip."

"Thanks. And thanks for taking See-Dog for two nights." She headed for the door.

Selah raced to the door and tried to go with her. Cliff held her collar as Julia slipped out. Her heart broke a bit at Selah's cry on the other side of the door.

GLARING at her alarm clock early the next morning as it blared music at her, Julia waited for a moment for Selah to come over to say good morning. It took a second for her to remember she was alone. It was weird waking up alone. She laughed when she realized she missed the dog's morning greeting more than Cliff's.

After a thankfully uneventful flight and cab ride, she arrived at the sleek Los Angeles office with plenty of time to grab some lunch and get to her meeting. She set up her notes file and double-checked the acceptances for the first meeting. Nine people had accepted, which meant she would probably get about seven.

She looked up from her laptop when the door opened. It was Dave, looking radiant as usual in another tailored silk suit. This time he sported a yellow and light blue pocket square.

"Hey, I heard you were in town," he said.

"Yep. Executing Phase One of Operation Fix-It."

"Operation Fix-It?"

"That's right. Fixing what happened in the leadership team meeting in December. I'm hanging out with the Sales team to build credibility and trust." Julia closed her laptop to avoid distractions. "Phase One is a Listening Tour where I show up and get yelled at for a few hours. Then, within two weeks, I'll follow-up on key action items and show I'm listening and I care about their input. In Phase Two, I'll be able to implement the changes. If I'm able to keep it up for a couple of months, I'll win credibility with the salespeople which will make it easier to get my policy changes through and adopted."

"Wow, I'm impressed. So you chose to stay."

"Yep. Jeff will have no choice but to work with me again due to the groundswell of respect, love, and support from his team." Julia beamed at him, making a heart shape with her hands.

"That's all well and good, but it sounds like a lot of work."

"Oh, it is," Julia agreed. "But join me in my fantasy-land for a moment. I have a great team, and we will do this!"

"I don't envy you," Dave said. "But thanks for taking my feedback to heart and doing something about it. We need changes around here to keep this business growing."

"Thanks, Dave," Julia said. "If you hear any scream-ing, come back in."

"Will it be you screaming or the salespeople?"

"Probably both." They shared a laugh before Dave slipped out of the conference room.

AT TWELVE-FIFTY, the first few people started filing in. By one, she had quorum.

"Hello, I'm Julia Winters, and I lead the Pricing Excellence Team. Now, I know you're probably thinking that's a dumb name for a team, because who would want to be on the Pricing Crappiness team, but that's the team name I inherited when I took this job."

The attendees laughed. She was off to a good start.

"I joined LampLight six years ago and used to be an Industry Analyst in the pricing space. I advised other companies how to set, manage, and enforce prices. I would love your input on what's working and what isn't." Julia looked meaningfully at the crowd. "I'd like to start with introductions. Would you kick us off?" Julia looked at the person closest to her.

The introductions showed there was a great cross-section of sellers from the largest accounts. *Perfect.* "Let's dive in. I'm here because I want to hear your feedback on how the pricing team is doing. I have a few questions I can ask, but if someone wants to bring something up, I'm all ears."

About three beats passed before multiple people all spoke at once.

"Why don't you approve more discounts?" Darcy from inside sales asked.

"Why does it take so long for your team to respond to our questions?" Henry from the strategic accounts team called out.

"Why does your team have to make everything so difficult?" Karthick from growth accounts yelled loudly enough to be heard over the first two.

Julia patiently answered each question. She wasn't learning anything new, but she diligently took notes and asked follow-up questions about how her team could improve.

After about thirty minutes, one of the more senior salespeople asked, "What're you going to do about all this?"

"Nancy, I have a lot of ideas, but I'm here to listen. My team needs your input. As my nursery schoolteacher used to tell me, I have two ears and just one mouth so I should listen twice as much as I talk." Julia paused for a laugh from the group.

"I want answers." Nancy's voice carried some heat.

"Okay, with permission from the group, I can share some ideas." Julia looked around the room for confirmation. She saw lots of nodding which meant she had exhausted their first round of complaints. *Go time.*

"Here are three things I'd like to do immediately. Two will make your lives easier and one will be harder. I'll make up for it by creating a new field empowerment guideline so managers can approve more discounts themselves."

"I want to hear about that," Nancy said as others nodded.

"Okay then, here we go." Julia explained her first set of recommendations.

The ninety-minute meeting flew by. With five minutes left, Julia summarized the action items and asked for any closing comments.

"I've been with LampLight for three years," said Kenny, an inside sales rep, "and I've never met anyone from your team in person before. Please don't let the fact that we yelled at you mean you won't come back."

Julia laughed. *She was creating allies!* "No, of course not. There's a lot of frustration across our teams, and I want to deal with it head-on. I appreciate your honesty and passion."

"I thought this was going to be boring," Nancy said, "but I learned a lot and you made it fun. It was kind of like edu-tainment." Everyone laughed.

"Thanks for attending everyone. Please keep the feedback coming. You know where to find me if you have more ideas. My team and I look forward to seeing you in person again."

Julia had scheduled a thirty-minute break for herself to re-charge and check her email before the next group came in. So many people wanted to talk to her one on one that she missed the break.

She snagged a granola bar from her computer bag to keep her energy up for the next meeting. The second meeting mirrored the first. Yelling was followed by a collaborative discussion followed by an apology and a request for more meetings.

Julia jumped on a deal review call at 5:00 after ushering out the last happy meeting attendee. One more meeting and she was free for the evening.

She slogged through the open deals with the team, approving some, providing alternate recommendations for others, and giving her team a pep talk that Operation Fix-It would work and they should keep holding the line on discounting and policies. They listened.

"Good luck tomorrow, boss." Kate sounded elated after getting approval from Julia on the final details of the gnarly deal that had started before the holidays. "We're all with you."

"But glad we aren't actually with you in person for the screaming," Jamie, the senior inventory manager added with a laugh. Julia loved that her team was in a good place and could laugh together while getting their important work done.

⊏⊐

THE ROOM WAS at maximum capacity by the third and final listening session the next morning. The brave attendees of the first meeting spread the word and salespeople who hadn't been invited poked their heads in and asked to join. Julia even saw Dave sneak in to catch the last half hour.

He politely waited his turn after all of the sellers had thanked Julia for coming.

"You weren't kidding." Dave flashed his toothy grin. "You had them eating out of your hand. You are the Pricing Goddess."

"I guess that's better than being the Pricing Bitch, isn't it?" Julia kept her tone jokey, but her comment hit the target as intended.

"Aww, don't be like that. I told you that for your own good and look how you converted it into a major stakeholder-building opportunity!"

Julia inwardly winced since it sounded a bit like he was taking credit, but she reminded herself that he was a friend, and she needed him in her corner. "Thanks."

"How can I help?"

"It wouldn't hurt if you could tell Blane the meetings are going well. Jeff already knows, but some love from above would help. I appreciate it."

"Consider it done, Goddess." Dave bowed with a lofty flourish of his hand before backing out of the room.

Operation Fix-It was working.

———

JULIA TEXTED Cliff as she rolled her suitcase across the skybridge to her car to let him know she was on time to pick up Selah.

Cliff answered her knock and asked her in. "It's nice to see you. Want to come in for a drink?"

Julia didn't know what to say. She just wanted to get her dog and go home, but Cliff had done her a favor, so she should be nice to him.

"A cup of tea would be great." She sat at his kitchen table as Selah brought her a toy so they could play tug of war.

"How's work?" she asked Cliff, scratching Selah behind the ears. Julia flinched at her own question, wishing she'd been a little more sensitive and asked about something less fraught.

"It's going well. A lot of people have turned over from when I was there before, but a few buddies are still around, like Eddy." Cliff made two cups of tea and brought them to the table.

"That's cool. Wasn't he renovating a house?"

"Yep, and he and Jonah got married."

"He was nice when we met him. I hope they're happy."

"They seem to be, but you know how things change." He sounded angry.

"Maybe it won't for them." The mood turned awkward.

Cliff was the first to speak again. "How did we get here, Jules? Can we go back to the way things were? Have I been punished long enough?"

Shocked he wanted to have this discussion, Julia tried to be understanding. "How have you been punished?"

"You kicked me out. But I got a job, I proved I could

live by myself, and now I understand I left too much for you to do. I'll be better now. When can I come home?"

He had only been out of the house for a few days. And he thought he had proved he could live by himself? *Poor Cliff*. He didn't get it. Without trust, there was no getting back together. Setting up his apartment showed Julia she had a lot of work to do to break out of her caretaking pattern, and she didn't think he was worth the investment. Cliff's secret sex problem had unplugged life support on an already sick relationship. Their marriage was dead.

"Cliff, we aren't getting back together. Aren't you tired of pretending everything's fine?"

"How can you be so cavalier about this? It's our life we're talking about."

"I'm anything but cavalier. I was very sad, and I put a lot of thought into it, but I don't think we can fix this. The best we can do is be friends, close friends, and help each other move on." Julia tried to keep it straightforward and honest.

"But I don't want to be alone," Cliff said. "I love you and I want to be with you again. I want to have our old life back. I can break the lease or sublet the apartment."

Julia took a deep breath. "I don't want our old life back. I put too much time into taking care of you. We'd have to separate our finances. It's not fair to me to continue the way we were."

"Why would we have to do that? I make so much less than you."

She couldn't help but laugh. "That's kind of the point, Cliff. I could only do it if you lived mostly on your own salary. You'd have to make your own money, support your own lifestyle, help with the house, and do lots of things you didn't want to do before. Like have a satisfying physical relationship for both of us."

"I can change. I'll be better."

"Cliff, if you could have changed, why hadn't you already done it?"

"I don't know. Because it's hard, I guess."

"And it would be hard for both of us. We collectively ignored the issues until they became insurmountable. I blame myself for smothering you. I blame you for not dealing with your job loss and sexual issues."

"Why can't we try?"

"Because I'm done trying. It's not enough that you want to change now when you're freaking out at the reality. I can't live with scaring you into changing."

"I'm not scared. Maybe I just understand the priority better now."

"I'm angry and hurt, and I'm afraid I'll punish you. Or even worse. You saw how I set up your apartment for you. I don't know if I'm capable of making you stand on your own two feet while we're together. It's too easy for me to slip back into my old ways and it's easy for you to let me. I wish I could wipe the slate clean, but I don't have it in me to start fresh."

Cliff started to cry.

Did he have to do this when she had just come from a grueling couple of days of meetings she thought, and then chastised herself for being cold.

"I'm seeing a counselor," he added. "Doesn't that show I want to change?"

"That's great. I'm happy for you."

"I think you should see one, too. Then, I'd know you're serious about figuring your side of this out," he said, regaining some of his composure.

"What do you mean, Cliff? I'm clear on what I want."

"My counselor says you're going through a phase. You'll come around and want to be with me. If you ever loved me, would you please go see a counselor and see if this is just a midlife crisis or something? Maybe you're just scared about turning forty."

After her initial flash of annoyance, Julia considered. She knew when she was overly convicted about a certain position at work, she would seek alternate opinions to test her own analysis. Why wouldn't she do it now?

"Okay, Cliff. If it'll help you get closure, I'll see a counselor." They sat at the table sipping tea, lost in their own thoughts for a few moments. "I guess I should go now." Julia spoke softly, getting up from the table and putting her cup in the dishwasher. Selah was right on her heels.

"Uh, one more thing. Band practice is tomorrow night. We can still rehearse at the house, right? I haven't told them, and we don't have another place to go."

"Fine. But don't expect me to wait on you and the band."

"Okay." He sounded defeated.

"Thanks for taking care of Selah." Julia clipped Selah's leash to her collar and walked out the door without looking back.

Chapter 16

Julia had one more meeting and an email to write before she could finish work for the day. She owed the team in Los Angeles an update about the actions she and her team were taking based on her meetings earlier in the week. It was important to follow-up and show progress so Jeff's team knew she took their feedback seriously.

True to her word, she had made an appointment with a relationship counselor and scored a same-day appointment due to a cancellation. It was a free benefit with her health plan. She wouldn't be out anything but the time, and perhaps she'd learn something. She didn't know what to expect. She figured it would be like it was in the movies with a lot of "how does that make you feel?" questions.

She shut down her laptop and headed out the door. It was a beautiful, sunny, and crystal-clear day. She was sorry she would have to spend an hour of it in a psychologist's office, as these midwinter dry, bright, and crisp days were rare in Seattle.

She chastised herself for having a bad attitude. *It might actually help.*

She turned into the driveway of the office park and looked for the counselor's office. Passing through the faux brick façade and across the gray carpet, she walked into the office and gave the receptionist her name.

"Thank you, Julia. The therapist will see you in just a few minutes."

Julia took a seat and considered the large stack of fashion and health magazines on the wood end table to her right.

"Julia? He's ready for you," the receptionist called out as she opened the door.

Julia was shown into a room that looked like a living room. She saw a soft-looking cotton covered sofa with a side table and a brass lamp. The counselor sat in an over-stuffed brown leather library chair across from it.

"Hello, I'm Doctor Ravi Malik. Please have a seat." The counselor had kind brown eyes and a gentle smile on his round face. He set a calm tone for their discussion.

"Nice to meet you, Doctor Malik." Julia sank into the plush sofa and looked at the doctor. "Okay, what would you like to know?"

"Let's start with the basics. Why are you here?"

"I broke up with my husband of fourteen years and he asked me to talk to someone before telling him it's absolutely over."

"Tell me why you want to end your fourteen-year marriage."

Julia took a deep breath. "We have a bizarre co-dependent relationship where I take care of him, and he lets me."

"I see." Doctor Malik steepled his fingers as he rested his elbows on the arms of his chair. "Tell me how you got to this place."

"We met on Wall Street when we were both on the

leadership track eighteen years ago. We got married, he got laid off a few years later, and he never went back to work. It was like his confidence was shot."

"Go on," the doctor said when Julia paused to take a breath.

"I supported him for almost ten years as he tried various training classes and careers. Then, just after Christmas when he went away for a week, I realized I was enabling his dependent lifestyle and decided to break the pattern. I asked him to move out and get his life together."

"That sounds like a good approach. Is that where you are today?"

"No, there's more." Julia raised an eyebrow. She decided to lay it all out there. "Our sex life was almost non-existent for the last several years. He refused to deal with it when I tried to talk to him about it and revealed to me on New Year's Eve that he participates in online group sex."

"When did this start?" the doctor asked in a mild tone. *Clearly, it wasn't the first time he had heard this tale,* she thought.

"I don't know," Julia admitted. "When it all came out, he told me he used to buy porn when we lived in New York City in the nineties.

"How did it make you feel when he told you that?"

Julia smiled inwardly at the question. "Like something broke inside me. I couldn't believe he hadn't shared this with me and could keep such a long-term secret from me. All the resentment of the previous ten years filled me up to the point of bursting. I told him I wanted him out of the house. I told him it was over between us."

Julia looked at the psychologist intently.

"How do you feel now?"

Julia thought for a moment. "Liberated. Free to make my own choices without him weighing me down. And I guess deep down there's guilt over hurting him. He's not in a good place and wants to get back together."

"Do you want that?"

"No. With the way I'm enjoying my newfound freedom, I don't think I have it in me to do the work necessary to rebuild the trust."

"Trust is the foundation of every solid relationship."

"I agree, which is why I want this to be over. I don't think I'd be happy with the result even if I put in the work."

"If you go into it with that attitude, it definitely won't work."

Julia didn't like where this was going. She prepared for a lecture about digging in and having a positive outlook. She braced herself, knowing that just because he said it didn't mean she had to do it. *Here it comes,* she thought.

"Julia, this one seems pretty clear to me. You're dealing with someone with an addiction problem. If he tells you it's once a day, it's probably more like two to three times a day, or even more. And if he promised to stop, he can't without help."

"Of course he promised to stop."

"You're correct in your self-diagnosis. You're enabling this behavior by supporting him. It's bad for both of you to stay in this relationship."

"Wow," Julia said. "I didn't expect you to give it to me so succinctly. It's nice to hear you agree with me."

"Why do you need someone else to tell you what you already know?" When Julia didn't answer, he continued. "You're convicted for a reason. It seems cut-and-dried to me. He's acting out of fear and promising you things he hasn't been able to do for the last ten years. He won't be able to do them now either unless you cut off the enabling behavior and he gets some help."

"That about sums it up," Julia said. *What an interesting experience.*

Doctor Malik looked at his watch. "We're twelve minutes into our time. What would you like to discuss for the next forty-eight minutes?"

He was her kind of counselor. Julia struggled to come up with anything. Then it hit her.

"Actually, there is something else I'd like to ask about. How do I stop repeating this pattern when I start dating someone new?" *When had she decided to start dating again?*

"You can start by coming to see me weekly to help you build new tools so you don't repeat the pattern."

Julia hoped her face didn't show her reaction to his marketing pitch.

He continued. "The first thing is to pick someone who has a job and can keep up with you intellectually so they don't need the extra care."

"That makes sense."

"But everyone needs care. Even if they're more self-sufficient than your husband, there are still pitfalls you can encounter by not practicing self-care."

She bristled at the term husband. "I get that, and what you're saying makes sense. Are there any guidelines for how long I should wait before I start seeing someone, I mean, to make sure it's not just a rebound thing and to get used to a new pattern?"

"There are no rules about that. Just be careful to date people who are true partners rather than the mother-child role you have with your current husband. Then all I can tell you is to have fun and enjoy it for however long it lasts, if that's two weeks or twenty years."

"It's just that simple?"

"It's just that simple. I do still think you should come

back and see me, though, as it's imperative you don't repeat the enabling behavior with anyone else."

Doctor Malik looked at Julia and waited patiently for her to respond. "I guess that's it for today then. Thank you."

"It was nice to meet you, and I hope to see you again so we can help you develop new tools for caretaking."

She shook his hand and walked out the door.

The sun was just starting to set. It was still a beautiful, clear day outside. She took a deep breath of fresh air that filled her with calm from head to toe.

New year, new life, she reminded herself.

Chapter 17

"Dinner time," Julia announced to Selah who dutifully sat before Julia delivered the goods. Julia was in an exceptionally good mood after a successful day of executing Operation Fix-It and looking forward to dinner with Melanie and Lesley so she could be out of the house during band practice.

The phone rang. Usually only her mother and telemarketers called her home line. Everyone else used her mobile number. But since she was near the phone, she glanced at the caller ID. It was Rob.

He probably wanted to know something about Cliff or band practice tonight, and she didn't feel like talking about Cliff. But, then, she remembered the way Rob always made her laugh, and she was in the mood to laugh.

"Hey Rob," she said. "Long time no talk. Are you looking for Cliff? He's out grabbing snacks for the band."

"Oh, hello." She sensed discomfort in his voice. "No. I called to talk to you. Um, I was kind of hoping I'd get your voicemail."

"Would you like me to hang up so you can call back? I won't answer." She thought she was hilarious.

"No, that's okay. Since I've got you, I'll just ask. I mean, why not, right?"

This was not the usual Rob, Julia thought. He was usually confident and funny.

She started to get nervous. Was he calling to say Cliff was dead? Julia prompted him as the awkward silence stretched more than a few seconds. "What can I do for you?"

"I was having a beer with Cliff after our last mountain bike ride, and we got to talking about you."

Oh God, here it comes, Julia thought. *A lecture about getting back together with Cliff. Great.* She rolled her eyes in preparation for a speech about how they could work it out.

She heard Rob clear his throat. "Yeah, we were talking, and I asked him if it was really over between you two." Julia waited for the punch line. She pictured Cliff crying in his beer and playing darts with Rob at a bar. At least Cliff was out and about. "He said it was all over. Is that how you see it, too?"

"Yes." Her conviction was evident in her tone. "It's definitely over." Julia wondered where he was going with this. Just making sure she knew what she was doing? She already had a professional opinion on that, and the answer was an emphatic YES. It was approaching the time to head out the door to meet the girls. "Yep, that's what I said. Rob, I don't mean to be rude, but I'm on my way out." She didn't understand what he was getting at with his questions.

"Wait. I have something to ask you." Julia heard him take a deep breath. "I think you should go out on a date with me. What do you think?"

Julia was floored. This was Cliff's friend, a member of

his band. Sweet, funny Rob who came to the house every week to chug a few beers, eat guacamole and chips, and play somewhat rough blues tunes. He was also the Rob with the hunky body, easy laugh, and great attitude about life. *Go out with him?*

"Wow. Really. Go out with you? Do people our age do that?" She tried to fill the gap so she could think. She turned the idea over in her head. He was awfully cute. But he was Cliff's friend.

It was Rob's turn to let the awkward silence stretch out. "Yes," he said. "Cliff said it's okay."

Julia's eyebrows shot up. "You and Cliff talked about it?" *Bold move.* "You asked his permission?"

"Of course," he said. "Bros before hos, as they say."

That was more like the Rob she knew. "So, I'm the ho in this particular situation?" she joked.

"No, of course not. I can't believe I said that. Well, unless you want to be the ho."

Julia laughed and set her keys back down on the counter. "Let me ask Selah. She is all-knowing." At the sound of her name, Selah looked up at Julia. "What do you think, Selah? Should I go out with your boyfriend?"

Selah stared back and thumped her tail as if to say, "Yes, I approve." But, actually, Selah thumped her tail whenever Julia looked at her. Julia realized she wanted Selah to say yes. It scared her.

"I can hear Selah's tail thumping on the floor over the phone," Rob said.

"She's easy," Julia joked, trying to get her thoughts together. "You know, Rob, I really appreciate it, but, ah, I really need to think about it, and I really need to go now." *How many times could she say "really" in the same sentence,* she wondered.

"Okay, I understand. It's a bit weird. I know it's a little

fast, too, but I just had to be sure someone didn't get to you before I had a chance." Rob didn't sound too deflated. "How about this? You think about it, and I'll check in with you tomorrow, because I'm free tomorrow night."

"Okay," Julia managed to get out. "We'll talk tomorrow."

"Don't think too much, just do it. Goodbye." He clicked off before she could even say good-bye.

"Well now. Doesn't that just kick you in the ass?" she asked Selah, who, as usual, thumped her tail in response.

▭

SHOULD *she or shouldn't she?* Rob was Cliff's friend. Julia had always enjoyed talking to him at band practice. She could admit she had an intermittent crush on him, but who wouldn't with all that flirting? Go out with him? New territory. She went back-and-forth and around and around during the seventeen-minute drive to the restaurant.

Julia checked the bar for Melanie and Lesley before grabbing a booth.

She was about halfway through her mental list of pros and cons when Melanie arrived. After exchanging hugs and compliments on each other's hair, Melanie ordered her Jack and Coke while they waited for Lesley.

"You look kind of stressed," Melanie said, folding her manicured hands on the table. "Is everything okay at work?"

"We'll talk about me later. What's new with you?"

"Work is actually the least of my worries right now. I'm in the middle of fixing a big issue that takes a crapload of energy, but I have a solid plan. I just need to execute. The jerks are out there trying to pull me down, but we're all used to that."

"There's a reason they call it work, Mel," Julia pointed her finger in the air.

"Hey Les!" they both exclaimed as she slid into the booth. Lesley's long brown hair was beautifully curled today and she was more dressed up than usual.

"Sorry I'm late," she said. "A friend tried to fix me up on a coffee date, and it turned into a therapy session. For him," she added before they could ask. "I got back to work late, and it was tough to get out."

"That's why I don't fix friends up anymore," Melanie added.

"He was one of those 'shhh, don't speak' types." Lesley made a closed mouth motion like she had a puppet on her hand. "After explaining to him why it wouldn't work out for us, I gave him a few pointers on how to be more successful next time. I wished him luck and left. Good karma points for me." Lesley ended with a flourish. "What's up with you?" She extended the "ou" in "you" so it sounded like youuuuuuuuu.

"Melanie was just telling me about a work sitch."

After several minutes of updates from her friends, Lesley looked directly at Julia. "You're being kind of quiet. That usually means something's up. So, what's up?"

"You two know me so well. I need some advice, ladies." Julia faked a serious tone. "It's about Rob."

"What's that hottie up to these days?" Melanie asked. She had sat in with Cliff and Rob's band for a few rehearsals when Stephen their singer was sick. Having attended a rehearsal or two as a trial audience, Lesley knew him, too.

"He asked me out," Julia blurted.

"What did you say?" her friends asked in unison as they leaned closer over the sticky wood table.

"I didn't answer. I told him I'd get back to him tomorrow." Julia looked at each of her friends. "I knew I needed your advice first."

Melanie shook her head of short, highlighted blond hair. "There are so many guys out there. Do you have to start with one of Cliff's friends?"

"I asked myself the same question about twelve times on the drive here. Things are tenuous between me and Cliff right now with him wanting to get back together. I don't think I should start dating so soon, especially one of his friends."

"I agree with you," Melanie said. "There are so many others out there. Pick one of them."

"I don't know." Lesley looked pensive as she picked up her margarita. "I saw you two work through that new bass line when I stopped by during band practice." She took a sip of her drink before continuing. "He got frustrated and you worked it out. That says a lot about your compatibility."

Lesley didn't miss a trick.

"You don't think it's cheating to go out on a date when you're still married, do you?"

The three of them each picked up their drinks and sat back to contemplate Julia's question. Melanie was divorced and remarried herself. She understood what Julia was going through. Lesley, on the other hand, had successfully dodged marriage.

Lesley spoke first. "No. It's over. Just because you're married according to a piece of paper doesn't mean you're married."

"I see your point, Les, but she's still married. And they just broke up a few weeks ago," Mel said. "Couldn't you wait until everything is settled with Cliff?"

"That would be very prudent." Julia leaned toward Melanie. "How long did your divorce take?"

"About six months from start to finish. We kept it pretty amicable and got through the process without a lot of fighting. Not having kids helped."

"I want it to be straightforward with Cliff. I've gotten a lawyer. I'm going to offer him forty percent of everything. Given that he hasn't worked in almost ten years, that seems fair. He'll probably counteroffer at forty-five percent, and we'll be done. He certainly can't expect more since he's been unemployed for more than half of our marriage."

"That seems more than fair – I just hope he agrees with you."

Lesley took a deep breath before giving her opinion. "Six months is a long time. And I don't think Cliff is going to be reasonable. My Spidey Sense says he's going to put up a fight." Melanie nodded thoughtfully at Lesley's statement. "You like Rob, he clearly likes you, and you are definitely getting a divorce. Cliff has no claim on you, and you should have some fun. I think you should just do it." Lesley nodded her head with finality.

Julia had spent the last several years not having much fun. Lesley's point spoke to her. Yes, she should have some fun without always worrying about protecting Cliff. She'd spent years watching out for him, his ego, his problems. *It was her turn, damn it.*

Melanie spoke next. "But you could have fun with other guys first and then go out with Rob in six months or so when things have quieted down and Cliff has had time to get used to it. Didn't Rob just get separated a few months ago himself? He shouldn't move so fast either. It's not cheating, but it's not very comfortable either."

Melanie was right, Julia thought. There were plenty of other guys who had shown interest in her when she was married. She hadn't thought much about starting to date again yet, but that question was clearly in her subconscious since she blurted it out to Doctor Malik. Rob's call had prompted her to think about it more. It didn't have to be Rob.

"I keep agreeing with both of you." Julia chewed on her lip. "You know my situation – it's still super fresh. This is tough."

Always one to lighten a mood, Melanie changed the angle of the topic. "Okay, so let's say you go out with him. How do you think he'd be in the sack?"

"Melanie! I'm talking about going on a date, not banging him."

Ignoring Julia's protest, Lesley jumped right in. "I bet he'd take care of you first. He seems like the type." She tipped her glass back.

Melanie agreed. "And he's probably one of those elusive guys who actually likes going down on women." They laughed a little too loudly for the people nursing their beers at the bar.

"That'd be nice. Let me remind you of my sex drought."

"You didn't get that vibrator we discussed?"

"No."

"You're missing out," Melanie added. "But let's get back to the question at hand. Do you want to get back out there?"

"Yes. Definitely. And I want to have great sex. New year, new life, new vibrator doesn't have the right ring to it," Julia added with a smirk. "I would even settle for okay sex. It doesn't have to be mind-blowing."

"Then you're doing it wrong." Lesley slammed her glass down on the table. "You need to get laid."

"I want to feel attractive, sexy, and desirable again. And an orgasm or three would be nice."

"You make a great point, Jules." Melanie raised her glass. "Forget my advice and go for it. What was that mantra again? Oh right. New year, new life."

"Let's update that. New year, new life, great sex."

They clinked glasses to seal the deal.

Chapter 18

"Let's try that again." Julia turned the volume down on her headset as the advertising agency executive on the line raised her voice another ten decibels in her first meeting Friday morning. This was a particularly tricky deal with an agency that demanded a lot of concessions.

Julia was simultaneously trying to balance her company's bottom line with the need to close this big deal while not introducing new price floors by accident that she would have to grant to other advertising agencies. Complicated.

She felt her sweat penetrating the fabric under the arms of her crisp white shirt as she leaned in. It was a delicate dance, and several levels of salespeople had failed to close the deal before it was escalated all the way up to her. She stared at the view of Mount Baker through her office window as she listened to the latest outburst in the negotiation.

"I have the list of the nine requests." Julia spoke with calm professionalism. "I can grant numbers three, four, seven, and nine. One and six are absolute non-starters. Let's talk about two, five, and eight."

Julia found that people appreciated when she stated her opinion up-front and quickly identified where the key negotiation points would be. The ad agency rep was a tough negotiator, but they were making progress as each of them recognized a worthy opponent in the battle but also had a shared goal of closing the deal.

They were agreeing on next steps to seal the deal by the middle of the following week when Julia heard a rustle behind her.

She turned around and found a huge bunch of sunflowers on the table in her office. She tried to wheel her desk chair toward the door to see who'd left them, but the cord of her headset jerked her attention back to the call.

"Great, Gloria. This is a good plan. Let's regroup again on Tuesday after we have each done some more analysis based on this discussion."

She wrapped up the call and read the card.

You deserve more sunshine in your life. Hope you're thinking about our date.

Rob

She stuck her head out of her office doorway, but there was no sign of him. All she saw was the next group of people waiting to come into her office for their meeting. She couldn't remember the last time she had been given flowers. And he remembered she liked sunflowers.

━━

JULIA'S mobile phone buzzed later that day as she walked down the hall to her next meeting. It was Cliff. She didn't want to talk to him but hoped he had an answer on her generous offer. "Hey Cliff, how are you?"

"I'm fine," Cliff said, not sounding it. "But something happened that's bothering me. I wanted to tell you."

"Is it about the offer? I'd like to figure out our monetary plan."

"No, it's not about that." She heard annoyance in his tone. "I wanted to let you know Rob asked me if he could ask you out. I told him no fucking way."

"Really? That's what you said?" Julia was amused at the difference in his version of the story compared to Rob's.

"Well, I didn't say it like that. It was more like, 'if that's what you want to do,' but clearly he should know I don't want him dating my wife. Anyone could get that from our conversation."

Typical, thought Julia. *Say one thing but mean another.* Getting angry had no value for either of them, so she tried to stay cool. "Thanks for the warning, but I don't want to talk about him." That was nebulous enough to still be factually correct. She didn't want to discuss it with Cliff.

"Good."

"I have to run to my next meeting, Cliff. Did you want to talk about the settlement terms?"

"Yeah, sure. My lawyer will be in touch." He hung up.

He didn't even give her a chance to say goodbye. At least he had a lawyer now. Progress.

⸻

HALFWAY THROUGH HER NEXT MEETING, she received an instant message from Rob.

R U free to IM?

Julia's heart raced. Why was she getting an adrenaline

rush? She wasn't even sure how much she liked this guy. Apparently, her subconscious felt a little differently.

> Thanks for the flowers

> U R welcome. I'll be at City Grille Steakhouse at 7 tonight dining with or without you. Hope it'll be with you. Have a good afternoon.

Before Julia could type her response, Rob logged off and was no longer available via instant message. *Tricky*.

She had about two hours to ponder her final course of action. She wanted to start dating, but was Rob the right guy to start with? She thought they were just going to talk about it today and here he was asking her to take the plunge.

She was wearing her typical work uniform of a white cotton shirt and a pair of black pants. Nothing sexy or fantastic, because she hadn't thought she would be on a date when she dressed for work that morning.

As her meetings wrapped up for the day, decision time came nearer and nearer.

She got in her car still unclear of which way she was going to go – home or the City Grille? Damn it, she was going. As long as her dog sitter could stop by and feed Selah. A quick call confirmed she could. It was settled. Julia steered through cross-town traffic to her first date in eighteen years.

▭

JULIA OPENED the heavy glass door of the restaurant and was greeted by the warm smell of grilling steaks and the hushed tones of dinner conversation. The atmosphere calmed her, even though she should have been nervous.

She gave Rob's name to the host. He took her to the bar where Rob was waiting. Rob gave her a huge ear-to-ear grin as she slipped onto the stool next to him. "I was hoping you'd come."

"I'm a bit surprised I'm here, but happy, too."

Impressing her with his security in his manhood, Rob ordered a Lemon Drop Martini. Julia had a glass of wine. They didn't say much for a few minutes. Talking to Rob had always been easy. *Just be normal,* Julia thought. She said the first thing that came into her head.

"Thanks again for the flowers. They're beautiful. I can't remember the last time I got flowers."

"Glad you liked them. I remembered you like sunflowers because they're my favorite, too. I remember lots of details about things you've said." Rob looked down at his drink. "Just to get this out there, I've liked you a little too much for a long time. I used to stay late after band practice just to talk to you. You're so interesting and accomplished."

Julia's heart raced. He was doing it again – giving her that special feeling as if she were the most important person in the world.

She sat at the bar sharing high-end pub mix with Rob and opened herself up to the feelings she had about him. She had always enjoyed his company and had flirted right back with him. Harmless, light-hearted flirting.

But now there was a current of possibility underneath the banter. Julia was torn about whether or not she could actually follow through on it. She was surprised at how much she wanted to, but her desire made her feel guilty.

"Sorry to talk about Cliff, but this will be the only comment about him tonight." Julia cleared her throat.

"He's not happy you asked me out. He would be even more unhappy if he knew I said yes."

"Well then, he shouldn't have told me it was okay. And I was just asking him as a courtesy because I have some class. It's our choice."

"Good point. You're here, and I'm here. I guess we've made it." Julia's tone conveyed confidence she didn't quite feel.

"But let's be clear." Rob pointed his index finger. "He regaled me with an hour's worth of stories to try to scare me away. It didn't work."

The host appeared to show them to their table. He took them up the lush, maroon-carpeted stairs. Julia trailed her hand along the dark wood banister as he walked them to a secluded table for two. A bottle of champagne was already at the table chilling.

Julia let out a breath she didn't know she was holding. *What was she getting herself into?*

Settled at the table, Julia realized she didn't know much about Rob's history other than the highlights and wanted to change that. "How long have you been a pilot?" Julia asked.

"Ten years or so. Camille is a pilot, too, so we decided she can keep our plane. I want something a little more powerful anyway. When did you start playing bass?" He turned the focus back to Julia.

"I was eleven. It's actually my third instrument. I started on the harp at nine and took up the drums at ten. I wanted something different. When I told my band director, he said he needed a bass player and that I was a good fit because I was tall and already knew how to read music. He sent me home with a bass for the summer and love was born. It's way easier to carry around than a harp!" Julia giggled. *She never giggled.*

She knew she was staring at him. She tried to stop. But she found him to be so much cuter as they spent more time together. She hadn't noticed the way his eyes crinkled at the corners when he smiled all the way. Or how his already deep voice turned even deeper when he told a story. It all got Julia's juices flowing.

THE EVENING FLEW BY. They talked about everything from religion to politics to movies. They had a lot in common, especially their senses of humor and musical tastes.

"I think we've eaten everything we're going to eat," Julia said after they'd shared each other's steaks and polished off the champagne. "Let's call it a night."

They both reached for the check.

"I asked you to join me, so this one's on me." Rob gently pulled the vinyl folder from Julia's hand.

It had been such an automatic response. She hadn't even given him a chance to pay. It was nice to be with someone who could pay their own way. "Halvsies?"

"Julia, really. My treat."

He held her arm as they walked down the stairs. "Where are you parked? I'll walk you to your car." Julia's face flushed at the embarrassment that she was driving a Toyota Camry. No offense to the very reliable car, but it was not the car a thirty-nine-year-old single woman should be driving.

Cliff had asked for the SUV that was in her name and the convertible she had bought him for his fortieth birthday while they worked through their settlement. She was stuck with Cliff's sedan. She added buying a new three pedal manual car to her mental list of post-divorce expenses.

As they approached the car, her mind changed gears to the goodbye. Would there be a kiss, or would they just smile and walk away from each other, content with sharing a fun evening?

As they neared the silver door of her car, Julia tried to concentrate on the idle chatter, even as her brain continued to toss around the idea of kissing him good-night. Did she want to? Surprisingly, yes. Or not so surprisingly. She had just had a great date with an interesting, virile man.

It had been a while, but Julia sensed Rob was giving off the signals he was interested in participating in the "great sex" part of her new mantra.

"It's good to be prepared," Julia said in response to a joke Rob made about being an Eagle Scout. Of course he was an Eagle Scout. It fit with his style and approach to life.

And then they were there. She unlocked the door with a click and reached for the handle. As she did, her hand met his as he tried to open the door for her. She pulled her hand back at the tingle of the skin-on-skin contact. "I thought things like that only happened in movies." She paused to let him finish the task.

With her door wide open, she turned to say goodbye and to see just how sweetly this lovely evening would end.

He was standing about as far away as his six-foot arm span would allow and still be touching the door handle. Julia looked up at him and thought about how nice it was to have to tilt her face up to look into his eyes given his height.

"Can we do this again or was it awful?" he asked.

"Well, it was tolerable, so I'm willing to give you another chance." Julia laughed at her own joke. *Again*.

"I'll take you up on that. Until then."

Julia found herself looking at his back as he hurried away.

"Okay. Good night. Thanks for dinner," she called out after him.

She was sure he was going to come in for a kiss. She was ready for it. She was waiting for it.

Perhaps she had misread his signals. She chose to think of the positive as she pulled out of the mall parking lot. She had been on a date. Even without a kiss goodbye or specific plans for a second one, she had popped the cork on her dating life.

Chapter 19

Julia's Monday morning meeting turned out to be the type of meeting that spawned about five other ones. She was working on a new monetization strategy for a services offering, and the models were not turning out to be detailed enough.

The team didn't have the data needed to run a solid predictive model. She had to make the tough call to launch the service in three markets at different price points and test the market that way. She had to get a measurement tool set up quickly so she could capture the sales data and mine it for trends before rolling the final answer out to over two thousand salespeople. And all before she left for the next step of Operation Fix-It.

She was doubly annoyed because her trip to New York had been delayed by two weeks since the New York Sales team was pitching a bunch of deals to their top agencies, and they had to focus on that.

Julia was deflated at the delay. But she was in it for the long haul. At least she could combine the trip to New York with her Atlanta visit.

Dallas and Chicago had been postponed because once the sales leaders figured out she would be in town, they wanted her to meet with agencies and local accounts, pretty much to be a punching bag. But hey, if that's what it took to gain their respect and trust, she would do it.

As much as she tried to focus on her work, thoughts of Rob kept infiltrating the corner of her mind. Just like they had all weekend as she arranged and rearranged her house to her liking while packing up Cliff's belongings since he hadn't bothered to yet.

It had only been a date – there was no reason for her to be concerned he hadn't called. They both had lives, right? And they weren't children. She could always call him, or maybe a casual instant message was better.

She took a deep breath and opened an IM window. As her fingers touched the keyboard to send a jaunty morning greeting, her screen lit up with a red exclamation point email from a member of her team. An important escalation on a deal required her immediate attention. Rob would have to wait.

Julia's entire week went like that. Every time she thought she would get a minute, something else came up.

Julia frequently had calls at six or seven in the morning. She worked late into the night on Wednesday. Thursday included meetings with a branch of a US-based agency in Europe in the morning and Asia at night. And she certainly wasn't at the house for band practice.

By the conclusion of Friday's early morning meeting, she was tired and having difficulty not taking her bad mood out on her co-workers. She was burning the candle at both ends and needed a night in with Selah.

An incoming instant message caught her attention. It was from Rob. It was just one word.

Dinner?

She wasn't sure she was up for a date that night, especially because she had just completed a fantasy that involved her bathtub, some ice cream, and play time with Selah after the series of meetings she knew would be difficult that afternoon.

Can't tonight. Tomorrow?

Yes to Saturday but I don't want to wait that long. Lunch today?

She only had a small window between meetings.

Available from 12:30 to 1:30

C U out front at 12:30

It was that simple. No games, no controversy, just a straightforward exchange. Julia basked in it for a moment. Then, her attention was pulled back to the work she had to crank through to make the 12:30 lunch possible.

―

ROB WAS WAITING outside her building in his gray SUV right on time. She had seen his car pull up in front of her house a bunch of times but had never ridden in it before. She slipped into the passenger seat. "It's nice to see you again. Thanks for getting in touch." That sounded too formal. *Just be normal!*

"Sorry it took so long. Family drama over the weekend that bled into the week."

"Everything okay?"

"Yeah, just time-consuming, so I didn't have a chance to call."

"That's okay, I was busy too." She didn't need to tell him just how much he was on her mind.

"Where do you want to go?"

"Anywhere fast is good," Julia responded.

"What are you in the mood for?"

"Whatever you like."

"I'm easy."

Julia realized neither of them were going to express a preference. Rather than being the pleaser, she decided to take bold action and make the call. She laughed at herself for thinking it was pushy to choose the restaurant. "Have you been to the French Bistro down at the strip mall?"

"Nope, but I guess I wanted to aim a little higher than the strip mall."

"That's because you haven't tried it yet." Julia smiled in anticipation of the food. "Their pastries are the closest I've found to Paris, including bakeries in New York and Boston."

"Well then, let's go."

They shared a *Croque Monsieur* and a salad so they could leave room for an exquisite apple turnover. Forty-five minutes went by quickly. He was easy to talk to and he made her feel interesting. He had great stories to tell about the people at work and always found a way to solve the problem that was blocking him. That skill had been missing in Cliff as of late, and Julia realized just how much Rob's independence appealed to her.

Julia licked the apple filling off her finger and smiled.

Rob looked uncomfortable as he shifted in his seat. "You said you only had until one-thirty, so as much as I would like to stay, I have to get you back on time."

Julia appreciated that he was on top of the details and invested in her success.

They pulled up in front of her building. Julia thought back to the other night when Rob high-tailed it away from her. She had been thinking about kissing that adorable mouth all week and decided it was go time. *Stop being awkward*, she commanded herself. *You are a grown-ass woman, not some junior high teenager!*

Rob interrupted her preparation. "I'm going to kiss you now."

Julia froze. It was just a kiss. Not a big deal. But she was sitting in front of her building.

She realized she was not giving him the signal she meant to, especially when he added, "Unless you don't want me to."

"Well, I know it's going to happen eventually, so we might as well get it out of the way." Julia's smile was mischievous.

They each leaned in to close the distance. Lips poised to meet for the first time, their glasses clanked together and made them pull back laughing. Rob slipped off her glasses and put them on the dashboard. He did the same with his own. "Let's try that again."

His eyes looked even bluer now and seemed to sparkle at her. He put both of his hands on her face, perhaps because he couldn't see her anymore, but she decided it was to be romantic.

Their lips met in a soft and warm kiss. They lingered over it just a bit, mouths opening to take it a little deeper. Julia pulled away first but didn't get very far because Rob's hands were still caressing her face.

"That was nice." They stared at each other for a few seconds before Julia broke the spell. "I have to go, or I'll be late for my meeting." Her cheeks felt the cold January snap as he gently removed his hands from her face.

"Thanks for meeting me for lunch. I'll pick you up tomorrow at six. Where do you want to go?"

"You picked our first date. I'll take care of our second." Julia smiled as she retrieved her glasses.

She closed the car door and turned to wave at him as she approached the glass door of the building. Then, she smartly walked right into the edge of the door, stubbing her toe.

Catching herself before falling over, she turned back to the car hoping Rob was already pulling away. Instead, he was laughing just a little too hard. She couldn't help but laugh, too. *Classic.*

Chapter 20

Seattle was more happening than the staid East Side location of their first date. Julia's good friend Brent had introduced her to a fabulous speakeasy with no sign. You had to know how to get in.

Julia thought Rob would enjoy the pageantry, so she texted the bar. She was able to get a table for one hour. That was perfect. One or two drinks and she would then take him to her favorite French Bistro up the street. She made her reservation at Les Abeilles and smiled at a job well done. It would be a good night.

Julia tried not to agonize over what to wear that evening, but she was stuck. She wanted to be casual but sexy. She hadn't been casual but sexy in years.

She thought of a sweater and pair of jeans Melanie had picked out for her on a recent shopping trip. The sweater was a soft gray with a boat neck collar, so it would slide off her shoulder. Julia had good shoulders and that would be a subtly sexy way to show some skin.

Of course, her strapless bra was uncomfortable and the

lovely grandmother-style shade of nude. Oh well, he wouldn't see it anyway, as this was only their second date.

She paired the sweater with the jeans Melanie called her Bart jeans. Bart was short for Butt Art, as the jeans had jewel-covered back pockets. They were a size ten which was a size Julia hadn't seen in a while. She felt sexy in them. She added tall black boots to complete the outfit, also courtesy of a shopping trip with Melanie. She would have to thank her later.

Next, it was time for hair and makeup. She decided not to load on the makeup. She just went with light eyeliner, a bit of eye shadow and mascara. She painted her lips just to make them look healthy since they were always so chapped. She fluffed her curly hair and was ready.

Thankfully, it was not raining as it usually was in Seattle in January. She decided to add a slim-fitting suede trench coat she had picked up at a thrift store in New York City. Rain was in the forecast, but she would risk the twenty-dollar thrift store find for the right look.

She had just fed Selah and given her some solid petting time when she heard Rob's car in the driveway promptly at six.

This time, he wasn't coming over for band practice. On those evenings, he had learned to just walk in the door, but tonight, he knocked and waited for Julia to answer.

Selah beat Julia to the door as Rob said "hellooooooo" from outside to get the dog's tail wagging with excitement at the play session she knew was coming.

Julia opened the door to a different Rob. This one was dressed for a night on the town. His navy pea coat was buttoned up over jeans and he was wearing a fedora to match his coat. He smelled amazing. They shared a tentative kiss at the door while Selah flopped down on her back for belly rubs.

Rob knelt down to be near Selah saying, "Who's my little pumpkin," like he always did when he greeted her.

Julia left them alone for a minute while she grabbed her purse and a treat for Selah which she gave to Rob to give to her gleeful dog. Getting the treat gave her a minute to calm herself down. *When had she turned into a high school girl, getting all fluttery just because she enjoyed his cologne?*

Selah immediately sat and patiently lifted a paw while waiting for Rob to deliver the goods. Dog cookie devoured, he opened the front door, waited for Julia to lock it behind her, and walked her to the car to open her door.

"Where are we going?"

"Did you bring your passport?"

"Uh, no, I didn't. Are we driving to Vancouver? I could stop and get it." He mistook her joke for reality.

"No, no, that's not necessary. We aren't heading to Canada, but I've made plans for us in Seattle. You know how East Siders joke about having to take their passport when they cross the lake to the big city."

He was trying so hard. It was adorable.

They chatted about work and his most recent mountain bike ride as they drove the twenty-five minutes to the Capitol Hill neighborhood.

The speakeasy was located at the corner of an old building that ended in a point between two cross streets. It was unmarked and there were no other shops right near it. Julia instructed Rob to park nearby.

"I know this neighborhood really well – there aren't any restaurants down here. Sure you don't want to park closer to the action?"

"Oh ye of little faith," Julia chided. She led him toward an unmarked door. Rob looked confused. Julia enjoyed the mystery.

Two people in front of them approached the door. Julia

held back and Rob followed suit. The couple knocked on the blue door which was promptly answered by a woman who looked like she had stepped out of the fifties, complete with the Bettie Page dress. Her dyed black hair with pink streaks gave her away as being from the neighborhood.

"Can we come in for a drink? There are two of us."

Amateurs, Julia thought. She wondered what would happen next, as she hadn't seen anyone get denied before.

"No," the black-and-pink haired woman closed the door in their faces.

Couldn't have planned it better, Julia thought. It added to the mystery.

"What a jerk," one man said to the other after the door closed. They walked away dismayed and cursing the hostess. Julia would have explained the rules to them, but they walked off too quickly.

"Are you sure we're in the right place?" Confusion was evident in Rob's tone.

Julia shot him a jokingly defiant look. "Trust me."

Just like the people before her, she knocked on the nondescript door. The same woman opened it. "Hi, I'm Louise."

"Welcome, Louise, your table is ready." The hostess led them to a table in the corner.

"Your server will be right with you to take your drink order. Enjoy your evening." She sashayed back to her station at the door.

Julia watched Rob take in the slightly rundown rococo interior. It reminded Julia of her great-grandmother's house, except hers was the real thing back in the day. This was a cheap imitation, but the lights were low so you couldn't tell. They sat at a table near hipsters sipping their libations.

Their server showed up a minute later with a drink

menu about fifteen pages thick. "I'll give you some time to look it over." She moved to another table.

Rob looked up from the seemingly endless drink menu. "I can't believe you've taken me to a great place I've never even heard of when I've been living in the area for almost thirty years, more than twenty of them over the legal drinking age."

"I'm full of surprises." Julia hoped it was true and was happy to have scored.

"Listen to the description of this one. It's called the French Floozy. House made grapefruit-infused vodka with lemon liquor, elderflower liquor, and rosemary."

"I'll have to try that." Julia raised an eyebrow. "I've lived in France, and I'd like to become a bit more of a floozy." *Sassy*.

"Just let me know how I can help with that." Rob found another description to share. "How about the Brandy Sex Kitten? Spiced bourbon, apple brandy, allspice dram, spiced pear vodka, honey, and egg white."

"I'll start with the French Floozy and see how it goes from there." They both laughed while staring at each other over the menus.

"What's the secret for getting in here?" Rob asked, breaking the moment.

"If I tell you, then you'll bring all the girls here."

"Doubtful."

"You text them with the time you want to come and the number in your party. You also give them a name to use. My friend Brent used his middle name, so I did too. Makes it easy to remember."

"Tricky, tricky. That's cool."

"You heard the others who didn't get in. That's because they asked to come in. You have to just say your fake name," Julia explained.

When the server came to take their order, Rob ordered for both of them, remembering she wanted a French Floozy. She watched him flirt with the server as he placed their order. He looked so cute in his hat. His eyes sparkled as he laughed with the server over one of her recommendations. It was nice to be out with someone who brought joy to other people's lives.

"When did you live in France?"

"During college. It was only a semester in Paris, but I fell in love with the city. Of course, I was on a student budget, so I can tell you where all the cheap places are."

"I don't get how you can be so accomplished yet not seem to have a conceited bone in your body. We'll go back now that you can treat yourself a little better."

Did he just ask Julia to go on a trip with him? She started an intricate fantasy about what she would do with Rob in the City of Lights. He continued, pulling Julia out of her daydream. "It must have been interesting to live in another country. I've gone on a lot of extended business trips, but I've never lived out of the country. Camille and I once thought about moving to Copenhagen." He trailed off.

Julia waited for Rob to continue, but he didn't. She sensed he might be thinking about Camille and tried to put him at ease. "I went to a conference there. I thought it was pretty sterile, but then again, I didn't have much time to see anything other than the conference center."

"Ah, yes, the windowless conference room tour." Rob chuckled.

"Oh hey – the time went fast. We need to head to the restaurant." Julia asked for the check.

As the server set the check on the table, both Rob and Julia reached for it.

"Ah ah ah." Julia joked and wagged her finger at Rob. "My turn."

IT HAD GOTTEN a little colder outside since they'd gone into the bar, and they were hit with a blast of chilly air as they stepped outside and headed up the block. But still no rain. Julia was glad her suede coat would survive.

Dodging scaffolding and construction debris as they went, Julia noticed Rob had moved to her outside so he was closer to the road in an old-fashioned display of protection. It was a short walk to the restaurant. He held her hand the whole way.

The buzzing bees on the sign always made her happy. She had enjoyed several great meals at this restaurant over the years. "This is the place," Julia announced.

"I've never been here either," Rob said. "You *are* full of surprises."

"Continuing our earlier discussion, I hope you like French." Rob held the door open for her. "At least it's a little different from our lunch yesterday." Maybe she should have picked something other than French.

Through the wooden door, there was a cozy bar to the left and a small dining room to the right. The bar had a few people in it, but the restaurant was dead empty.

"Are you sure this is the place?" Rob looked worried.

"Oh yeah. We're in the trendy part of town. The hipster kids don't eat until nine or ten. By the time we leave, it'll be jumping."

Rob hung his hat on the coat tree in the entranceway. They were shown to a seat near the back corner of the restaurant. Julia looked down at the scuffed wood floor as she took her seat.

"I've never had a bad thing at this restaurant. The crêpes are the closest to French crêpes I've found stateside, and the French onion soup is amazing."

"What're you going to have?"

"Soupe à l'oignon and a crêpe amandine." Julia's voice went dreamy. "It might sound like an odd combination, but when they melt gruyère cheese on a crêpe and then add almonds, it totally works. Oh, and I have to get the gratin du jour, whatever vegetable it is." Julia's laugh had a twinge of nerves in it. "I sound like a pig. It's been a few months since I was here."

"That's good – I won't feel bad about having a nibble of everything at the table."

There it was again – a flirty comment that could mean the food or her. "Thanks for making me feel better about wanting to stuff my face." Two could play at that game.

"I'm thinking of the cassoulet and then I'll have a dessert crêpe. I haven't eaten all day in preparation," he said.

"Good planning."

"Comes from being an Eagle Scout." Rob blinked both eyes.

"What does that mean?"

"What do you mean what does that mean – I winked at you."

"No, you blinked both eyes. I noticed you do that a lot."

Rob laughed with gusto. "That's so funny you noticed. My grandmother couldn't wink. She could only blink both eyes even though she thought she was winking. Over the years, my family kind of adopted it as an homage to grandma. Now I automatically wink with both eyes."

Why did he have to be so damned cute? He was making it hard to not want more.

Chapter 21

"Clearly, we hated it," Rob joked with the server as she removed the empty plates.

With a final sip of their French Press coffee, they decided to give up their table. A line of people waiting had formed in the bar. It amused and pleased Julia that Rob was just as worried about that sort of thing as she was.

A light rain had started to fall while they were in the restaurant. *That's the good thing about a twenty-dollar thrift store suede coat,* Julia thought. "Did you like it?" Julia asked.

"Oh yeah, definitely. I don't think I've ever had a better crêpe."

"Wait until you have one in Paris." She settled into the seat for the short ride home.

He was just so interesting, with multiple facets and experiences. She felt very boring compared to his escapades in car and motorcycle racing, flying, mountain biking, hundred-mile bicycle rides, and stories about camping. All she did was work, play a few instruments, and take her dog to the dog park. She hoped she could keep him interested.

The closer they got to Julia's house, the more she wanted to invite him in for some alone time. She worried she was moving too fast, but she was eager to make progress on her plans for using her lingerie.

They pulled into her driveway. Just as she was going to bite the bullet and invite him in, he asked if he could say goodnight to Selah.

"Of course." Julia smiled inwardly, glad he didn't want the evening to end either. They repeated the Selah greeting ritual when they walked in the door.

As Julia stood up from scratching Selah's belly, Rob grabbed her face with both hands and kissed her. At first, Julia was so impressed that he just went for it without having all of the awkward moments of second date navigation, she realized she was not doing her best work.

She changed the angle of the kiss and teasingly traced his lips with her tongue with lovely results.

Rob's hands slowly moved down her shoulders and rested just above her hips. It reminded her of high school when she would wonder if her date was going to bring those hands up and try to cop a feel.

Rather than keeping her arms at her sides for protection as she did in those days, she wrapped her arms around his neck, giving him free access to her breasts if he wanted it. His hands started a tortuous journey up her torso.

Oh no! The granny bra, she remembered with horror. She had to think quickly.

Julia broke the kiss. "Let me hang up your coat. I'll meet you on the sofa."

After checking to see that Rob wasn't looking, she reached around and flicked her bra open. She leaned into the closet, pulling the granny bra out from under her sweater with one hand while hanging his coat with the other. Julia tossed the embarrassing undergarment on the closet floor out of sight and went to the couch. *Smooth,* she thought.

Julia straddled him on the sofa, going with instinct instead of letting her doubts block her actions. He put his hands back where he had placed them before and this time, she let him explore.

He groaned when he found her breasts unencumbered. "If I had known you weren't wearing anything under your sweater, I wouldn't have been able to keep my hands off you at dinner." She smiled to herself at her creativity. *Grandmother bra disaster averted.*

Julia didn't know how fast or slow adults were supposed to take the physical side of their relationships.

Movies had people screwing on the first date, but Julia wasn't into that, and it was too late anyway since this was their second date. Or maybe it was their third if she included the lunch date. Isn't that when sex usually happened? Oh shit. She hadn't shaved or worn the right underwear. And maybe he wasn't interested anyway.

Focus, she thought and put her attention back on Rob. He was a great kisser and knew his way around a set of lips. She heard a low hum. It took a moment for her to realize it came from her.

She was enjoying the way Rob pressed his lips to hers and danced his tongue along the edges. She was getting as much pleasure out of kissing him as she had ever gotten out of full-on sex with Cliff. *Damn it. Why did she have to think about him?*

This was it, she thought. She was going to reach southward. She felt a bit awkward, but all she had to do was focus on the sounds Rob was making, and she became much more comfortable that he wanted that, too.

She reached between his legs, using the palm of her

hand to apply a little pressure. She cupped her hand and rubbed his entire length, pleased with what she found.

He trapped her hand in between them and started grinding against her. He moaned a bit and pulled back.

"You first," was all he said.

He reached for the button of her jeans and undid them as he pulled her zipper down and laid her back on the sofa. As her breathing grew harder in anticipation of what was next, he reached in and played with the edge of her panties. She loved that she had lost enough weight his hand fit.

He was driving her crazy. And he hadn't even made contact with anything important yet. She threw her leg over the back of the sofa to give him more access. Hairy legs be damned. This was too fun to stop.

His hand crawled deeper and deeper toward her center. She could feel his fingertips brush her clit and she started moving against his hand.

It had been so long since anyone had touched her with this much care and attention. That was just as much of a turn-on as the actual contact. She tore herself away from thinking only about herself and reached down to unbutton his jeans.

As she opened his zipper, she was amused to find that he was sporting tighty whities. *When did those come back into style?* She filed that away for later and got back to the business of freeing him so they could have some more fun. She closed her hand around him and squeezed.

He grabbed her wrists with one hand and put them over her head as he reached back down into her pants with the other. "Not so fast. I'm not done with my task yet." He found her center and teased the opening.

He was kissing her and working her pants off at the

same time. She still had enough operational brain cells to appreciate his technique.

"Are you okay?" he asked in a gruff voice. "I don't want to move too quickly, but I want you."

"Yes, I'm good," she answered, appreciating the care he was taking.

He slipped a finger and then two into her. She cried out and started moving instinctively against his hand as he drove her.

She was glorying in his touch. She felt her muscles start to gather and she knew she was getting close. She threw her head back, enjoying the newly remembered sensations as Rob feasted on her neck while driving her to the peak.

A sound at the door broke her concentration before she finished. The moment collapsed.

A second, more impatient knock echoed through her living room. It was ten-thirty at night. Who would be out there at this hour?

Chapter 22

There was only one answer. Cliff. And he still had a key. Julia panicked.

What if he opened the door and found them?

"Shit, I think it's Cliff," Julia hissed. They both jumped up like guilty teenagers. Rob hastily tucked his shirt back into his pants as Julia zipped her jeans and rearranged her sweater. Selah ran to the door.

Julia took a deep breath and started toward the door as she heard the key in the lock. It opened just before she reached the doorknob. The open door revealed a mutinous Cliff on the other side.

"I saw his car and knew he was here," he said before Julia could say a word. "I want to talk to you."

"Now's not a great time." Julia's calm voice belied the fast beat of her heart, portraying calmness she didn't feel.

"What's he doing here?" Cliff demanded.

"We're just back from dinner." *The truth is best,* she told herself. It was technically accurate while also an evasion.

Rob stayed near the sofa and didn't come to the door.

Cliff pushed it open and yelled, "Are you here trying to fuck my wife?"

Julia was horrified. *Was he drunk?* Rob didn't answer. Julia jumped in.

"Cliff, you need to calm down. We aren't doing anything wrong. You and I are over."

"That's what I came over to talk about. I don't want us to be over. I prepared a whole speech I wanted to share with you. You weren't home. I thought I'd just come back. And then I did and found HIS car here."

Julia didn't know what to do. She was horrified and embarrassed. *Why did he still have a key? Why hadn't she changed the locks? Why was he under the impression there was a chance of reconciliation?* Even Selah seemed uncomfortable and slinked back to her bed in the living room.

"I'm going to go. See you later." Rob pushed past Cliff at the doorway.

Cliff looked like he was going to take a shot at Rob. Julia hoped he didn't, as Rob would have laid him out in one punch. He had a lot of martial arts training, twenty pounds of muscle, and four inches of height on Cliff.

"I'm so sorry," was all Julia could get out before Rob closed the door behind him.

"What the Hell are you doing here?" Julia yelled at Cliff. "You have no right to be here."

"You're my wife. Why are you cheating on me with my best friend?"

Julia didn't know which topic to cover first. Unfortunately, she was upset enough to choose the wrong part of the sentence. "When did he become your *best* friend. You guys are just friends at best." *Nice going,* she thought, wishing she hadn't pointed that out.

"When did you become such a slut?"

"Wow, Cliff, that's out of line." Julia worked to regain

her composure. She thought of Rob driving away in a rage and almost burst into tears. "First of all, we were not having sex." She could feel okay saying that because she wasn't going to sleep with him that night. Obviously, she would have stopped him because she hadn't shaved. *A little fingering with pants mostly on was one thing, but full access to hairy legs? No way.*

"Then why was he here?"

"This isn't about him. This is about you and me." Julia tried for a redirect. "Our marriage is over. There is no us anymore." She gentled her tone. She could see now Cliff was upset, but not drunk. "Come into the kitchen. We can talk about this. I'll make you some tea."

All the way back to the kitchen, she wondered why she had made that offer instead of kicking him out. He had called her a slut, yet she was being kind to him. *Old habits die hard.*

As Julia led the way to the kitchen, Cliff took his customary seat at the kitchen table. Julia sat in a different seat than usual, a small display of rebellion.

"Why do you have to jump into bed with him?" he demanded. "Can't you wait? Or choose someone else?"

"I thought about it a lot before I went out with him, and it was hard for me to choose to do what I want after putting other people, especially you, first for so many years. After a long battle with myself, I didn't see why I should wait. I don't mean to sound crass, but you had your chance. You chose to not have sex with me for years. It's almost like now that someone else wants to, you want to come back and claim your territory. It doesn't work like that."

Cliff just stared at her. She stared back until Cliff started to cry. "Oh geez, Cliff, don't cry." She sipped her tea now that it had cooled to give him a minute.

"I ruined everything," Cliff wailed. She had never seen him cry like this. He was sobbing. *Should I comfort him or throw him out,* she thought. Eighteen years of training had her consoling him.

"Cliff, look at me. You didn't ruin everything. We'll still be friends and we'll still be part of each other's lives. We just won't be living together. And we won't be married anymore."

Cliff looked at her with a tear-streaked face. "I'm so sorry," he blubbered as more tears rolled down his cheeks.

She hated seeing him like this. "Let's talk more tomorrow when you come to pick Selah up for your afternoon with her."

"I can't do that. I'm going mountain biking with some new friends." He got his crying under control.

"Oh, okay." Julia was annoyed. He kept saying he wanted time with Selah and then he bailed. She had made plans to be out all day. "Why don't you head home now? We can talk when you're calmer."

"It's weird being back in the house. It feels like the scene of a crime."

"Whose crime?"

"Yours. Being here with Rob. I couldn't live here again."

If kissing was a crime, what did Cliff call all of his time in the Masturbation Station? Setting her annoyance aside, Julia was happy to hear he didn't want the house. She loved her house and knew that Cliff couldn't afford the mortgage on his own anyway. She decided to let his comment pass rather than getting into a whole new argument.

"It's late, and I had a long day. You probably have to get up early tomorrow."

"Yeah, you're right." Cliff stood up. "We're going to be okay, right?"

"Things will work out the way they should," she answered, being purposefully non-committal. Her priority was to get him out of the house.

She shut the door behind him and made a mental note to have the locks changed.

After letting her breath out in a long whoosh, Julia looked at her phone. Two texts from Rob.

Don't worry about me

Call me after he leaves

She had wasted her time talking to Cliff when she could have been finishing her evening with Rob.

She was annoyed with herself. Even though it was late, she thought Rob would have waited up for her. He answered on the first ring.

"Are you okay?" he asked instead of saying hello.

"Yeah, but that was pretty awful."

"I'm sorry I didn't stick around to defend you, or to at least stand with you."

"It's not your battle, and it was easier for me without you here."

"I know you can handle anything, that's just my guilt talking."

"Thanks for your belief in me." His words sunk in like the balm she needed.

"Are you getting back together with him?" Julia appreciated his straightforward question.

"No." She let it hang for a few seconds for emphasis. "I'll never go back to him. And that has nothing to do with you. I wouldn't get back together with him even if you weren't in the picture. I'm ashamed I fell out of love with him so quickly, but there it is. I don't love him, and I don't want to be with him."

"I'm glad to hear that, although I'm sorry for him."

"Hell of a second date." Julia laughed a bit awkwardly.

"You have to change the locks. Regardless of whether or not you have me over again, I don't think it's safe to allow him to have access to your house."

"You're right." She was suddenly very tired. "He gave me his key but apparently had another. Who knows how many copies he made."

"Is there anything I can do?"

"Give me a couple of days to deal with this, and then I'd love to see you again." Two could play the straightforward game.

"I'd like that."

"Thanks for a great evening…up until that last part," Julia said with a watery grin.

"My pleasure. Really. Up until that last part," Rob joked back. "Good night."

What the heck was she going to do now? Her mind was swirling.

Chapter 23

"Hi, Cliff." He called her Wednesday evening. She thought about not answering, but that would just delay an inevitable conversation.

"Hello, Julia. My lawyer says the next step is to divide up our stuff. Can I come over tonight to do that?" Her lawyer, Marty, had said the same thing. She had already sent over all of the financial paperwork for Marty to share with Cliff's lawyer.

"Okay. Selah will be happy to see you." Julia caught herself in the lie. Selah didn't seem to care if she saw Cliff at all. "I already had dinner. Have you?"

"Yes, but a drink might be nice."

"Head on over, and I'll see you in a few."

JULIA HAD a list of all the household items and noted who would get the obvious things like Cliff's recording equipment and her musical instruments. They would decide on everything else together.

Cliff pointed at the table where they were sitting. "I want the kitchen table and chairs."

"Okay." The process was relatively painless because Julia made it that way.

Cliff wanted a few things Julia also had her eye on, but she didn't want to fight. She was generous, giving him everything he asked for from the house.

She was happy they could be cordial to each other. It was a sign they could be friends through this process. "When do you want to come and get all of this?" she asked him, pointing to the divided list.

"How about Saturday? I'd appreciate it if you weren't here when I come to get it all."

Julia didn't like that idea. What if he took property he shouldn't? Well, she could get it back – they had just agreed to the list and signed it. "Okay. You'll have to enter through the garage using the code since I've changed the locks." Although she could see him cringe at that statement, she had to say it. "I'll change it back to the code we used to use so you can remember it." *And change it back when I get home,* she added to herself.

"Okay."

"Are you still planning to take Selah for the weekend?"

"I'd rather not. I miss her, but I'll be in and out so much she won't have a very good time."

"Fine." Julia felt the tension in her jaw from her clenched teeth. "I'll plan to be gone all day on Saturday so you can move everything out."

"Sounds like a plan."

She walked him to the door and said goodbye. Selah didn't even come to the door when he left.

Julia couldn't help but contrast the way her dog interacted with Cliff and Rob.

HER DATE with Rob had only heightened Julia's sexual frustration. She knew she was on the path to breaking out of her sex drought and was impatient for the rain to fall. Her work schedule impeded her progress on that front. Late meetings combined with executing the necessary design work on Operation Fix-It ate into her evenings, and now she had to figure out plans for being away on Saturday. That would create a further delay in her path to great sex, but it was more important to get Cliff's stuff out of the house. And she had a plan on the sex front.

JULIA PREPARED METICULOUSLY for her next date with Rob. This time, she went all out. During her multi-hour pampering session, she slathered her smooth, freshly shaved legs with scented lotion that matched her perfume. Rob's cologne did such a number on her that she dug her French perfume out of the back of her bathroom cabinet and sprayed some on. She hoped it had the same effect on him.

She selected her best red lace underwear, designed to both drive Rob crazy and to help her feel sexy. It did the trick. She struck a pose in the full-length mirror and liked the confident, sexy woman who looked back at her. *Tonight was going to be a great night.*

Julia put on her lowest cut black dress with a slit up the side and leopard print stiletto heels before applying a flash of red lipstick with a flourish. She hardly recognized the sex goddess who looked back at her. Rob wouldn't know what hit him.

At his knock on the door, Julia opened it and looked directly at him, giving him a chance to admire her. "You take my breath away," he growled as he pounced on her, pulling her to him and kissing her like he was dying and she was the only thing that could save him.

She responded in kind, throwing her leg around his waist and grinding against him. She could feel his hardness against her center.

He grabbed her ass and began pumping against her. She wanted him to strip her down so she could feel skin on skin. She reached back to unzip her dress and let it fall at her feet. She stood before him in her red lace bra, panties, and garter. "What do you think?" she asked him as she reached for his belt buckle.

"Actually, I'm not sure I'm in the mood after all." He backed away from her.

The cold air slapped her exposed skin as the horror of his rejection sent a wave of hot embarrassment up her entire body. She was standing there offering herself to him and he turned her away. Had she forgotten how to be sexy? Was she actually the ugly, unattractive person Cliff made her feel she was?

"I'm sorry, I thought this was what we both wanted," Julia squeaked out in a voice that sounded nothing like her own.

"No, I'm sorry if I led you on. I thought you'd be better at this seduction routine than you are. I guess it was the mystery of it that was interesting rather than the actual act. I'm going to go."

Suddenly, Julia was looking at the open front door asking Rob to stay. "Come back, come back! I'll be better! I'll get it right!"

The door closed and she stood on the other side banging her fists against it in embarrassment and rage. Cliff was right. She was no good at sex.

· · ·

SHE WOKE from the nightmare with her fists clenched and her heart racing. It was a dream. A bad, bad dream. Rob hadn't rejected her. *She didn't even own leopard print stilettos.*

But the dream had rocked her world.

Here she was with this fantasy about jumping into bed with Rob when she was terribly out of practice and was probably too flabby to even keep the lights on while they were doing it. What was she thinking?

What if this was a premonition instead of a nightmare?

Not able to go back to sleep, Julia got up to splash some water on her face and wash away the remnants of her nightmare. She better work on a plan for making sure she didn't turn that nightmare into reality.

Julia indulged in a few morning pets on the floor with Selah, seeking comfort after the nightmare. She held Selah close as the dog happily rolled over and snuggled in for a big spoony cuddle. The big yellow dog started snoring as Julia stroked her belly.

JULIA SAT with her friend Margaret at a coffee shop on Saturday after a trip to the dog park. She had a series of get-togethers planned while Cliff moved his belongings out of the house.

Margaret and Julia had worked together when the two of them still lived in Boston. After Julia started at Lamp-Light, she found the perfect gig for Margaret. She and her husband moved to the Seattle area.

Margaret was one of the few people in Seattle who knew Cliff long enough to know how he used to be. Julia had been avoiding Margaret for the last few weeks, but it was time to come clean. They were better friends than that.

"Hit me with the story." Margaret slapped her hand on the table. "I want all the details."

Julia recounted the tale.

"Wow. You've had a rough couple of months. Full disclosure, Peter and I talked about how different Cliff has become over the years. It's like he just faded away."

"Yeah, that's a great way to put it. I kept waiting for the color and life to come back, but—"

"It's not going to. Jules, it's over, and I'm happy for you."

Julia was shocked. She thought that out of all of her friends, Margaret would be the hardest to convince she was doing the right thing. "Thanks, Margaret. I just feel bad because I've fallen out of love with him so quickly." They each stared into their coffee cups for a moment until Margaret broke the silence.

She lifted her cappuccino. "To the next one! And let's hope he has a healthier relationship with porn. It has its place in a relationship, if you know what I mean." Margaret wiggled her dark eyebrows. Julia laughed.

"Yes. New year, new life, great sex." They clinked mugs.

"I like that mantra."

"Thanks. Mel, Lesley, and I came up with it a little while ago."

"Oh, I would love to see them!"

"I should get a dinner party together for us."

"Name the date and I'll be there. I love those two." Margaret steepled her fingers on the table and leaned in. "Okay, you're a swinging single gal and you haven't had decent sex in a while. What's your plan for getting laid?"

"There's this guy. Rob." Julia launched into a description.

"Ooh, he sounds hunky and interested." Margaret's eyebrows shot up again.

"Yeah, but…"

"No buts. That's all you need." Margaret sounded emphatic. "You deserve great sex."

"Yeah, BUT," Julia said again. "Part of me says it's too soon after my break-up with Cliff to be hopping into bed with someone else."

"Granted, it's only been about a month, but you've said yourself you have no intention of getting back together with Cliff."

"Yes, BUT," Julia smiled. "Shouldn't I be in mourning or something out of respect for a dead relationship?"

"I don't see what you're waiting for. You like him. He likes you. You're both unattached. And you're horny. Hell, he probably is too from what you told me."

"I hear you, but Cliff is already upset. We're trying to reach a peace accord, and I don't think that doing his friend is going to help with that."

"I get that, but you can't put your life on hold because Cliff is dragging his feet. He's moving his stuff out as we speak, and you're convicted you don't want to get back together. I can be very black and white like the books I love to read, but it seems pretty straightforward to me."

Julia thought about it while she sipped her second coffee. It tasted wonderful because of the company.

Having Margaret on her side emboldened Julia. Her friend's support felt great. "I don't know if I actually agree with you, or I just want to agree with you because you're right that I'm horny."

"Honestly, Jules, what's the difference?"

"What if I'm not any good at it? I had this crazy dream where I got all dolled up and Rob walked out."

"Ha! You said he has a pulse, right?"

"Yes."

"And he likes women, right?"

"Yes."

"Just act interested, give him a blow job, and you'll be off and running! It's like riding a bike. A lovely, hard, muscly bike. Just get back in the saddle and pedal. You'll both get to the destination, if you know what I mean." Margaret's eyebrows wiggled again.

"You're right. I'm letting the itty-bitty shitty committee that lives in my head drown out the sex goddess."

"My work here is done." Margaret tipped her mug back and tapped the bottom to get the last bits of frothy milk.

"Thanks Margaret. You're a good friend. Now tell me all about your new job."

"First, you have to hear about what Peter just did for our anniversary. Classic."

<hr>

JULIA HEADED HOME. It was on the early side, but she took her chances. She could always take Selah for another walk if she needed to kill more time.

Rob called while she was on her drive. "Hey, I didn't expect the pleasure of hearing from you today."

"Yeah. Something happened at band practice on Thursday that I thought you should know about. Did Cliff already talk to you?"

"Nope. I haven't heard from him."

"Okay. Um. This is awkward. You know we started rehearsing in my mother's basement to get out of your house. I was the last one to arrive on Thursday since I was running late. Leenie let them in. When I got there, I found out Cliff had just told Lisa, Frank, and Stephen he found us together at your house."

"Oh shit. Did you get a chance to explain?"

"Not really. From what I could tell, he let them believe he found us having sex rather than just together. He also suggested we'd been having an affair prior to your separation. The band broke up."

"Oh, I'm sorry. And with the Showcase coming." Julia felt terrible.

"We're a regular Fleetwood Mac."

"Thanks for joking about it, but this is bad news."

"The interesting part is that Frank and Lisa want to keep playing together. We met up at the brewery right afterwards so I could explain. Stephen just left in a huff. I don't like that he thinks the worst of me, but it's pretty telling he wouldn't give me a chance to explain."

They were both silent for a moment as that sunk it. "Think you could still pull a set together for the Showcase?"

"Yes. Lisa's going to try to sing, and if she can't, we'll just do instrumental versions of a few of the tunes. It's still a go. All good."

"All good? Really? Are you okay?"

"I'm not gonna lie. It was rough to walk into that with no warning. But I guess I shouldn't be surprised. Cliff's not exactly a stand-up guy and we knew he was pissed. We were in a bit of denial it wouldn't blow up."

"Good point. I'm still working on figuring out the truth versus stories I tell myself."

"Aren't we all." Rob chuckled into the phone.

"Thanks for the update. Selah and I are just about to

get back to the house after a fun day out. Hopefully he's gone along with all his stuff.

"Will I see you soon?"

"Yeah, when I get back from the East Coast at the end of the week."

"Have a great trip."

"Thanks."

Julia pulled into the driveway. The coast was clear. She was able to go inside.

With Selah trotting after her, Julia looked around the house and saw that Cliff had taken the kitchen table and chairs and some artwork off the walls.

The antique hat tree shaped like a musical lyre that used to live near the front door was gone. The dust bunnies behind it were still there, but she could fix that.

She went upstairs feeling lighter than she had in weeks. She had Margaret's support and reminders of Cliff were no longer all over the downstairs of her house.

Her joy was short-lived.

Anger filled her when she looked into his office. Everything was still there. She had neatly packed up his clothes in carefully labeled boxes and put them in the Masturbation Station. There they still sat, undisturbed. "Oh no he didn't," she yelled into the room, startling Selah.

Julia ran back downstairs to the shop off the garage and was dismayed to find everything still in place. His massive power tool collection was there – the drill press, radial arm saw, chop saw, planer, band saw, and all of the equipment that went with the tools.

She called him. "Cliff, I thought you wanted me to be away today because you were moving all your stuff out."

"I was busy. I wasn't able to rent a truck and get my friends over to move the big stuff. I'll get it another time."

"Are you kidding me? We had a deal."

"Yeah, and you said you'd be with me until death. Bummer, huh." The sarcasm dripped from Cliff's words.

"Hardy har har." Julia matched his tone, but she didn't rise to the bait. "Call me when you have your friends lined up. Good night." She clicked off.

Agh! She was angry. She could feel her blood boil as she thought about what she had gone through to pack up his things and arrange her day away. She stormed into the kitchen, a concerned Selah trailing after her.

She changed tactics and plopped down on the floor with her beloved dog for a cuddlefest. Her time with Margaret was exactly what she'd needed. Margaret had known Cliff before he went through the big change, and she had noticed the difference. Talking to someone who "knew him when" made her feel better about her decision to end things.

It was like everyone but Julia knew it was time to go.

She remembered to change the code on the garage door. Cliff couldn't get into the house without her permission again.

Chapter 24

"You're in the executive conference room down the hall."
The receptionist of LampLight's New York City office
pointed to a sleek glass door. *Fancy*, Julia thought as she
entered the room usually reserved for important customer
meetings.

It slowly but surely filled up with salespeople and Julia
started her pitch just like in Los Angeles. Feedback started
coming in immediately. She was off and running with the
New York team!

That evening, exhausted, but excited about the positive
outcome, Julia looked forward to seeing Harry, one of her
mentors and friends.

Julia and Harry had first worked together right after
she married Cliff. She was working at a Big Five
accounting firm and was just coming back from her honey-
moon when she was staffed at a major television network
on a project Harry managed.

As she walked down Madison Avenue to the restaurant
they had chosen, Julia thought about how Harry had saved
her from her horrible boss, Marla.

Marla was the type of manager who took credit when things went well and loudly blamed others when they didn't, even if the problem had nothing to do with the person at whom she hurled blame. None of the other more experienced consultants would work with Marla, and it was Julia's turn as the newbie.

When the three of them met in the lobby before a customer pitch, Marla made a nasty comment to Julia about her wardrobe. Julia had gotten so used to Marla's insults that she barely noticed. But Harry's eyes almost fell out of his head as he looked at Marla.

She remembered his words like it happened yesterday. "Did you really just say that to her? Julia is a professional and doesn't deserve to be insulted like she's at the play-ground. What's wrong with you?" He hadn't bothered to give Marla another look.

They closed the deal, and Harry was put in charge. Harry staffed Julia on his projects for the rest of her time at the company. No more Marla.

Harry taught Julia to always stick up for people when they were being treated badly. It was one of the many management lessons he taught her.

HARRY WAS jawing with the bartender when Julia arrived. She joined him at the long wood bar and slipped onto an oxblood leather stool careful not to snag her skirt on the brass studs around the base. He was sporting his trademark suspenders and as usual, his curly gray hair was just a little too long. "What're you drinking?" he asked in his strong New Jersey accent.

"You can choose for me, as long as there's booze in it. I had a long day."

He asked the bartender for a Lemon Drop Martini for her and a Scotch for himself.

"Why a Lemon Drop?" Julia asked, thinking a lemon martini sounded perfect that evening and it was the same drink Rob had ordered on their first date.

"Because it's kind of how I think of you. Part sweet and part sour." It sounded like "sawah."

"Nice one." Julia gave him a slow nod of approval.

"So what brings you into town?"

She filled him in on what had happened to create her need for Operation Fix-It.

He took a sip of his drink. "Good for you. It sounds like you're making progress. And, I'm glad to hear the angry guy – what's his face - didn't cause you to back off. That'd be bad."

"Yeah," Julia agreed. "As you taught me years ago, don't let the assholes get you down."

"I'll drink to that." Harry nodded and lifted his glass.

AFTER SLURPING DOWN HALF a dozen oysters, Harry got to the punch line of his latest story. "So there he is, pleased as punch with himself, standing in front of the shitty little cubicle they have me sitting in for this project, and he asks me how *we're* going to fix the delay." Harry pointed his finger to emphasize each point. "I told him, you caused the delay, and you're the one who decided not to mention it when you knew it would cause a problem, so when you ask me how 'we' are going to fix it, all I can say is…"

Harry paused so Julia could complete the line he had taught her years ago. She put on a New York accent. "By 'we' do you mean you and the mouse in your pocket?

Because you certainly do not mean me." They laughed at their hilarity.

It was always great spending time with her mentor.

———

DAY two in the New York office was as successful as day one. Meeting attendance grew as more salespeople found out what was happening.

Julia ended day two with a one-on-one meeting with the head of the New York sales office. Matthew, not Matt, was a tough nut to crack. A native New Yorker with a chip on his shoulder from being from a working-class background, Julia was able to bond with him through stories about public school in Cleveland.

"Why are you spending all of this time in the field when you could be happily bestowing your brilliance upon us from the safe confines of HQ?" Julia noted the sarcasm in Matthew's voice.

She decided to match it.

"You know, Matthew, New York is so lovely this time of year." She gestured to the February rain and snow mix that fell outside the window.

Matthew's belly laugh rang through the hallways.

"I like you." He pointed at her as he pursed his lips and gave her a nod.

Julia changed her tone. "But seriously, I want our teams to work together. I want to fix issues and streamline processes. I want our products to be valued in the marketplace. I want your sales team to have the tools, skills, and mindset to be competitive and exceed their quotas."

Matthew nodded his agreement. "Where do I come in?"

"I'd be happy to get your feedback as well. I can either share what I've already learned, or just hear it straight from you. Whichever is easiest for you."

"Hit me with the summary, and then I'll add my comments." Julia recited the top five areas of improvement off the top of her head. "You mean it. You aren't just going through the motions. I like your straightforward approach. Very New York. Not the passive aggressive bullshit we get from most people who come out from HQ."

Julia blushed at the praise. Getting Matthew on her side was big. Really big.

"Thanks Matthew. My time in Manhattan has been invaluable. If Jeff asks, perhaps you could share the progress with him."

"I'll do that. And I'll even read the email update. If you want to bounce ideas off me at any point, just give me a call." He stood to signal the end of the meeting.

Another success!

IN THE HOTEL that night after savoring a slice of New York pizza, Julia crafted an email to everyone who had attended her listening tour in New York and those who had been invited but didn't make it to the meeting. She gave a special shout out to Matthew for his time and listed her action items. She cc'ed Jeff on the email so he would know she was gathering feedback from his team.

She knew it was the right thing to do. She also knew he wouldn't read it.

She felt good about her accomplishments for the day. She had definitely built some credibility with the team. She just had to keep going.

Julia stretched her arms over her head. Her shoulders

cracked and popped as they were released from the hunching position over her laptop. She was tired, but it was a good kind of tired. She'd had a very productive trip so far, made tangible progress on Operation Fix-It, and had a great time catching up with Harry.

Atlanta was up next. She combined the visits to New York and Atlanta into one trip to maximize the impact and minimize the travel costs.

Breathing deeply for the first time in a couple of days, Julia thought about Rob. He had managed to squeeze his way into her subconscious awfully quickly. She decided to give him a call. The time change was in her favor.

"Hey, I was just thinking about you." She could hear the smile in his voice.

"What're you up to?"

"Since you're out of town, I had dinner with my other best girl."

"Your mother or your sister?" Julia asked with a chuckle.

"I love that I can say that without you getting jealous, knowing I mean my family. This time, Leenie was the victim. We went for Italian."

"Sounds fun. I'm looking forward to seeing her again." Julia hoped that wasn't too forward.

"I'm looking forward to seeing more of you when you get home." She pictured Rob raising one eyebrow suggestively.

"And I look forward to being seen." Julia felt naughty flirting like this.

"Don't start something over the phone you aren't ready to finish."

Julia froze. Did he want to have phone sex? She didn't know how to do that or what to say. She let the moment pass, feeling relieved when Rob continued. "When will you be home?"

"Late Thursday."

"Okay, I'll check in with you then."

Julia smiled at the phone after they hung up.

———

ATLANTA WENT JUST AS WELL as Los Angeles and New York. Turnout was high, and Julia continued to make progress. By the time she got off the plane in Seattle Thursday evening, she was just plain worn out. But she felt good about progress on Operation Fix-It.

Her first stop after she landed was to pick Selah up at the kennel. At home later that evening, Julia reflected on Margaret's sex pep talk from Saturday. It was time for action. Margaret would approve.

ROB'S ONLINE STATUS SAID "AVAILABLE" when she got to work Friday morning. She pinged him with a chirpy message.

> Good morning, can you IM?

> For you, of course

> Dinner tonight?

> Yes, I'm planning on having it

Always the jokester. Julia kept typing.

> Let me be clear - with me

> Oh, then definitely yes. Where and when?

New cantina on Market Street, 6PM

I like a woman who takes charge. C U there
and then

166

Julia had trouble concentrating on her meetings that day. Jet lag from the time change was part of it, but the other part was thinking about her upcoming evening with Rob.

One meeting in particular was going to be tricky. Jeff had requested a one on one which was not very typical. They usually just interacted during leadership team meetings. But given the amount of energy she was putting into developing relationships and building respect with his team, she had a solid agenda and progress to share.

She hoped for the best but planned for the worst.

She would be polite but not deferential.

Firm, but not bossy.

Informed, but not a know-it-all.

She would listen. Even when she wanted to scream.

It was only a thirty-minute meeting. She could handle anything for thirty minutes.

Jeff had, of course, had his admin schedule the meeting in his office for home field advantage. Julia practiced deep breathing on her way there.

He wasn't in. His admin told her to have a seat on the

tiny guest chair in his office to wait. *Another power play*. Julia got out her laptop and kept working. She wasn't going to lose time just because he was late.

He breezed in about ten minutes later followed by his usual cloud of cologne. He sat across from Julia, all smiles. She returned his smile. "Hey Jeff, nice to see you." Pleasantries should eat up another minute or two.

"What's this I hear about my sellers sitting in conference rooms with you when they should be out selling?" He laced his fingers together and cocked an eyebrow at Julia.

So much for pleasantries.

She kept her tone light, trying to hide the defensive response she wanted to give. "The meetings aren't mandatory – they're attending because they want to share feedback about me and my team."

"Well I have some feedback, too. Stop talking to my team and let them sell."

"Jeff, I completely understand your concern that I'm taking them away from their day jobs." She thought it best to agree with him even though she didn't. "Please understand that the hour they spend with me will increase their seller productivity. And it's having a positive impact on morale. They told me."

"And I'm telling you to stop. Cancel your trips."

"What would I tell the people who've set up agency meetings with me in Chicago and Dallas? Wouldn't it be worse to cancel? What reason would I give?"

"I don't care – tell them you have some sort of important pricing emergency, whatever that could be." She ignored his derisive snort.

Julia wondered why he was concerned. She also knew asking questions that started with the word "why" could exacerbate his already bad mood. *Elbows in,* she thought. "What would have to happen for you to view this as a positive thing for your team?" She was very proud of her question. She kept her cool and didn't rise to the bait.

"You'd have to end each meeting lowering the prices that you charge. And you don't need to talk to them to do that."

Her tactics weren't working. She would try deferential next. It was not her strong suit. She knew if she wasn't careful, her tone would sound condescending. "What would you have me do instead? I'm trying to build rapport with your team so we can solve problems together. My goal is to improve their jobs, not make them more difficult. You told me I have a lot to learn, so I'm learning." She saw the flash of victory on his face.

"You're doing this because I said you should?"

"Yes. At the last leadership team meeting, you told me I didn't know anything. I heard you and I'm taking action."

"Okay then, you can finish your little tour, but only because you're learning more about what you need to fix."

She had to get out of there. Continuing this conversation would only increase the chances of slipping up and letting her true thoughts come out of her mouth.

She reflected on advice she got from a colleague a million years ago that was brilliant but hard to follow. He told her that if it feels good to say it, she probably shouldn't say it. As annoying as it was in the moment, it was great advice. She always tried to follow it – *tried to*, being the operative words. "Then we're aligned. Thank you." Julia left his office.

SHE STOMPED BACK to her office the long way, hoping to burn off some pent-up energy. What the hell? He couldn't tell her what to do. And she hated that her response had been to back down instead of telling him to fuck right off.

Was she learning to be a better corporate citizen or was she just being a wimp? If only her divorce were settled, she could be freer with her comments and actually defend herself without worrying about the consequences.

She felt more like herself by the time she got back to her office. She didn't need to take her frustration out on her next meeting attendees. She was better than that.

JULIA FINISHED her meetings at four o'clock which gave her some time to get home, take a shower, shave her legs, and change into something a bit more flattering than her work wardrobe of a gray jacket, blouse, black pants and heeled Mary Jane shoes. It would also give her time to get Jeff out of her head. She hated that his voice stayed there, taunting her.

Julia wanted to try the new Mexican place that had opened up earlier in the month in her town. She liked the idea of taking Rob there since she and Cliff had gone to most of the local places together. She wanted new memories.

Julia arrived at the Cantina at five fifty-five, and Rob was right behind her at six o'clock on the dot. On time, as usual.

"Tell me all about New York. I have to admit I was glad you didn't tell me where you were staying because I would've shown up at your door."

Julia believed him. "Next time, maybe I'll take you with me."

"I'd like that."

As a bowl of guacamole and a basket of chips arrived at the table, Julia abruptly changed the subject. "I made some good decisions while I was gone." She pointed at him with a chip. "Mostly about you."

"Care to elaborate?"

"Well, for one thing, I want to give this a go, I mean give it a try instead of skirting around it. I've been holding back because of all the Cliff weirdness, but I missed you when I was traveling. Are you in?"

"You have to ask?" Rob grinned.

"I hope it doesn't make you uncomfortable, but I had some blood tests recently and they added an STD check. I'm clean." *Thank you Doctor Winkyface.* "Would you mind doing the same before we take things further physically?"

"Good news," he said. "I just had my pilot physical for the FAA and added some bloodwork for myself, hoping that we would be taking it to the next level. All clear."

"Always good to plan ahead and be prepared." She hoped her excitement didn't show through too much. "It must be the Eagle Scout training."

"Or maybe I was making sure I was ready when you were." There was a gleam in his blue eyes.

They shared some tacos while continuing their light banter. But something had shifted between them, and Julia was in a hurry to get back to her house. She ate quickly. He was waiting with his credit card out when the server came over with the bill.

Julia took one last sip of water. "I'll open the garage so you can park inside. I'd rather not be interrupted by another Cliff visit. I changed the locks, but let's not tempt fate if he swings by again.

"Sounds like a plan." Rob wiped his mouth with his napkin, never taking his eyes off her.

"Ready to get out of here?"

He threw his napkin onto the table. "I thought you'd never ask."

Chapter 26

"I've never used this line before," Julia said when they were in her living room, "but let me slip into something more comfortable." It was black lace body stocking time.

She could feel his eyes follow her up the stairs.

She literally could not remember the last time she'd had sex. She was hoping she wouldn't be saying that tomorrow morning. *New year, new life, great sex.*

She rolled the stockings up her legs and slipped her arms through the arm holes. She turned around and craned her neck to see herself from behind. She took a few more seconds to straighten out the crooked seams, which turned out to be a little harder than she thought. The black lace stretched across her breasts and showed a hint of pink nipples through the thin fabric. If his eyes just stayed on her boobs, she'd be fine.

Doubts stemming from her nightmare started to flit around the edges of her mind, but visions of Margaret's wiggling eyebrows pushed them out. She took a deep breath and squared her shoulders in the mirror. It was go time.

"Rob, want to come upstairs?" As Rob turned the corner and looked up the stairs, he stopped dead in his tracks.

"That screams sex, Julia." Her heart raced at the guttural grunt he made as he bounded up the stairs two at a time. His arms were around her and his hands were on her backside pressing her to him before she could even figure out what happened. "You better be sure you want to do this, because I can only stop myself for another three seconds having seen you in that."

Julia nodded at him. "I'm sure."

He swung her into his arms, whisked her into the bedroom, and placed her on the bed in one effortless motion. He slipped off his shoes and joined her.

Julia had to admit that as smoothly as he had moved her onto the bed, it felt weird to be almost naked while Rob was fully dressed. She wanted to even the playing field. She rolled over on top of him and unbuttoned his shirt, appreciating the contrasting collar and cuffs. Rob leaned forward. She slid it over his shoulders.

God, he was beautiful. His smooth and muscular chest narrowed into a trim waist. She couldn't see the rest because he was still wearing his jeans. Julia got to work fixing that.

She tried to slow down the pace to get a good look, but he was on top of her again, kissing her neck and rubbing seductively against her. His caresses became more urgent as she reached down to unzip his pants and free him so she could take him in her hands.

Rolling over again, she helped him remove his pants and ran her hands back up his chest. She felt the black lace strain across her breasts and hoped Rob was enjoying the view.

She moved over to one side and reached down to

stroke him. Based on his reaction to her touch, Julia quickly replaced her hands with her mouth. He groaned as she slid his length in and out.

Julia savored the feel of him, licking his head as Rob tried to keep control. He sounded like he was getting close. She started to release him. "Please keep going," he said through gritted teeth. "I recover quickly." She did as he asked, and he climaxed in her mouth.

She lay down next to him giving him time to collect himself before round two. It didn't take long.

"You're so beautiful." Rob's voice was husky with desire. "I've got to get you out of this thing. I want to see all of you."

"Actually," that was all Julia could get out before Rob started sliding the first strap off her shoulder. "It has like a little hatch down there, so you don't need to take it off. It's for peeing, I guess." She sounded lame, even to her own ears. Julia was uncomfortable about being naked with him and preferred to keep the thin lace barrier.

She couldn't believe she was making such stupid comments while trying to be sexy. Before she could think of a second, more appropriate comment, Rob pushed all thoughts of awkwardness out of her head as he trailed his hand down her body and found the opening in the body stocking. He traced the edge, making her shudder and crave more.

He gently opened her folds with his finger and danced his fingers around her clit as she tried to keep still. Soon, she was rubbing against his fingers encouraging him to enter her.

After what seemed like an eternity, he plunged two fingers into her core.

It had been a long time since she had been excited like this, many years actually. She decided to focus on herself and get the most out of the pleasure Rob was giving her.

She felt her muscles tightening as she moved against his hand. This was going to be a good one.

"I love how responsive you are," Rob said. "It helps to know you're enjoying this." Julia was happy to learn Rob didn't need any coaching. He sensed when to go faster and when to change the angle.

Just when she started to worry he was going to think she was taking too long, he hit just the right spot and sent her soaring. It was the longest orgasm she'd ever had. Something that had been tightly wound uncoiled in her core.

"I loved watching you come. I don't think I've ever been as turned on as I am right now." He moved on top of her.

Julia basked in her post-orgasmic glow, feeling loose as she came down from the waves that rocked her. But she wanted more. More of him. She wanted to feel him inside her.

She opened for him as he moved between her legs. He pushed her knees up to her shoulders and slid into her with one fluid motion. "You're so wet."

That almost made Julia laugh. She had never seemed wet enough to make things comfortable in the past. The fact that he slid right in following the orgasm she had just experienced showed her that her parts were in fine working order.

He began his glorious slide in and out. Julia had almost forgotten what it was like to be filled by a man. Each thrust increased her excitement as she rose up to meet him, fervor growing.

Rob pulled the top of the body stocking down to reveal her full breasts and bent to take one in his mouth.

The last few weeks of tantalizing play without fulfillment had whipped her into a frenzy of need, and she felt like he was right there with her. "I've fantasized a lot about this moment," he said between kisses, "but nothing compares to actually being right here, right now. Damn, you're sexy."

Julia was lost in the moment. Lost in him and the feel of his body pressing hers to the bed. Going on instinct, she pulled her legs down and wrapped them around him, tilting her pelvis down for maximum clit contact as she moved with him.

She grabbed his ass with both hands and matched his pace. She felt the gathering of muscles and the warmth in her core that preceded another orgasm. She had never come during actual sex before. Yes, mouths and fingers had worked, but never a dick. She wondered if this could be the time.

Perhaps focusing on her body instead of over-thinking it would help, she thought, trying to get out of her own head. She ground his hips into her and felt the need building.

Floating on the sensations she had never experienced before, Julia climaxed and bucked in rhythm with his thrusts. She felt proud as she came – proud that she could get there and proud of him for taking her there on his first try.

This is what sex is supposed to be like, she thought. *No wonder everyone talks about it so much.*

She moaned out loud. "Your turn." She lay back to enjoy the aftermath of her second orgasm of the evening. Rob's thrusts increased as he started to make his own set of noises.

"Here it comes." He was a talker, Julia was amused to discover. She felt the ripple of muscle to muscle and reveled in it. He dropped on top of her, breathing hard. "I'm powerless against that lingerie."

Julia was alive. She had just been thoroughly loved by a

man who couldn't control himself at the sight of her wearing black lace. It wasn't her problem after all. It was Cliff's.

She pushed him out of her mind so she wouldn't ruin the moment. Julia cuddled up to Rob to give him a chance to rest, even though she thought she had another orgasm or two inside her.

He took three deep breaths. "Okay. Your turn again."

When they were both spent, they lay together on the damp, twisted sheets. "You have to warn me before you put that on again."

"I might have it bronzed," she purred.

JULIA LAY in bed the next morning renewed and energized, enjoying the soreness in places that hadn't been sore in years. Another step forward in her new year, new life, great sex mantra.

She smiled as she thought of Rob's departure around midnight. They had lingered at the door for several minutes hugging and kissing before he headed home so he could get up early for a Saturday morning mountain bike ride. She basked in having avoided the awkward morning after scene.

Plans had been made for a date that evening. She had started looking forward to it as soon as he pulled out of the driveway. She had reverted right back to a college girl with a crush.

Guilt tried to creep in, but Julia pushed it right out again. She decided to enjoy the moment rather than punish herself. Lesley, Melanie, and Margaret would be proud.

· · ·

IT WAS CLOUDY AND DRIZZLY, but Julia was so alive after her night with Rob it didn't dampen her mood on her walk with Selah in the cold morning.

Work thoughts crept in as she walked. She mentally flipped through her plan for the week. She was leaving Monday to visit Dallas and Chicago on her next trip to collect feedback as she blazed through all of the US offices.

She hadn't let up for a second at work and she had to keep Operation Fix-It on track.

Nothing could stop her now, she thought.

Chapter 27

"How goes it in love-land?" Lesley asked later that day. They would cap off brunch with a trip to the mall. Julia needed new lingerie. Finally.

Julia tapped her index finger to her lip. "I would say it goes well."

"How well? Like well enough you're still exploring or well enough you think you'll keep this one?" Lesley raised her eyebrows in anticipation of the answer.

"I'm keeping him for now."

"Excellent. Have you done the deed yet?" Julia couldn't stop herself from smiling. "That's what I believe they call a 'shit-eating grin.' I assume the answer is yes then?"

"Yes." Julia nodded and blushed as she remembered her evening.

"And how was it? Did the earth move? Did he ruin you for all other men? Did he take direction well?"

Julia kept her voice low. "I've never had such great sex. No direction needed."

"Woo hoo! Points for Rob! I thought you two would have some fun."

"You were right, as usual. Thanks for encouraging me to go for it. I knew my inner sex kitten was in there somewhere, and he has lured her out to play. In fact, it's hard to think about anything else."

"And what about the other guy?" Lesley asked referring to Cliff.

"It's bad. He's angry and won't move his stuff out of the house."

"I hate him."

"I am trying not to, but it's tempting." Julia sipped her mimosa. "What's new with you? Any new dates to update me on?"

"Actually yes. You better order another mimosa, because this is going to take a while."

▭

ROB WAS TAKING her to his favorite pizza place for their Saturday night date. That was a risky move given her time in Manhattan. Her recent trip to New York only proved that point further.

But more important than the pizza, Julia was looking forward to what happened after dinner. Rob awakened a sex-crazed teenager inside of her. And she loved it.

As usual, Rob was right on time. She opened the door to let Selah bask in his attention. He looked fabulous in his blue sports coat with a flowered pocket square peeking out. She caught a whiff of his cologne as he bent over to greet the dog who was as happy to see Rob as Julia was.

"Hi." He straightened up and handed Julia a bouquet of daisies, alstroemeria, and roses. "I thought you might like these. Sorry they didn't have sunflowers."

"They're beautiful. All flowers are beautiful — not just

sunflowers. Please don't think you have to bring me flowers every time we go out."

"Listen to us." Rob laughed. "I'm apologizing for not getting you the perfect flowers and you're demurring and saying I don't need to bring you any."

"There's something wrong with us." Julia smirked. "Let me try again. Thank you." She gave him a kiss. He took her face in his hands and deepened it. Julia went right along for the ride.

Finally breaking away, Julia pulled back for a moment while his hands still held her face. "Keep it up and we'll miss our reservation."

"They can wait." Rob leaned in again.

"I'm going to assume that the guilt you would feel from messing with the restaurant outweighs your desire to keep kissing me."

"You got me – let's go." He let go of her face.

THE RESTAURANT WAS in the artsy part of town where the air smelled faintly of marijuana while aging hippies with dreadlocks strolled past shops selling incense and Rastafarian hats.

The aroma of sautéed onions and marinara sauce wafted through the air to greet them when they opened the heavy wooden door. The restaurant was full of people happily munching on salads and pizza while drinking one of the many beer selections they had on tap.

"Pizza and beer. No better combination." Rob helped Julia off with her coat. "For food, anyway." He winked at her with both eyes.

They were shown to a booth covered with red vinyl that matched the placemats on the scarred wood table.

"The pizza is amazing here, but the ambiance… not so much. I know you like French restaurants and champagne bars. Did I miscalculate?"

"I was thinking it reminded me of a restaurant I used to love going to as a kid. If the pizza is as good as it smells, there's nothing to worry about." Julia silently commended herself for being able to compliment Seattle pizza. Clearly, she was growing.

"What do you like on your pizza?"

"I'm a traditionalist," Julia answered. "Pepperoni or sausage and onions. I wouldn't mind if a green pepper fell onto the pie as well. Maybe even some black olives."

"I go Hawaiian, all the way – ham and pineapple. Our first area of incompatibility," Rob joked.

"Yep, looks like it's over between us," Julia said with fake solemnity. "Or, we could go half and half and make the best of a terrible situation."

"Glad that's settled."

Laughing their way through another fun meal, Julia threw in the towel after her third slice of pizza. "You're right – that's good stuff."

"It's my favorite. I'm glad you liked it. Maybe you'd let me bring you back again."

"Without a doubt." Julia looked at her watch. "It's still early. Want to take a walk? I don't get to this neighborhood very often."

"Love to."

They strolled down the street hand-in-hand taking in the sights. They passed a couple of bars, and Julia thought about asking Rob in for a drink. But it was a pleasant night, and she was enjoying the walk. She didn't think she could eat or drink anything else for a while anyway.

"Gelato," Rob announced with childlike glee. "Want

some?" He stopped in front of a small shop with beautiful mounds of gelato made from a rainbow of fruits and nuts.

"I don't think I could fit anything else in right now."

"Oh, come on, there's always room for ice cream. It fills in the cracks."

"Good point. Let's do it." Julia decided to live a little.

The woman behind the counter smiled around her various piercings.

"We haven't been in before. What's good?" Rob checked to see that there was no line behind him.

"They're all great. And the best news is you can have more than one. A small has two flavors, a medium has three, and a large has four. I like the coffee and pistachio combo. It tastes like a cookie together. Vanilla fig with dark chocolate is another winner."

Julia was determined to not completely blow her diet. "Tough choice. I should get a small, but I can't decide."

"Get a medium. It's date night!" Rob wiggled his eyebrows at her.

"You sold me." Julia logged a requirement for an extra twenty minutes on the elliptical the next day. "I'll go for a medium with dark chocolate, espresso, and pistachio."

The woman behind the counter smiled as she started to scoop. "Good call. How about you, sir?"

"I'll have a small with peanut butter and dark chocolate."

"A small?" Julia yelped. "Now I feel like a pig!"

Rob just looked over and put up a finger to silence her. "I will *also* have a small with dulce de leche and fig."

"Great choices all around. I'll get those going for you."

"Good save," Julia laughed. "You managed to put me in my place and make me laugh."

.   .   .

ROB OPENED the car door for her. "Where to now?"

"I was kind of hoping I could entice you to come home with me so we could pick up where we left off last night."

"I am putty in your hands, my sweet. Your wish is my command."

"Did you have anything specific in mind?" Julia asked as Rob pulled out of the tight parking space and headed to the highway.

Julia was not used to talking openly about sex. She was surprised she felt a bit shy. But this was probably a rebound thing. She should enjoy it and not get her ego too involved. "I've lived a pretty sheltered sex life. Perhaps you could teach me something new."

"You mean like a backward cowgirl?"

"Maybe. If I knew what that was."

"It's you on top but with your back facing me. It can be fun for you, a little less so for me, but I get to watch your butt go up and down."

"We'd have to practice." She decided to be honest. "I've never been on top."

"What? Ever?"

"It's kind of embarrassing, but I didn't fool around a lot in college because I didn't want to get pregnant, and then there was Cliff. You know the story there. He clearly wasn't into experimental stuff, at least with me, so I have very limited experience – mostly missionary position."

"I don't mean to embarrass you. I've tried a lot of approaches. I can show you some and we can find something you like."

"Then I'll try to get over my embarrassment and be a good student. What do you like?"

"Sex."

"Can you be more specific?"

"Sex with you." He snuck a glance at her before putting his eyes back on the road.

"Okay, I get it. You aren't going to tell me."

"Let's make tonight about you. That way, I can use your desire for fairness to ensure there's another date."

"Nice touch," she chuckled.

Julia started getting excited thinking about what they would do when they got home. "What if you had some fun first, and then we focused on me?" Julia asked.

"What do you have in mind?"

Julia felt naughty talking this way, but she wanted to experiment with being more open about sex. "I've been staring into those blue eyes all evening and it makes we want to lick you."

"If you keep talking like that, I'll have to pull over and get started right here."

"Really? It turns you on to talk about it?"

"Are you kidding? A hot woman talking about sex? Major points on the hot scale."

"I'm a hot woman?" Her voice rose about an octave from its usual timbre. "Nobody's ever thought of me that way before."

"Told you and thought about you that way are two different things. I'm glad we're almost back to your place." Rob shifted in his seat.

Julia was lost in her own thoughts about what they were going to do. As they drove up the hill to her house, she decided to take another risk. "I'm getting pretty hot thinking about what happens when we get back to my house."

Rob groaned through his teeth. "I'm already speeding – don't make it worse."

Julia enjoyed her new-found freedom to talk about sex

and have some verbal foreplay before they got home. She didn't know that people, well Rob anyway, liked that.

She opened the garage door as soon as she was in range and was unbuckling her seatbelt before the car was in the slot.

Rob reached across the front seat toward the buttons on her shirt. "Nope, not yet. I get to work on you first." Julia pushed him back on the seat and got busy opening his fly. Once she freed him, she bent over the center console and took him into her mouth. She had to adjust to avoid the drink holder, but she found a decent position after a few seconds.

Rob rocked back and forth into her mouth. Julia hadn't done this much since college, but the skill came back to her quickly and she could tell Rob was enjoying it.

Julia's left leg started tingling as it fell asleep from the awkward position needed to avoid the center console. She chose to focus on the new sensations she was feeling as she saw Rob's response and felt her own reaction.

With a call of triumph, he exploded into her mouth.

Recovering quickly, Rob reached under her skirt. "I need to get you into the kitchen for part two." He pushed the lace aside and plunged two fingers inside of her. Julia moved against his hand.

"We can start act two out here. That feels so good."

He continued to caress her as he watched her start the rise toward her first orgasm of the evening.

Not even sure what she was doing, Julia found herself on all fours in the front seat while Rob did magical things to her. Even in this awkward position she was going to come faster than she ever had before.

As soon as she crested, Rob was out the door and ready to get her into the kitchen. On trembling legs and enjoying fun aftershocks, Julia made it through the door.

"Now what?" Julia asked, breathless with excitement.

"Lie down on the table with your legs hanging off the side." Rob pushed her skirt up and slid her panties down her long legs.

Rob nestled between her legs and bent down to kiss her mouth. After indulging in deep, wet kisses, he started moving down her torso.

Julia started to get nervous. She thought of the shower she took that morning and wondered if she would be stinky. When she was sure he was headed in that direction, Julia tried to stop him. "I'm not exactly fresh and minty if you know what I mean." Embarrassment filled her.

"You smell like a woman,"

"I don't like that smell."

"That's because you aren't a lesbian. I'll stop if you like, but I'd like to have some fun down here."

"Okay, but I warned you." He was awfully good at this, Julia thought before all thoughts were pushed out of her mind by his quick tongue and active fingers.

While she was coming down from her second orgasm, he slipped out of his jeans. "Okay, now wrap your legs around me."

Julia did as she was told. Rob pulled her to him using her legs. She had never had sex on a table. She was perplexed by how the angle was going to work out since she was several inches lower than him.

A patient teacher, Rob didn't make her feel like a novice. Instead, it was like he loved showing her new things. He placed his hands under her butt and lifted her to the right height. "God, you're gorgeous."

She let his words fill her with happiness. This hot, sexy man thought she was gorgeous. She savored these new feelings and appreciated she could be sexy while learning a lot about what she'd been missing.

She wanted him inside of her but waited for the next instruction.

He positioned himself at her opening and entered her in one fluid motion. She went taut in his arms as she enjoyed the sensation. He began to thrust slowly. "How's that angle?"

"All good here." She was hot with desire after her last orgasm and was eager to feel the next wave of sensations. At this angle, she could take almost all of him in. She felt him touch the back as he made soft contact with her clit.

Rob's thrusting became more energetic as he got closer to the edge. Julia watched as he enjoyed himself. *She was having sex on her kitchen table.* She wished for a pillow for her head but didn't feel like it was the right time to say so. *Next time.*

He let go of her butt with one hand and brought it around to the front, placing his thumb on her clit. He drove himself into her while stroking her to her next orgasm. *Three? Three orgasms?* With a manly groan, he climaxed right after her and they took a moment to savor the latest waves of pleasure.

Out of breath, he placed his hands on each side of Julia. "How was that?"

"It was great, and it seemed to work for you." She was still catching her breath, too.

"That's an understatement."

"My head hurts a little bit. It would be good to sit up." Rob immediately wrapped his arms around her and pulled her up off the table.

"Can I get you something to drink?" he asked, sounding concerned he had hurt her.

"I wouldn't mind some water. But then we're going upstairs to finish this, because I've had more orgasms than you and I'd like to even the score."

"I love your attention to fairness. I like that idea."

Julia stopped about halfway up. "I'm sorry to be weird, but would you mind brushing your teeth before we keep going?"

"Sure, no problem," Rob laughed as he continued upstairs.

She handed him a toothbrush and he rinsed his beard before they fell into bed for more.

Chapter 28

Julia watched Rob sleep. It was his first sleepover, and she found it odd to see someone other than Cliff in the bed next to her.

Setting that aside, she let the joy of waking up with Rob after a wonderful night of sex fill her. Her body felt delightfully used. She rejoiced in it as she reflected on the way Rob had instructed and guided her the night before.

Rob stirred and opened one eye. "How long have you been up?"

"Just a few minutes. Why don't you sleep a bit more while I take a shower?" Julia tried not to let him smell her morning breath.

"What time is it? I'm supposed to meet Carla at nine for our monthly brunch."

"It's only seven. You have plenty of time."

"How about I join you in that shower instead?"

Julia tried not to be shy as she stood in the shower facing Rob. He had already seen every part of her, but that was in dim light. *Does water hide cellulite?* She took a stand

and decided to envision the water rinsing her negative thoughts away.

"Let me help you with that." Rob massaged shampoo into Julia's curly locks. She tilted her head back and enjoyed the feel of his hands on her. He gently turned her around to put her face in the water. "Don't want you getting shampoo in your eyes."

Rob cupped her breasts and pulled her soapy back against him. She could feel his muscular frame from head to toe as he gently pulsed against her. She rested her head on his chest while he continued the journey down her body with his slick, soapy hands.

She clasped her hands around his head to give him full access to anything he wanted to touch. Julia breathed in the scent of shampoo and felt her skin heat up, not just from the hot water, but from what Rob was doing to her. She writhed against him as his fingers found her center.

"I love being with you like this."

The storm gathered in Julia's body. "Yes!" she cried out as he teased her over the peak. "Don't stop," she moaned as she rode the wave. She fell back against him as he continued to caress her with one hand. "Mmm, that was nice," she murmured, turning around to look into his blue eyes. She liked the look of pure desire she saw on his face.

He picked up her leg and held it to the side as he slipped inside of her. He took his time building up the speed of his thrusts. She wrapped her leg around him to hold him closer as they moved together.

"Can you put your other leg around my waist?"

Julia was confused. She would fall over if she did that. "Think you can hold me up?"

"I know I can." He pressed her back against the shower wall and shifted her up as she wrapped her other leg around his waist.

Another new position, Julia thought. But soon, all other thoughts were forced out of her head by the warm feeling of another orgasm building. He pressed her against the wall as he continued to thrust into her.

Julia clutched him close as the next orgasm ripped through her, accelerated by pressure on just the right spot. His hand was trapped between them as he increased his thrusts and emptied into her.

Pinned against the wall, Julia took a few deep breaths. "You must be getting tired of holding me up."

"That's the best part of this. The wall does a lot of the work."

They grinned at each other under the spray of the water.

"How do I, um, dismount?" Now that they were done, Julia's novice embarrassment reared its ugly head.

Rob put his hands in her armpits. "Unwrap your legs and just stand up."

"Duh."

"Julia. I love that you're open to trying new things and I want you to ask questions. I'm happy to be on this journey with you."

Oh what a journey it was.

JULIA SAT at the kitchen table sipping a steaming mug of coffee while staring at her phone and a text from Cliff.

She was swirling on the juxtaposition of the fun she was having with Rob and the stress she felt about Cliff dragging his feet about their divorce settlement. What if being with Rob was making it worse and that's why Cliff wasn't moving his stuff out of the house or accepting her offer?

"What's on your mind? It looks serious." She looked up at Rob and was instantly transported back to the shower. She wanted to hold onto that feeling.

Julia sighed. "I got a text from Cliff asking to meet up. It's making me think too much." Julia hated that a message from Cliff could erase the warm fuzzy feeling she had after gliding into the kitchen on a sexual high.

"About what?"

"Is the fun I'm having with you worth the potential pain it's causing Cliff? Is the fact that we're together fueling his anger and inability to let go?"

"What're you saying? What's going on for you?"

"I was just sitting here wondering if it's worth it. I feel so selfish. I don't know what this is. Is it a rebound or is it real and does it even matter? I know I don't want to be with him, but I wonder if we should cool it for a bit and wait until everything is settled before we continue our exploration. Waving the red flag of us being together in his face is only going to fuel his anger. If he escalates, it could get really expensive. And my job isn't secure right now. I'm working really hard to prove I'm a good leader, but Jeff is still angry. He might continue to try to get me fired."

"Oh, I see. Now that you've had your way with me, you toss me out like yesterday's newspaper." He winked with both eyes. "But seriously, you're scaring me a bit. You and I are good together. We have fun, and we're happy. It's foolish to not choose happiness when it's right in front of us because you're worried about how it makes other people feel. It'll all work out."

"How can you be so calm? Camille hasn't signed your agreement either. What if you can't meet her terms?"

"Then we'll have to change them until I can meet them. Yeah, I might wind up paying her alimony for a long time. And yeah, I might not get my money back out of our house. It'll all be okay eventually."

"I have no idea how you can just bob along and not be worried."

"We don't have the assets you do. We're just going to divide things fifty/fifty and I'm going to sweeten the deal with the plane. No big whoop." Rob bent down to kiss Julia on the top of her head. "I'll call you later."

"And I'll see you when I get back from my next trip."

Julia sat with her cooling coffee, contemplating the words Rob had said – and hadn't said. He didn't disagree with her that this could be a rebound. He hadn't said he liked her. She was deeply programmed to consider how her actions affected others. Guilt from being selfish gripped her.

And how was he able to be so blasé about money?

Rob and Camille were splitting their assets fifty/fifty. But they were both employed so that made it easier to divide things in half.

Forty percent was more than generous given her situation for the last ten years. Julia had done the math. Her portfolio had shot up once she started being successful at LampLight. She had worked hard to earn her money. All without any contributions from Cliff. She had hundreds of thousands of dollars in vested stock. And he would get a big chunk of it.

It made her angry. It made her sad. "Fuck Cliff!" she yelled into the empty room. Selah came running in and laid her head on Julia's leg. She stroked her loving dog's head and calmed down.

The only way Julia knew to snap out of it was to switch gears back to work. Her next trip started the next day, and she had to get a bunch of work done since she'd be out of the office in meetings with the Dallas and Chicago teams.

She used that as an excuse to set her ruminations about Rob aside and focus on work. Protecting her financial future was more important than protecting her heart. *Or was it?* She wished she knew.

Chapter 29

"Thanks for coming everyone. Great stuff. I'll follow-up soon with actions." Wrapping up her second day of meetings in Dallas on Tuesday early afternoon, Julia felt the strain of her long days and the exhaustion of little sleep.

She'd repeated the process she'd perfected in Los Angeles, New York, and Atlanta. She collected a few more action items and validated some of her new approaches.

Now she had to hurry to the airport for her flight to Chicago. Once arriving in the Land of Lincoln, she'd walk right off the plane into a late dinner meeting with Brian, the head of Sales for the Midwest team.

If Operation Fix-It was going to work, she had to curry favor with Jeff's direct reports. Brian, like Matthew in New York, was key as he was one of Jeff's favorites. Then she had a day of internal meetings and a morning with agency clients before heading home.

Long days. She hoped it would be worth it.

. . .

AT DINNER THAT EVENING, Brian delivered a monologue on the virtues of his strategic account approach. "And that's how I'm going to grow this business," he ended with a flourish. His floppy light brown hair bobbed with the exaggerated movement.

Julia thought most of his plans paved a path for getting his entire team fired, but she kept her most negative thoughts to herself. *Elbows in.* "How are you attracting the mid-tier agencies and advertisers?" she asked. "They have less negotiating power in the market, so you can command higher prices from them."

"Oh no, Julia. You don't get it. It's the same amount of work to get a big deal at a huge agency as a medium-sized deal at a small agency. We're going after the volume play."

There was only so much coaching Julia could do. Anyone could tell you a diversified portfolio was better in a volatile market, but he didn't want to hear that feedback. Julia focused on her meal and just let him talk. She was supposed to be proving she could listen, *right?*

Keeping her inner monologue firmly in place always tapped her energy. She could almost feel the physical sting of biting her tongue for so long.

Dinner finally ended, and Julia was able to escape. Even more exhausted than before dinner, she was ready to check into her hotel, give Rob a call, and head to bed.

Opening the door of her room, she was surprised to see a bouquet of sunflowers smiling at her when she set her suitcase down near the bed. She didn't remember this hotel chain being fancy.

She texted Rob to let him know she was safely in her hotel. He called her within a minute.

"How's the weather in Chicago?"

"It's colder than Seattle."

"Is it *sunny* there?" he asked.

"Not really – it was pretty cloudy today during the few minutes of daylight I could actually see from the plane window." Julia was confused about why Rob was interested in the weather.

"Anything unusual about your room?"

"Yeah, actually. There's a huge bunch of sunflowers." And then it hit her. She felt like an idiot. "Those are from you, aren't they?"

"Why yes they are."

"Are you kidding me? You sent me flowers in my hotel room?" Julia was floored.

"Yes. It's funny you didn't figure that out."

"Thank you!" Julia was horrified she hadn't known he'd sent them.

"I hope you like them. I wanted you to know I was thinking about you."

"You certainly accomplished that. They're just beautiful. But so expensive! With our divorce petitions still unsettled, we should be careful with our money." She was met with silence. *Why was she letting her monetary insecurity color her appreciation of Rob's gift?* She should focus on the act of kindness as a symbol of his feelings for her. *Shouldn't she?* "What I mean to say is, thank you."

"You're welcome. I know it's after eleven there. I won't keep you. Have a great day of meetings tomorrow." They both hung up.

Julia sat there for a minute feeling both loved and a little bad. She thought it was a very sweet gesture. But she also thought it was a lot of money for something she couldn't get back to Seattle with her. *You're being a fool. Just enjoy a nice gift.*

Why did she have to make that stupid comment about money? She had hurt his feelings when he was trying to be nice. Why was she so fucked up about money? It was just that with so many open questions about their finances, she would rather they saved their money for more important things.

She was being an idiot. If her boyfriend wanted to buy her flowers, she should let him and not be a jerk about it.

Boyfriend? Where had that word come from? They'd only gone out a few times. They were having fun in bed, but did that make him her boyfriend or just her fuck buddy?

She didn't know the categorizations. She stopped that train of thought and decided not to get wrapped up in labels.

But how did she feel about him? Great sex was clouding her brain. Or was it more? She felt all warm and gooey inside when she thought of him. She got nervous and excited when he called her, smiling every time she was reminded of something they did together. She had trouble keeping her attention on her meetings if she let her thoughts drift in his direction.

Was she falling in love?

No – she didn't have time to complicate her life with love.

She had to give all her attention to dealing with her work situation. This was just a rebound thing with some great sex thrown in. Great sex. Yes. She fell asleep with a smile on her face.

THE CHICAGO SELLERS proved to be a tough crowd. It was a difficult day, but she stayed calm, practiced patience, and let them work through their anger before she helped them see new ways to get their jobs done.

Brian set a nice tone by joining the morning's sessions. She had built some credibility with him at their dinner. That good energy continued into the agency meetings where Julia helped move a deal forward that had been stuck for a few months.

"That was amazing, Julia." Brian beamed at her in the car on the way from one meeting to the next. "You had them eating out of your hand."

"Thanks Brian. I know the value of our products and how to explain it."

"It was more than that. You got the agency talking about what they wanted and then made it sound like what we had was tailored for them, even though it was the same products they've been buying for years."

"Some of that is just my title. A monetization person can say the same thing as a salesperson but the customer believes the monetization person because we don't sound like we're selling. We're just talking."

"But you were just talking. You didn't push them to sign the deal or anything."

"Oh, I was selling. I was just being subtle about it."

"Wow, Julia, I have a lot to learn. Maybe you could mentor me. I'm going to hit my quarterly target because of that deal. Thank you."

"I'd love that, Brian. And it would be even better if it was a two-way street. I need your feedback on how we can improve."

"Done and done. I'm so glad you came to Chicago."

▭

AS USUAL, her first stop after her flight was the kennel to pick up Selah. She was already snoozing in the back seat after a few action-packed days with her doggie friends at the boarding facility. Julia would be home early enough that she could invite Rob over for dinner.

She had missed him, and she wanted to do something to thank him for the beautiful flowers. She thought of the Chicago office receptionist's face when Julia offered them to her.

Clearly, Julia couldn't get them home on the plane, and the receptionist had been ecstatic to take them off Julia's hands. Everybody won. Julia liked that.

She thought Rob might be a little miffed with her over her reaction to the flowers. She hoped she had thanked him enough and had made up for her blunder. She'd let Rob decide if he wanted to see her or not.

It was late enough that he should be off work by now, but not too late to catch him before dinner.

"Hey, you're back," he answered cheerfully. That was a good sign.

"Yep. And I was wondering what you're doing tonight."

"It's the last band practice before the Showcase next Wednesday."

"Oh right. How could I forget?" It was easy to forget because they now practiced in Leenie's basement.

"How about tomorrow night?"

"I'm too tired to work out tonight after my trip. I need to do it tomorrow after work."

"I guess I was thinking about getting you hot and sweaty in a way that doesn't involve a machine." She pictured him winking with both eyes.

"Saturday morning could be just as good for hitting the elliptical," she answered with a grin.

"I would love to cook for you tomorrow night, but I don't actually cook. How about if I bring a pizza over instead? I'll buy it before it's baked, so it'll be like I cooked for you."

"Okay, I should be home from work around six tomorrow. And thanks again for the flowers."

"Sounds good. I'll be there soon after that to pour you a glass of wine while the pizza cooks.

"See you tomorrow."

She was glad he wasn't angry. Maybe, just maybe, she had dodged a bullet or at least smoothed things over enough to make it okay.

She was good at that.

Chapter 30

Julia put in a full day at the office on Friday even after her grueling trip. She synthesized all the feedback from her five office visits and prepared for the final meetings next week with the Seattle-based team. And then she had the report-out to Blane. *Whew!*

She decided to wash off the vestiges of work with a shower. She was just zipping her jeans when she heard Rob open the front door and give Selah some love. She met him halfway down the stairs.

"Hi, beautiful," Rob greeted her as he wrapped the arm that wasn't holding the pizza around her for a welcoming hug.

"Hello to you, too. I missed you." Julia hoped she didn't sound too clingy. He came in for a kiss.

"How about if I get you a beer while we wait for the pizza to bake?"

"How about if I pour you some wine while I hear about your trip?"

"Okay, compromise. We each get our own drinks while

you tell me how the band is doing. Ready for the Showcase next week?"

They headed to the kitchen. "Stephen was there last night and apologized for jumping to conclusions."

"Better late than never."

"Yeah. The music school running the Showcase is over capacity for the two hours. We were cut down to three songs. Lisa was thrilled because she still couldn't get the middle section of *Heartbreaker*. With Stephen back, she's off the hook. We're doing *Gimme One Reason*, *Crazy Little Thing Called Love*, and *Don't You Know You're Riding with the King*."

"That's a great set. I can't wait to hear you. Are Leenie and Carla coming too?" She looked forward to seeing them again.

"Yeah. About that. Stephen let me know Cliff joined another band and he'll be playing, too. I don't think you should come."

Julia was torn. She wanted to be supportive of Rob's music, but she didn't want to throw it in Cliff's face that she wasn't there to see him. "Good point. I think I'll skip this one."

"That's for the best. How was your trip?"

"It gets harder and harder to sit there and listen to people bitch about my team, but I know it'll serve us in the long run. I didn't learn much new feedback, but I got the heads of the Dallas and Chicago sales teams on board with my plans. I even helped close a deal."

"That's great. When do you get to start telling them what to do?"

"Oh, I've got some work to do before then. The big reveal will be in New York at our leadership team meeting with Blane next month. In the meantime, I have to show real progress to the teams so they back me up and start telling Jeff – enemy number one – that my team and I are doing good work that helps them."

"How do you deal with staying quiet when all you want to do is yell at them that they're wrong?"

"It's an art – one I've had to perfect over the years. No one wants to listen until they've gotten what's bugging them off their chests. It feels a bit manipulative, but I just paraphrase their words back to them so they know I heard them before carefully weaving that language into my recommendations for change."

"That must take a lot of energy."

"It does, which is why I'm exhausted, but it'll be worth it in the end when the results of our efforts are realized, and I get that promotion."

Julia sat back as she munched on her pizza. She had felt the support in the room in both Dallas and Chicago and could pinpoint the shift from anger to people being enrolled in the process. *Now she just had to deliver.*

"Enough shop talk." Rob interrupted her thoughts about the next phase of Operation Fix-It. "I'm going to clean up while you sit there and look beautiful."

Ignoring her protests, Rob cleared their plates, rinsed them, and put them in the dishwasher. Julia squirmed in her chair watching. She tried to live in the moment and appreciate it, but it was uncomfortable. Nobody had ever waited on her in her adult life.

When the kitchen was clean, Rob pulled Julia up from her chair with an outstretched arm. "Ready to have some fun?" he asked with a grin.

"Why yes, sir. I believe I owe you for the beautiful flowers."

"You don't owe me anything. I wanted to get them for you."

"Okay then, I just want to do something nice for you

that has nothing to do with the flowers." Julia was a little nervous to ask but decided to go for it. "I enjoyed our training session the other night and I'd like to be a good student. Is there something in the sex department that you particularly like or are in the mood for tonight?"

"That's hard to say. I'm not good at dictating what we should do."

"Even when I ask you to?"

"Actually, it's a real turn-on that you're interested in having sex and aren't shy about telling me. How about if I just kiss you and we see what happens from there?" Rob reached for her and began caressing her lips with his. "I've thought of something." He took her hand and led her upstairs.

JULIA WASN'T sure what she was in for, but she felt safe with Rob. She wanted to be sexy and satisfying for him in bed. She was a little intimidated by stories of his sexually active past.

She was certainly reaping the benefits from dating a reformed slut. His vast experience in his early days was paying off for her. *But was she enough for him?* Could she keep him interested so she didn't repeat the Cliff pattern?

She caught herself. Rob didn't need to know how she was feeling inside about this. She had to put on a confident front and go where he took her.

God, did they need a safe word? What if he wanted to do something she wasn't comfortable with?

There it was again – that self-doubt. *Stop it!* She told herself to just be in the moment. To take this opportunity to learn from him rather than making everything a big deal. She snapped herself out of her negative thought pattern.

She could be anyone she wanted in the bedroom. She didn't have to be an aging ex-wife with baggage.

No! She could be a sex kitten with great lingerie and a healthy appetite for experimentation.

She started charging herself up to be this new Julia. A gamer. A baller. A sexual goddess. Yes!

Rob stopped at the edge of the king-sized sleigh bed when they got to the bedroom.

"Please lie down across the bed, on your back, with your head toward one side. If you don't like this, just let me know. Having sex with you is fun, even if we just do it vanilla style."

"I know. I'll tell you if it's too much, but I'm looking for new experiences." She got a zing of power from letting her sexual energy find its voice.

"Scoot down a little bit so the curve of your neck matches the edge of the bed."

"Wait a second. Didn't we forget something?" Julia asked with a playful tone.

Rob stopped mid-motion. "What do you mean? What's wrong?"

"Nothing bad," Julia reassured him. "It's just that I'm wearing some nice lingerie, and I'd like you to see it. Mind if I take my clothes off?" She was getting into this sex goddess identity.

"I don't think any heterosexual man would say no to that, but no – I don't mind at all, as long as you don't mind me removing that lingerie pretty soon. I'm sure it'll look lovely on the floor, too."

Julia sat up, unbuttoned her shirt and slipped her jeans down her curvy hips before resuming her position across the bed.

Rob used that time to strip.

She took a moment to appreciate Rob, admiring his

six-foot naked, muscular frame standing near the bed. As she watched him, she had all the proof she needed that he liked his view as well. It encouraged her to be freer. "You look like you're trying not to drool."

"Who could blame me? There's a beautiful woman in blue silk lying in front of me."

Julia felt herself blush. His words sent a thrill through her. No one had ever talked to her like that before, and she liked it. It made her feel sexy and wanted.

All worries about if he could see her fat through the lace fell away, and Julia fully became the sex goddess she wanted to be right there on the edge of the bed. "Bring yourself over here and tell me what to do."

"You're doing it right now. Just go with what feels good." He slipped himself into her mouth and started slowly moving in and out.

Julia adjusted her head a little lower and made sure her lips were curled over her teeth so she didn't hurt him.

Rob leaned forward and cupped her breasts, teasing the sensitive peaks.

Julia put a hand around the base of his cock. Having her hand there made it so he could go deeper without her gagging – *that would not be sexy*, she thought.

Because she felt like it, she reached around behind him with her other hand to push him into her mouth. The noises Rob made encouraged her to keep experimenting.

Julia felt Rob's hands creeping lower and lower until he reached the top of her lace panties. He toyed with the waistband driving her a bit crazy as she mentally urged him to go lower. He leaned forward just a bit more and found her center.

Julia began moving against his hand. She worked to concentrate on letting him finish before she gave into the ecstasy he was creating inside her. It wasn't easy.

Her patience paid off as Rob emptied himself into her mouth. His thrusts slowed and he leaned over her. He balanced on one arm while he continued to pleasure her.

Her movements became more frenzied as she rode the wave toward her first orgasm of the evening. Taking her higher and higher, she erupted in his hand.

He joined her on the bed for a cuddle.

"How'd that work for you?" he asked.

"I love learning from you and I'm pretty sure I just proved to be a good student."

"Straight As across the board, or in this case, across the headboard."

Julia loved being able to laugh in bed. *Everything about this was different.* She loved building on the *great sex* part of her mantra.

She hoped there was more to learn.

Chapter 31

Maybe I should just burn it all, Julia thought. She wished she could do as her friends suggested and just throw Cliff's boxes into a pile in the cul-de-sac and have a celebratory bonfire.

She didn't have it in her to be mean-spirited. *Well, most days anyway*, she thought as she stood frowning at the neatly packed, stacked, and labeled boxes. She might be able to muster the strength to do it today.

She couldn't believe he still hadn't come to get his stuff out of the house. She decided she had waited long enough. Over three months had gone by since he'd moved out and only a few of his belongings were out of the house.

She headed downstairs and grabbed her phone. She sent him an email stating, as nicely as she could, that he had two weeks to come and get his stuff or she would move it to storage.

She didn't have to wait long for Cliff to respond saying he would come that weekend to get his remaining items from the house.

Finally, Julia thought. She started the process of moving

everything to the garage. She didn't want him coming into the house any more than was absolutely necessary.

Julia was relieved. One more thing checked off the list.

She thought of Cliff's belongings as the physical representation of the baggage she carried from their relationship. So much of it was negative. The feeling of being unattractive and unfulfilled. Having to be a parent in the relationship instead of a partner. Carrying all of the financial burden. It had done a number on her.

And now, after all her hard work, her money was in jeopardy. If Cliff wanted more than the forty percent she offered, she would move farther away from financial security and happiness.

But he wouldn't do that to her. He had to have at least some self-respect left.

She tried to tell herself to be more like Rob and to self-soothe by thinking that everything would be fine. That was better than taking her anxiety out on him like she had done with the flowers. That was bad. Her baggage had opened up and spilled all over the floor of that Chicago hotel. She wanted to make it up to him. But how?

She sat with her feelings about Rob. Julia loved the way Rob always looked for the happy part of any story. She loved how he made her feel when they were together. She loved that she missed him when he wasn't around. She loved the way he liked to have honest conversations about real issues.

Shit, she loved him. She. Loved. Him.

The thought caused a zing of energy through her body. How had she not seen the signs?

Even if it was too soon and he didn't feel the same way, she wanted to tell him – was almost bursting with the need to share her feelings.

She would go for it.

ROB WAS RIGHT ON TIME, as usual, for their Saturday night date. She could barely see him through a big bunch of tulips.

"Oh, they're beautiful. Just beautiful. Thank you."

"Happy Valentine's Day," he smiled.

"But it's not Valentine's Day. It's March."

"I know, but I didn't think it was appropriate to buy you Valentine's Day flowers when it was actually Valentine's Day." She thought that was cute. "And I know I'm taking a risk buying you more flowers even though you snapped at me about the sunflowers in Chicago."

"Yeah, about that. Sorry again. I'm just worked up about money since I don't know how things will be divided with Cliff. I guess I'm projecting that onto you since you and Camille haven't settled either."

Rob looked uncomfortable. "You shouldn't miss out on flowers because of short-term financial uncertainty. It'll be fine."

"You're pretty adorable."

"I try." Rob smiled.

Julia returned the smile and took the bouquet into the kitchen.

ONCE THEY WERE SEATED in the restaurant, Julia took Rob's hand. "I have something I want to tell you."

"Is it bad? Did I do something?" Rob looked startled by her words.

"No, it's not bad. It's good. I think," she added hastily as the server approached the table.

After they'd placed their orders, she began again. "About that thing I wanted to tell you."

"Are you breaking up with me?" Rob blurted.

"No, you big silly. I can't believe you thought that!" Julia heard his sigh of relief. "If I may continue." She paused for dramatic effect. "There are only a few people any one person gets to love in a lifetime." She stopped to appreciate his kind face and sparkly eyes. She continued after a deep breath that filled her with strength. "I know you're one of those people for me. We haven't been together for very long, but I want to share something with you."

"Is it about my bad breath?"

"Would you cut it out for a minute? I'm trying to say something important here."

"Sorry. I do that when I'm uncomfortable. You're scaring me a little bit."

"Hope this doesn't scare you more. I love you."

"Wow," Rob stammered. "I wasn't expecting that."

"I know, just like I know it's too soon, but loving someone is a gift, and I wanted you to know even if you don't feel it for me."

Rob looked her and wink-blinked a few times.

Julia enjoyed the shocked look on his face. She read it as happy, but definitely thrown for a loop. "Is this because of the flowers?" he asked.

"No, but they don't hurt. To prove it, here's a letter I wrote to you before I even knew you got them for me." Julia slid a beautiful ivory envelope across the table.

She told herself he was being silly because she'd made him uncomfortable, not because he was ignoring her statement. Rob opened the letter.

In the beginning, my feelings for you were like a pulsing, searing light I could contain in a nice little metaphorical box in one part of my heart. Lately, the power of you has spread through my whole life like a labyrinth of tree roots that are taking hold and will not be contained in a simple box. And, rather than trying to stop it, I unlocked the box and threw away the key.

I love you.

Rob looked up with tears in his eyes. One slid down his cheek. "Thank you," he all but whispered.

He reached into his pocket and pulled out a Valentine's Day sugar heart.

"Be mine," Julia read.

They both laughed as their butter chicken and chana masala were served.

Chapter 32

Cliff was due at the house any minute to pick up his belongings. "I'll see you later at the Cantina?"

"You bet. Just call me after Cliff is gone."

As time clicked by, Julia became more and more annoyed. Cliff finally arrived about forty-five minutes late. In his SUV. Alone.

"I thought you were moving your stuff out today." She hated sounding huffy.

"Yeah, that's the plan."

"Where's your van and people to help?"

"I figured I'd just make a couple trips. Mind if I get started?" Cliff pushed past her into the garage.

"Want some help?" she asked his retreating back.

"No, I got this." Julia followed him anyway to ensure he didn't take things he shouldn't.

Cliff started reading the labels on the boxes. He didn't even thank her for packing everything neatly. Julia tried not to get angrier. "Have you arranged a storage unit for your tools?" Cliff ignored her. "They won't fit in your car." Julia hated being Captain Obvious.

Still no response.

"Have you rented a garage for the convertible?" Julia's anger over storing the sports car and everything else was starting to show.

"Nope. You only have one car. I can't park a soft top outside in Seattle weather. You'll just have to keep it a little longer."

"The motorcycle?"

"Same thing."

"Cliff, it's been months." She desperately wanted reminders of him out of her space. "We had an agreement."

"Yeah, we used to have a lot of things you broke, so I don't see a problem." Julia thought he looked pleased with himself as he picked up the first box and headed to the car.

Even though he had said he didn't want help, she wanted him out of the house as quickly as possible. She grabbed the next box and followed him.

They loaded a few more boxes in the car without speaking.

"That's enough for today," he said, closing the door.

"That's all you're taking? Five boxes? None of your tools?"

"Fuck you, Jules. Deal with it." He got in the car and started it up. Julia stepped away from the car as he put it in reverse.

She was speechless as she watched him leave. She wanted him out of her space. But what could she do? Her friends kept suggesting she have a bonfire, but that wasn't Julia's style.

Time to have a chat with her lawyer, she thought as she stomped back into the house.

. . .

AFTER A QUICK EMAIL exchange with her lawyer, Julia notified Cliff she would move all of his belongings into storage and would pay for that storage space for one month. After that, Cliff would have to take over the payment or he would forfeit ownership, as per the storage facility's policies. It cost her some extra legal fees, but it was worth it. She was done with his shenanigans.

Julia got to the Cantina after Rob and found him holding court with the servers since it was a slow night. Three laughing servers encircled him as he sat on a high stool at a four-seat table in the middle of the room. Skulls painted in a Día de los Muertos theme grinned from the restaurant walls adding to the festive mood Rob created around him.

Julia liked that he could entertain himself. Cliff would have been sitting there sullenly, pretending to read the menu over and over.

"Hello everybody." Julia took her seat on the stool across from Rob. "What'd I miss?"

"Diane and Tess were just telling me about their latest horrible customer."

"He was awful, and after all that, he didn't even leave a tip!"

"His punishment is that he has to live with himself for the rest of his life. And you know the next time he comes in here, just give me the signal, and I'll take care of him." Rob gave them a two-eyed wink.

"My hero," Tess and Diane beamed at him. "Can I get you another drink now that your lady love is here?" He nodded. "Julia?"

"I'll have a scratch to go with his house margarita, and I'll make sure to tip well." Diane laughed at Julia's comment and walked back to the bar.

"Are you going to yell at me for flirting with them?"

"Ah, no." Julia slanted her eyes. "I know you like making people feel good. It's harmless."

"Phew. I'm still adjusting to being with a woman with an in-balance ego. I'll catch up." He laughed.

Julia didn't think she should be worried about it. The way he made her feel like the center of the universe was one of the things she first liked about him.

His flirting didn't mean anything. *Or did it?* Was she his lady love?

"I WISH you'd listened to me and burned it all," Lesley said as she hauled the high-end smoker up the ramp of the moving van Julia had rented. "It's not too late. Clearly, he doesn't want it that badly."

Melanie and Lesley had volunteered to help her move everything to the storage unit when Julia explained the plan. They were happy to help, but furious she had taken such care with Cliff's possessions.

"I'm still trying to end things amicably." Julia realized it might be time to admit the truth that it wasn't going to end well. "I'm treating his stuff the way I would want him to treat mine."

"Yeah, I get it, but the difference is he wouldn't treat it like this." Lesley was right.

"Everything in the shop goes?" Paul took off his baseball cap and scratched his head. Rob also enrolled his friend Paul to lend a hand. He brought his wife Gertie along.

"Yep. I moved everything that's mine into the mudroom. Everything in the shop can go."

"You're one hell of an organizer." Gertie was about five feet tall with piercing blue eyes. She was also incredibly ripped, so Julia was happy to have her additional muscle this morning.

"Thanks, Gertie. And thanks for coming to help. Kind of a weird way to meet. I really appreciate you helping out a total stranger."

"Any friend of Rob's is a… well, a mild acquaintance I don't mind being a beast of burden for. You seem cool. I'd like to get to know you better." Julia smiled, thankful for Gertie's help and her offer of friendship.

It took three hours to load everything up, drive it to the storage unit and unload it again. But when they were finished, Julia had her house back.

It was also fun to pop open the champagne and heat up the hors d'oeuvres she'd made the night before. The six of them hung out for a couple of hours celebrating the emptiness of the house and their sore muscles. Julia had great friends. And some new ones.

JULIA AND ROB waved them goodbye around three in the afternoon.

Rob turned to her. "It's a beautiful afternoon, just right for a drive through some of Seattle's old neighborhoods on the winding and twisting roads. I wish I had a motorcycle we could take out for a ride."

"Cliff came back for his motorcycle, but we still have his BMW." It was the last remaining item of his still at the house.

"Think he'd let us take it?" Rob asked.

"We just unloaded all of his crap into a storage unit. If he didn't want me taking his car, he shouldn't have left it here." Julia had agreed not to drive it without his permission, but she was feeling rebellious. "Let's make it a happy hour picnic."

They packed a basket and headed to the Seattle Arboretum. Selah loved the convertible, and even though it was a tight fit, she didn't mind sitting on the floor in front of the passenger seat with her head hanging out the side window.

Julia drove on the way out, appreciating the way the tight stick shift responded to her commands. She hadn't bought herself a new car because of her financial insecurity. She reminded herself to do it once things were settled.

After their al fresco snack, Julia and Rob packed up their basket and whistled for Selah.

"It's pretty warm. I don't need my jacket. Would you like it?" Rob was always thoughtful.

"No, thanks. I'm good. Just throw it in the trunk."

They took a different scenic drive home, this time with Rob at the wheel. He certainly liked to go faster than Julia. She pressed back into her seat to enjoy the rush of wind on her face as her floppy hat danced in the wind. Selah looked like Julia felt. Happy, relaxed, and enjoying the moment.

Cliff must have sensed she had taken the convertible out because he called that night to say he would be picking it up. Julia was elated to get the final piece of Cliff out of her house. They set a time for the next day.

<hr>

"HAVE YOU SEEN MY JACKET?" Rob asked as they got ready to take Selah to the dog park the next weekend.

"Which one?" Julia opened another closet door to join the search.

"Good point. I do have a lot of jackets. The lightweight black one with the windbreaker lining."

"Haven't seen it." Julia picked up Selah's leash.

"Oh, I'll take a different one, but I've been looking for it all morning, and I can't find it."

Selah took her customary spot on the back seat. "When do you last remember having it?" Julia asked as he maneuvered the car out of the driveway.

"That's an excellent question. You know I wear it all the time. I love that jacket. I've looked everywhere I can think to look."

"Did you try the closet in the laundry room? Sometimes, when Natalie comes to clean, I throw extra stuff in there."

"I'm onto your sneaky plan to make things look neater than they are, so I already looked there."

They drove for a few minutes, each lost in their own thoughts, Julia trying to think of where his coat could be.

"Oh, shit," she said out loud. She remembered where the jacket was.

"What – what's wrong?" Rob sounded alarmed.

"You left it in the trunk of Cliff's car. You put it there after our picnic. Do you remember taking it out?"

"No."

"Fuck."

"He took the car last week, didn't he?" Rob asked. "Shit."

"No big deal, I'll ask him for it when I talk to him the next time." Julia tried to hide her annoyance that she would have to remind Cliff she was seeing Rob.

"You okay over there?" he asked.

"Yeah." No need to make a big deal about a stupid jacket.

Chapter 33

"I have a form you need to sign for my health benefits." Cliff only called her when he wanted something. "It's due tomorrow."

"Want to swing by?" She had just finished up on the elliptical machine and needed time to shower. "Give me fifteen minutes."

"Fine."

"And while I've got you, did you find a jacket in the trunk of the BMW?" She hated having to ask.

"Nope, no jacket." She figured Cliff must be in a hurry with his clipped answers.

"Hmm. You sure? A friend thinks they left one there. Could you take a look?"

"Were you driving my car? How would a jacket have gotten in there? I thought we had an agreement."

She was glad he couldn't see her eye roll over the phone. "Yeah, just to keep it in good working order. It had been sitting for weeks." A subtle jab back.

"Whatever. See you later."

. . .

JULIA HUNG out in the garage with the door open pretending to straighten up the already straightened gardening tools. When Cliff drove up, she picked up her pen and walked to the edge of the garage.

"Thanks for making time for me." She heard anger and sarcasm in his voice.

"No problem. Do you have the form?" Julia didn't understand why he was so angry. Because she drove his car? Well then he shouldn't have left it at her house for so long.

"Here." He stood there watching with an impatient look on his face while she read it in the light from the garage. "You don't have to read every word, it's just a form letter."

She ignored him and kept reading. It said that because they were still legally married Cliff could remain on her healthcare benefits. "Are you going to pay your part of the health insurance?"

"What do you mean? This form isn't about payments. It's about coverage."

"I know, but I'm paying your healthcare through my job, and you have a job now. I know what it costs for a single person, so I know how much I'm paying for your part. Are you going to start paying the difference?"

"Try to make me," he challenged her. "We'll see who has all the money at the end of this."

She wanted to throw the unsigned form back at him, but she knew that would only make it worse. And what did that last comment even mean? "Once the divorce is final, you'll have to pay your own way. Even this form says it's only valid until the day of the final divorce decree."

"Yeah, well, I'm looking forward to that day." Cliff looked disgusted.

She handed back the signed form. Cliff walked to the car without saying goodbye. Rather than getting in, he opened the side door, pulled something out, and came back toward her. Julia couldn't see what it was until he was two feet away. He dropped Rob's jacket onto the ground in a heap.

"Oh, you did find it. Thanks." Julia found herself talking to his retreating back as he stormed down the driveway to his car. *He couldn't have just handed it to her?* As she reached down to pick it up, the car door slammed, and the window rolled down.

"By the way, your boyfriend has herpes." He peeled out, tires squealing.

JULIA CALLED Rob and caught him just after band practice at his mom's house. "Guess who just dropped off your jacket?"

"Who found it? And where?"

"Cliff. In his trunk. And he said something strange. Apparently, you have the gift that keeps on giving."

"What?"

"Herpes."

"Herpes?"

"Herpes. Have you been talking to Cliff? Maybe at the Showcase?"

"No. He totally ignored me. And I don't have herpes. I can explain," Rob rushed to say.

"Rob, sweetie, I'm kidding. I don't think you have herpes. I'm just telling you what Cliff said as he was leaving after literally dropping off your jacket."

"No, really, I can explain. Don't be mad."

"Why would I be mad Cliff is making shit up?" Julia was unnerved by Rob's reaction.

"Can we talk about this? I'll come over right now."

"Okay." Julia was completely confused. He really wanted that jacket back.

She hung the jacket on the back of one of her new kitchen chairs.

She and Rob had never finished the exclusivity part of their conversation. Was she not seeing the big picture here? Did he just give her an incurable venereal disease?

She'd wait the thirty minutes and find out.

SHE WAS GETTING Selah some water when Rob drove up. He came in and skipped his usual Selah greeting. He looked shaken.

"What's all this about?" Julia asked.

"I'm so sorry. I can explain." Rob spoke very quickly, which was unlike him.

"Explain what? We were both tested before we got together. I know you're clean. Cliff is just being a tool. What's going on?"

"I didn't tell you this, and I'm sorry."

Julia felt a crackle of dread spark through her body. "Well if you have herpes, then we both do, and we'll deal with it." She didn't understand and wondered where he got it. Had he lied to her? *Had he slept with someone else?*

"No, no, no, it's not like that. It's Camille. When I was at our old house a few weeks ago doing some maintenance for her, we had a bit of a fight." He paused and took a deep breath, looking embarrassed. "As I walked out, she told me she has herpes and consequently, so do I."

"Oh no. Was she saying she had cheated on you while you were together? How would she have gotten it?"

"That doesn't matter because I don't care who she's been with since we broke up. But I went back to the doctor to get tested again, just in case." He paused and took a breath. "I'm clean. Camille just said it to be awful and scare me."

"Wow, that's really terrible."

"Since I was at the doctor's office for a suspected case of herpes, she gave me a pamphlet called 'Living with Herpes' before the results came back. I must have left it in my jacket pocket."

"Well, that explains it." Julia laughed as relief filled her.

"You aren't mad?"

"Of course not. I believe you."

"I need to get used to that. I'll just say others haven't been so trusting."

"Welcome to a well-balanced relationship with a trusting partner." Julia grinned, but then some doubt crept in. "But speaking of trust, we are exclusive, right?"

"Yes, of course. Why would you think otherwise?"

"Because you never actually said it." Julia was glad her intuition was correct but also a bit bummed it took a herpes scare to get the information. "It's weird, though," she continued. "Why would Cliff be so mad when he thought you had herpes? He can't be worried about me."

"Since he accused us of having an affair prior to your break-up, maybe he was mad because he thought he would have it, too?"

"No way," said Julia. "We hadn't had sex in forever. It's pretty funny that he went through the pockets in the jacket and lied about having it. He must've been planning just what to say for days. Whatever. Let's just chalk it up to divorce weirdness." Julia thought the subject was closed.

"Oh shit." It looked like all the blood drained from Rob's face as Julia watched him. "There was something else in my pocket." His expression was a mixture of sadness and realization. "Where's my jacket now?"

"In the kitchen. What's wrong?" Julia said to his retreating back as he went to retrieve it.

"Damn." He fumbled with the pocket and waved a tattered and worn-looking envelope.

Julia recognized it immediately. It was the letter she had written to Rob telling him she loved him. And Cliff had read it.

They looked at each other with horror.

"Well, I think that letter just cost me about a hundred grand in the divorce settlement. There's no chance he'll be reasonable now," Julia said with resignation and a bit of heat. "No wonder he's mad."

"At least I don't have herpes." Rob looked at her endearingly.

Julia couldn't help but laugh.

———————————————

Chapter 34

———————————————

Back at work on Operation Fix-It, Julia leaned back in her chair to work out the kinks in her neck. She felt the strain of the workday.

She'd spent the last forty-five minutes finalizing her latest Operation Fix-It newsletter to the sales team and it was ready to send. She knew most people didn't read it, but she did it nonetheless to keep her commitment to herself, her team, and Blane's leadership team. Progress on her recommendations was the real deliverable.

When she looked back at her screen, she noticed a new email from a name she didn't recognize. It was Cliff's lawyer and included the divorce petition. A wave of relief washed through Julia's body. He was actually moving forward.

There was a second attachment along with the divorce petition. Julia hoped it was his acceptance of her offer of forty percent of their assets.

She read the opening paragraph and froze, paralyzed by anger. He wanted seventy percent of their community property plus thirty thousand dollars in legal fees.

That was over a million dollars.

What. In. The. Absolute. Fuck!

How could he ask for that much money when he hadn't been working for almost ten years? He wanted seventy percent of her 401Ks and their retirement portfolio, two cars, and his motorcycle – and he didn't want any of the household goods to count toward the total value. That meant the thousands of dollars of recording, voice-over, band equipment, and power tools she'd given him over the years didn't count. And seventy percent of the equity in the house! And seventy percent of her next bonus and unvested stock, claiming she had earned them while they were together.

She felt an angry flush start in her toes and creep up her entire body until she was filled with a seething, bitter rage.

This had to be a nightmare. But no, she clearly would not have been able to sleep through this level of gut-wrenching anger. She growled in frustration.

This was too much. Here she was, thinking she'd been generous when she offered him forty percent of everything, and he hit her with this!

What if he got it? Even if he only got fifty percent, she would still be locked into the golden handcuffs of her LampLight job or she couldn't pay him.

She knew she should calm down, but she had dialed his number before she could think better of it.

He answered on the second ring.

"Hey Julia, I thought you might call." His voice had an ugly sneer, like the villain in a bad melodrama.

"This is your offer? I wait this long for you to give me a number and you throw out seventy percent plus your legal fees? Are you kidding?"

"My lawyer thinks it's fair."

"Cliff, listen to me. I'm trying to stay friends. You've disrespected me, called me names, accused me of lying, refused to get your shit out of my house, and have been awful to me." Julia took a deep breath before continuing. "If you continue down this track, you will irreconcilably break what's left of our relationship. I want to have you in my life. I want to be friends. None of your actions suggest you want the same thing."

Julia waited for a beat, then two.

Cliff broke the silence. "I'm angry at you, and you can't take all the money."

"I'm not taking all the money. I offered you forty percent of everything, even though you haven't contributed in ten years. That's fucking generous. Why do you think you should have more than that?"

"I just do. And so does my lawyer. He thinks I can get it."

"Cliff, this isn't about how much you *can* get. This is about what's *fair*."

"I'm going to get as much as I can from you for ruining our marriage."

Julia realized she was talking to a stranger.

Fear and panic had turned him into someone else. Someone she wanted nothing to do with.

"Last chance, Cliff. If you continue with this, we'll only talk through our lawyers." Julia spoke with deliberate emphasis. "We won't be friends when this is over."

"If that's how you want it, that's how it'll be. I want my seventy percent."

"Then we have nothing else to say." Julia shook with anger when she hung up. She couldn't believe it had come to this after everything she had invested in keeping the relationship going.

Her next call was to her lawyer. "I've seen crazier

things." Marty's calm tone did not help Julia settle down. "Marriage isn't like a lottery where Cliff gets more than half just because he chose well," Marty quipped. "Worst case is fifty/fifty. Just relax."

"That's still way more than he deserves."

"Yeah, I know, but you make plenty of money and you'll make more."

She hoped he was right, but it still stung.

SHE NEEDED something to look forward to. Time with her girls. She had told Margaret she would schedule a get together with Melanie and Lesley. It was time to make good on that. She would invite Gertie, too.

She sent a text inviting them for dinner. They were all available on Tuesday.

JULIA SET A BOTTLE OF BOURBON, a bottle of red wine, and a pretty dish of stuffed mushroom cap appetizers on the table. The steaks would go on the grill as soon as everyone was there.

Just as she was pulling the baked potatoes out of the oven, the doorbell rang, and the little party began.

Margaret was the first to arrive, followed by Gertie.

"Steak and bourbon. I like it." Margaret spoke around a mouthful of mushroom once she heard what was on the menu.

"It was Gertie's idea. I asked her what women eat." Julia explained.

"And I said, I don't know what *women* eat, but I like steak and bourbon."

"I love that!" Margaret exclaimed, "What was that, like

forty-five seconds, and I already fell in love with you? Welcome to the group!"

"Damn glad to be here," Gertie smiled.

"I loved it too." Julia raised her glass to the two of them. "No frilly little quiche for us! No! Red meat and hard liquor." They clinked glasses and turned to see Melanie and Lesley come through the door. Selah greeted them with excitement.

"Welcome to steak and bourbon!" Margaret yelled, extending her glass toward the door.

Julia needed this. Strong women making connections and enjoying each other's company.

She took their orders for how they preferred their steaks and put the meat on the grill. She returned to the table in the middle of a discussion of Hillary Clinton's decision to step down as Secretary of State.

"Speaking of bad marriages, how's it going on the divorce front?" Gertie jumped right in with the direct question. She was a lawyer after all.

"I had a chat with Cliff, who I will refer to as The Douchebag from now on. He shared his counteroffer with me."

"I can tell from your face it's not good. What did Mr. Douchebag ask for?" Melanie asked as she sipped her drink.

"There's no mister. He doesn't deserve that much respect." They laughed together. "Get this. He wants seventy percent of our community property. And since we were married for over ten years, everything is community property."

"What a douchebag." Lesley added.

"My sentiments exactly."

"What're you going to do?" Lesley's question was a good one.

"Nothing until mediation day. I emailed my lawyer, and he's adamant that the forty percent is a good offer because of the extenuating circumstances of Cliff quitting his job and not contributing. I don't feel very hopeful at this point that I'm going to come through this in a decent financial position."

"You'll be fine. With your salary, you'll make it back." Lesley always knew what Julia needed to hear.

"Thanks Les. That's what my lawyer said, but that's not the point. I worked hard, much harder than he did, to make that money. I went without vacations and things I wanted. After sharing my money with my family, I didn't have money left to buy fancy clothes or jewelry or shoes. I maxed out my 401k every year. I paid extra on my mortgage to build equity. I saved and saved. And now, it's pretty much for nothing and I'll be broke. That's eighteen years of savings gone if he gets seventy percent."

"To take liberties with a quote from Wesley in the Princess Bride," Gertie took a swig of straight bourbon before continuing, "life isn't fair, Highness. Anyone who tells you differently is selling something."

That was one of Julia's favorite movies. "Right again, Gertie. But he said pain, not fairness."

"Yeah, that too." Gertie raised her glass toward Julia. "I'm an employment lawyer, not a divorce lawyer, but I bet he gets his fifty percent."

Julia felt her shoulders droop.

"Want me to take out a hit on him?" Melanie made Julia laugh again. "I have contacts in Olympia who can keep it on the downlow."

"As good as that sounds, I'll stick with the legal process. I have to write an 'unemotional' letter explaining the situation for the judge in our divorce case." Julia used air quotes to indicate her feelings about being unemotional. "I guess

I'll have to do some heavy editing," she joked, starting to feel a bit like herself again.

"If you want me to look at your letter when it's done, just let me know," Gertie offered.

"Thanks Gertie. And that's enough about The Douchebag."

"Yeah." Margaret jumped in. "Tell us more about you, Gertie. What's the story behind those amazing biceps?"

"Hold that thought – time to check the steaks."

Julia arranged the steaks across the platter from rare for Gertie to medium well for Margaret.

"Now, where were we?" Julia sent the booze around the table again, thankful for her girlfriends.

Chapter 35

Julia stretched her arms over her head and rolled her shoulders on the plane to New York. The crick in her neck released with a light popping sound as she breathed out.

She had just put the finishing touches on her action plan based on her final feedback meetings for Operation Fix-It. She had completed the Seattle meeting, and everything was looking good for the Quarterly Leadership Team meeting the next day in the Big Apple.

She stitched the new strategy together with a phased approach for landing new policies. She was prepared with the results from the changes she was already able to implement. The sales teams respected her, and they had co-created the solutions. She had reams of positive feedback and support for the changes. Her list of blockers was being whittled down daily, and her team's morale had never been higher. Things were looking up and she had learned a lot about making sure she was bringing everyone along with her for the ride toward her strategy rather than lowering the boom on people.

She hoped she had made enough progress to impress Blane. She needed the money from that promotion even more now.

IT WAS EARLY for bed considering what time it was in Julia's head, but she needed to get a good night's sleep before the meeting that started at eight in the morning.

She was just about to shut off her laptop when an incoming email from her lawyer caught her attention. Cliff had finally agreed to non-binding mediation. It was scheduled for late April. She wished it was sooner, but at least she had a date.

A date.

She wondered what Rob was up to. She hadn't seen him in a few days since she'd been giving it her all at work. They had exchanged a few text messages. She knew he was in the thick of a gnarly contract negotiation for the hardware team.

She liked that they could have these breaks without it being a problem for either of them. She liked a lot of things about Rob. He treated her well. He respected her. Cared for her. Made her laugh. Didn't mind that she made more money than him. Taught her about herself. Helped her find her inner sex goddess. Had a job. These were all excellent items in the plus column.

On the other hand, he was the first person she had dated after her breakup. What if there were others who were better for her? She didn't know how he felt about her. He had never told her he loved her. Her declaration just hung out there. He flirted with everything that moved. They hadn't discussed where this was going. Did they need to, or could Julia just sit back and enjoy the literal and figurative ride?

Julia sometimes hated how analytical her mind was. Why couldn't she just stop analyzing and enjoy, especially when she was trying to sleep? *Because her brain didn't work that way.* It picked and poked and peeled things apart. Her relationship with Rob couldn't escape her debugging.

With the time change in her favor, she gave him a call to check in and calm her nerves for the big meeting the next day.

He didn't answer.

———

THE ALARM BLARED at her to get out of bed. Six thirty in the morning in New York felt a lot more like three-thirty when you came from the West Coast, but she was ready.

After the Quarterly Leadership Team meeting all morning, she had three meetings with Madison Avenue advertising agencies in the afternoon. She was already looking forward to her quick lunch with Harry while she was in town.

Julia put on her lucky orange panties, donned her favorite suit, and strode down the steps of her hotel and up the Avenue of the Americas to LampLight's New York City office.

This is what it had all been for – the trips, the action planning, the re-working of her strategy, the tongue biting, and the ass kissing. And it would all pay off today as she got her rewards for executing Operation Fix-It. Julia was filled with power as she checked in at the security desk and arrived at the conference room door.

IT WAS her turn to present. She had a two-slide executive overview that succinctly summarized her progress. She heaped praise on her colleagues and explained she couldn't have done it without them. She included positive quotes from emails she received from sellers including Brian and Matthew. She also described additional work to be done with a self-critical tone to make sure she didn't sound conceited or self-congratulatory.

"Thank you all, especially you and your team Jeff." Her smile was as genuine as she could muster. "We couldn't have done it without you."

The team erupted into a round of applause with Blane clapping the loudest.

"You're welcome, Julia." Jeff's smile didn't quite meet his eyes. "Hope you learned something about actually talking to people instead of just bombarding us with data." Jeff nodded his head as he spoke, like he had just given Julia a great gift of insight.

She clenched her teeth while trying to keep her face in a pleasant smile. She wanted to scream "bombarding you with data is exactly what I should be doing you ignorant asshole," but instead, she said "Thank you, Jeff. I appreciate that." She would process her anger later at the hotel gym.

"Thanks, Julia." Blane beamed at her. "Great job. And to top it all off, I just got a sneak peek at the quarter-to-date numbers. With the changes you've already implemented, we're back on track to hit our revenue goal. With a few more of your changes going live, we might even make up the entire miss we had last quarter. If we stay on this trajectory, we're going to have a great year."

The room burst into applause again. *What a relief,* Julia thought.

Her hard work had paid off. Listening to tough feedback from Dave and taking action on it while also remaining true to herself and her goals worked. It felt like she had addressed her mistakes and now she had the executive support she needed to make the rest of the changes necessary for long-term growth. And get that promotion. She couldn't wait to celebrate with her team and with Rob.

Blane interrupted her thoughts. "I have a meeting with my boss right now. We're going to have an extended lunch break. Those of you joining us for the executive briefing for UHY will join us in this conference room at one."

Julia had planned to meet Harry for a quick lunch at noon, but now she had more time. She hoped he did, too.

"SO, WHAT HAPPENED?" Harry asked as they walked into his favorite steak place in midtown. They had switched from the self-serve salad bar to a nice restaurant since they had extra time.

"Oh Harry, it was great. I undid all the damage from before and brought them along with me. It only took me four times as long as I thought it should." She rolled her eyes.

"Yeah, people stink. They just mess everything up, but at least some will come along with you when you bash them over the head with real leadership enough times." Harry laughed at his joke. "Now let's have a congratulatory soda since it's only eleven thirty on a Tuesday."

"Cheers to that," Julia said.

"Remember the first time we came to this restaurant?"

"Yeah, fifteen years ago with that network CIO. Can you believe it?"

"I feel old, so of course I can. Here's to the next fifteen." He raised his glass of soda.

"May we get everything we deserve," Julia added.

Harry pulled back his glass and blinked at her. "I won't drink to that – if I got everything I deserved, I'd be dead by tomorrow. Let's drink to your success today. I had no doubt you'd prevail." They clinked glasses, laughing.

Chapter 36

When Julia got back for the afternoon round of meetings, Blane pulled her aside. "Part of the meeting with my boss over lunch was to review the work you've done and the strong, positive impact it's had on our results." A picture of Randall came to Julia's mind. Blane's boss was a tall, balding guy who always seemed to be smiling when she saw him in the hallways. He had a good reputation, but Julia hadn't had much interaction with him.

"Oh wow, thank you. It was a team effort." Julia radiated her happiness at the praise.

"Yes, I know you had help, but these changes have only come about since you've been leading the team. Randall and I would like to add the global team to your scope. That'll allow you to make some of the same changes on a global scale. We haven't had a single global leader for the monetization team before. You're the first."

"This day just gets better and better." She beamed as she took it all in.

"If you accept, it'll be effective immediately."

"Oh, I accept! I'm thrilled at the opportunity to have a broader impact. Thank you thank you!"

"That's great. Congratulations. There's more."

"I'm listening." Julia eagerly anticipated news of her promotion and raise that must come with this expansion of duties. She was finally going to get what she wanted because Blane and Randall saw her true value.

"Julia, I want you to be the first to know I've decided to leave LampLight."

She took a sharp inhalation of breath. "Uh. That's unexpected." *Where is this going,* she thought.

"It's great to see the way you and Jeff have worked out your issues." Blane placed his hand on her shoulder.

Julia wanted to shift and dislodge his hand, but she didn't have room in the hallway. He meant it in a nice way, but Julia had her boundaries. "Thanks. I worked hard on that."

"I know. Now, details are still hush hush about my decision to leave, but there's one more thing."

Finally, Julia thought. *Blane is going to tell me about my raise and promotion.*

"Now that you and Jeff are on good terms again, I'm happy to tell you he'll be the acting lead of the team while they look for my replacement. That's why I wanted you to get closer to him."

A shot of adrenaline ignited Julia's body from head to toe like an electric shock. It was quickly replaced by dread. Jeff would be her new boss? Worst possible outcome. She was sunk. Her détente with Jeff wasn't strong enough to hold once he was in charge and had more power over her.

"Remember, Julia. Mum's the word. A few pesky details to work out." Blane pretended to turn a lock over his lips.

· · ·

JULIA'S TRIP down the elevator after her customer meetings felt very different from her last trip to the lobby. It seemed like weeks ago, but it was only a few hours. She had been full of hope and feeling the rush of forward progress. She was elated to be concluding Operation Fix-It and moving onto her real job of implementing the strategy.

Now all of that was in jeopardy until her new boss was hired. Even then, she would have to start all over. And what if it was Jeff for the long-haul?

Julia barely registered the honking horns and awestruck tourists as she walked through Times Square to her hotel. Even the bright lights, smell of the food carts, and the hordes of people were not enough to pull her out of her funk.

She had worked up to a full steam as she pounded the hotel elevator button for her floor. She stomped down the carpeted hallway to her room.

She was going to quit. There was no way she was going to work for that weak, scheming, sack of shit. "Why do the assholes always win?" she yelled out loud in her hotel room.

She wondered how long it would take Jeff to dismantle the changes she had implemented. A week? A month? He could do a lot of damage before they picked the actual leader, and it could be him. Or it could be an even worse choice if one existed.

Deep breath, Julia, she told herself. Maybe Randall had already done some succession planning, and they had candidates lined up. Maybe it wouldn't be that bad.

But then why had Blane told her to get closer to Jeff?

Of course it would be that bad, or worse. Jeff had the spotlight. All she had was a weak set of junior stakeholders and expanded scope for her role. More work at the same pay.

Back to square one.

No promo.

No Blane.

She remembered Dave's words to her back in December. *As long as Blane is around, you're safe.*

She missed yet another night of sleep tossing and turning as she tried to come up with a new plan.

CHECKING her email in the cab on the way to the airport for her flight back to Seattle in the morning, Julia saw the announcement that Jeff would be the acting lead for the team while they searched for Blane's replacement.

To add insult to injury, he was also being promoted at the same time. She stared at her name on the list of people who would temporarily report to Jeff. *No promotion for her.* The knot in the pit of her stomach grew larger.

They usually didn't assign acting leadership roles to people who weren't in line for the permanent gig and the promotion showed the executive team had confidence in him.

Unfairness swamped her and dragged her down into a funk.

She would have to add "new job" to her mantra.

Was she ever going to be happy? It was like only one part of her life could be on track at any given time. While her job was good, Cliff wouldn't move his shit out of the house. When the sex was good, she was worried she wouldn't be sexy enough to keep Rob interested. When she was happy out on a date with Rob, she felt like she was ignoring her work obligations. When she got expanded scope, it didn't come with more money.

"Stop, just stop," she said out loud as she tried to get a grip.

"Did you need me to stop for something, sweetheart?" the cab driver asked.

"No, sorry – just losing it back here after some bad work news."

"I find that a nice stiff drink helps with that." He turned around and gave her a wink.

She decided to joke back. "It's a bit early for that, but if I add orange juice, it somehow seems more appropriate in the morning."

"Exactly." He refocused on the traffic heading to JFK airport.

▭

SHE AND ROB were supposed to see each other after she landed, but she wanted to beg off. Her head was too full of what she had to do about Jeff to give Rob the time and energy he deserved.

Rob answered on the first ring. "Hey beautiful."

"Hi. I'm just driving home from the airport."

"Good meeting?

"Yes and no."

"How mysterious. Care to elaborate?"

"My part went well, and they expanded my role, but—"

"Wait, can we just stop there for a sec? That's big! I know you were worried, but it sounds like things were good."

"Yeah, they were for about an hour, and then Blane dropped a bomb on me."

"You got your promotion?"

"No."

"You got a huge raise?"

"No, Rob. And could you please just stop? I'm not in a great mood and you're pouring salt into an open wound."

"Sorry. Trying to be supportive. What happened?"

"Blane is leaving the company and Jeff is my new boss."

"Shit. Jeff? Enemy number one? That sucks. But you still got an expanded role. That's like a promotion, right? So that's good news."

"No, Rob. It's actually bad. They expanded my role without an increase in pay or a promotion. They just want more from me without giving me anything in return."

Rob was silent.

Julia started to feel the shame of taking her anger out on Rob. "Sorry. I'm angry. It's not your fault, but you're getting caught in the crossfire."

"Don't apologize," he said. "I didn't get it because it makes no fucking sense."

"I know." The silence held again.

"Want to have dinner?"

"Why would you want to have dinner with me when I'm in this mood?" Julia didn't think she was fit for company and fanaticized about cuddling up with Selah before taking a bath and crawling into bed.

"I want to have dinner with you *because* you're in this mood. I can help distract you."

"You're right. I'll just go home and wallow. Maybe a little distraction is just what I need."

"Be there in about two hours to fulfill my distraction duties."

JULIA CHOSE to stay active instead of giving in to her frustration. She went to her go to mood enhancer, cooking.

She stopped by the grocery store for chicken thighs and mushrooms for coq au vin. She picked up an excited Selah at the kennel and headed home to start dinner. Rob was due in about ninety minutes. She had enough time for a cuddle session with Selah, a shower, and prep time for the meal if she kept clicking at a good pace.

Rob was right. This was much better than sitting on the sofa with a glass of wine and wallowing. She could think through next steps while also being productive.

As she lit the alcohol for the flambé for her coq au vin, she thought of roasting Jeff's balls in the flames. She was on such a high after yesterday morning's meeting and now all hope was lost. She could have just cut her losses a few months before instead of going through all this crap just to have it blow up in her face.

She flushed with anger, using the energy to shake the pan as the alcohol in the cognac burned off in blue flames.

Taking a deep breath, she poured most of the bottle of red wine into the pan and brought the liquid to a boil. The angry bubbles matched her mood.

As she reduced the heat to allow the sauce to simmer, she knew she needed to do the same with her attitude or there would be another incident where Rob would be collateral damage.

Julia strolled to the living room with the end of the bottle of wine in a glass and installed herself on the floor to cuddle with Selah until Rob arrived.

"COME IN!" she yelled at the knock on the door.

"That's right where I like to find you – on the floor, petting Selah with one hand and drinking wine with the other."

Sensing that Julia needed her, Selah thumped her tail

and looked longingly at Rob as he walked over to join them. He crouched down to join the petting festival. Selah rolled over onto her back.

"It smells amazing in here. What're you cooking?"

"You're smelling bacon, onions, and garlic – the way to every man's heart. The coq au vin is ready to go."

"Cocoa what?"

"Chicken with wine."

"Yum! I just feel kind of bad you're cooking when you had such a rotten time in New York."

"Cooking helps recenter me. Selah and I were just talking about it."

"How can I help?"

"You can take over Selah petting duties while I put dinner on the table. See you at the table in five."

"So what happened?" Rob stopped to savor the taste of the chicken. "This is good."

"Thanks. At first, the meeting was amazing, and then it all just fell apart."

"Not all of it – you still have a great job and more responsibility."

"Rob, I know you're Mr. Optimism, but right now, I need you to just listen and say things like 'that sucks' and 'what a jerk.' Then we can move to problem solving."

"Got it. What a jerk! That sucks!" Rob spoke with dramatic emphasis to make Julia laugh.

Chapter 37

"Hey Jeff, what can I do for you?" Julia was wrapping up for the day at work when she saw his name on the caller ID. He never called her. Tempted to ignore it, she had reluctantly put her headset on and answered.

"Hello Julia. Blane scheduled a three-day sales leadership offsite before he announced his departure. We're going ahead with it. The international sales team is coming too, so with your expanded role, I thought it would be good for you to join us."

"Thanks Jeff, that'd be great." He was looking out for her. Was this a new beginning? "When is it?"

"It starts tomorrow out at the Cedar Lake Lodge."

"Tomorrow?" He was giving her less than one day of notice for a three-day offsite? Several hours from Seattle? *What a tool.* For a second, she thought he was extending an olive branch, but instead he was setting her up for failure. Infuriated, she tamped down her anger and kept her tone light. "I'd be delighted to attend."

"Oh." Jeff's tone said *I was hoping you'd decline.* "A bunch of us are grabbing the eight o'clock ferry tomorrow morning if you want to join us. I rented a van so we can carpool from the LampLight office at seven."

"Great. I'll see you there. Bye." Julia wanted to scream. Really scream. Just let it out and keep screaming. Instead, she threw her laptop and notepad into her bag and stomped out of the office.

Fuming on the drive home, Julia tried to talk herself into a better mood by focusing on the positive. It would be a great chance to get to know the international sales team. It would give her a few days in a nice resort.

Who was she kidding? Three days at a resort watching Jeff swing his big dick around and audition for the leadership job was going to take all of Julia's strength to endure.

She compiled a mental checklist of everything she needed to do. Getting Selah situated was at the top of the list. She called the kennel about ten minutes before closing. They were fully booked. Damn it.

As she was thinking through other options, Rob called.

"He just sprang this on me, and I have to leave early in the morning. The kennel is booked, and I need someone to take the See-Dog through Thursday late in the evening. What a pain." Julia mentally started her packing list.

"Would it be too forward of me to offer to stay in your house and watch her? That way she can keep her doggie play date routine. You know I love hanging out with her."

"Wow," Julia was shocked. "Would you really do that? I hate to ask you, especially on such short notice." Julia thought it was an awful lot to ask.

"Let me remind you that you didn't ask, I volunteered. And I live in my mother's basement. Not much of a sacrifice from where I'm standing."

"That'd be great." She felt some of the stress fall off her shoulders. "I have to leave around six fifteen in the morning to catch the carpool to the ferry, and Anna comes to pick Selah up for her play date at eight, so as long as you swing by to feed her dinner, she'll be fine all day."

"I'm actually working from home tomorrow and Wednesday since I don't have any in-person meetings. How about if I come over now, stay overnight, and then work from your house for the next three days. That way, Selah won't be alone at all."

"Are you using my dog to get sex?" Julia asked playfully.

"Yes." Rob answered without hesitation.

"Okay, we can stay in tonight. I'll order Italian and you can pick it up on the way here. You know the place on Front Street?"

"Yep. I'm already out the door."

JULIA HAD JUST FINISHED FEEDING Selah when Rob knocked. She hadn't even had a chance to change out of her work clothes or get plates out. She opened the door and hugged him as he came into the house. They stopped for a brief kiss. The smell of the food made her stomach rumble. She hadn't eaten since breakfast.

"I heard that. Did you skip lunch again?" He ran his hands down her arms. "Let's get you some food."

Julia walked back into the kitchen to set the table. She could feel Rob's eyes on her as she bent over the dishwasher to get clean plates and forks.

Rob came up behind her and pulled her toward him.

"You shouldn't bend over like that while wearing a skirt when I haven't seen you for a few days."

"Like this?" Julia asked, wiggling her butt into him.

"If you keep doing that, dinner will have to wait."

"I can wait for dinner if you can."

He cupped her breasts in his large hands while he

gently laid her down on the counter. He ground against her for a moment before releasing her breasts and pushing her skirt up around her waist. Julia quickly stamped out the negative thoughts about how much cellulite he could see when she turned her head and saw the look on his face.

She felt him reach between her legs and start to stroke her, pushing her panties to the side.

"God that feels great," she said pulsing against him. All thoughts of her upcoming offsite and hunger pangs were pushed aside.

"Tell me if this gets uncomfortable." She heard his zipper go down.

She had never had sex from behind before and she wanted to learn how it felt in this position.

The tip of his shaft brushed against her folds and then he was gliding into her. The high heeled Mary Janes gave her the couple of extra inches she needed to make everything line up. He grabbed her hips and started sliding in and out.

"Are you okay?"

"Yes. Keep going," Julia answered as he started to move. She could feel him go farther in using this position. She liked it.

"You have starred in several fantasies I've had of doing just this. Walking into band practice, seeing you in the kitchen, and just taking you right there." Rob's thrusts grew quicker.

He reached around with his hand and began to play with her clit. *His long arms certainly came in handy*, she thought. She started to move with him. The dual feelings as he filled her more deeply and kept the pressure on her clit had her coming quickly.

"I'm coming." She moved against his hand.

"Right behind you." He cried out as he continued to

pump into her. When he was empty, he lay down on top of her for a backwards hug.

Julia loved it. She'd thought she might feel cheap because when she saw this position in the movies, it seemed controlling and a bit violent. But it wasn't like that at all.

FINISHING THEIR ITALIAN FOOD, Rob and Julia headed to the sofa to cuddle and watch a movie.

"You saved me so much stress today. Instead of obsessing about my job and being worried about the changes for Selah, my evening has been great. Thank you." Julia leaned over and kissed Rob on the nose.

"You're welcome. I just wonder why you didn't ask me to help you."

"I don't want to take advantage of you or assume that you can help out. It's what Cliff did to me, and I hated it."

"We're partners, Julia. I'm here for you, just like you're here for me." He kissed her and gently knocked on her head. "Now please get that through your beautiful thick skull."

"I'll try."

Chapter 38

The next morning, Julia headed downstairs to make coffee before leaving for the offsite. Rob got out of bed with her even though his first meeting wasn't for a few hours.

"I don't want to go," Julia partially whined.

"At least the resort is lovely."

"You always look on the bright side." She gave Selah some vigorous rubs behind the ears before heading out.

Julia tried to be one of the gang on the van. She successfully turned questions about her into requests for stories about the other people. She gleaned a lot of excellent details on the ride to the ferry terminal.

Once on the ferry, she struck up a conversation with Florence who led the sales team in Europe.

Julia admired Florence's style. She was dressed in euro chic with a colorful scarf draped over a funky sweater and tight leather pants. Julia knew the same outfit on her would look entirely different because she just didn't have the flair to pull it off.

Florence was cut from a different cloth than the rest of the sales leaders. She came from a media and publishing background rather than a software background. That was intriguing as well.

Julia thought of a good conversation starter. "We haven't worked together before, although I've heard about how you always hit your numbers, so congratulations."

Florence laughed, a deep, throaty sound. "I'm so glad that a good part of my brand precedes me." She brushed her short, highlighted hair out of her eyes.

Julia didn't ask what other parts of her brand there were and instead waited for Florence to continue. "I'll tell you my little secret." Florence's French accent took Julia down memory lane to her time in Paris. "My targets are set too low." The laugh came again.

"How do you manage that?"

"First, I make lots of noise like ooh la la that's way too high, don't you understand we're all just little countries in Europe. Then, after I lure them into my trap, I close it and land smaller targets. Every year, I succeed, and my team succeeds because the men don't know what hit them." Julia loved the approach as well as the way 'them' sounded like 'zem.'

The announcement that the ferry was landing interrupted their chat. "I hear good things about you, too, Julia. I'm looking forward to getting to know you better over the next few days."

THE MEETING STARTED off with agenda setting. Julia couldn't believe this group of senior leaders had all gotten together without an agenda. Dave was doing the best he could to try to bring order to the chaos now that he was Jeff's Chief of Staff.

"We don't need all this process," Jeff interjected. "Let's

just create an issues list and go through them one by one until we run out of time."

Julia groaned inwardly. That was exactly how to waste time – focus on short-term, top-of-mind issues instead of long-term opportunities.

It was his meeting, and he was the acting lead, so she went along for the ride.

They started to craft the list. Prices are too high. Sellers don't have enough flexibility. The market is soft. Competitors have better tools. On and on it went until Julia couldn't stand it anymore.

"If I may, could I suggest we prioritize the list we have and then work on action plans for the top two or three?"

An awkward moment of silence held before the brainstorming of issues continued like she hadn't said anything. Julia gritted her teeth and fought the annoyance.

About fifteen minutes later, Dave jumped in. "Let's prioritize the top two or three issues and figure out action plans for each one."

"Great idea, Dave." Jeff pointed the dry erase marker at Dave for emphasis.

Dave raised his eyebrows at Julia which she interpreted as acknowledgement that she had said the same thing and had been ignored. Typical Jeff.

Let the games begin, she thought as she opened a new notes file. At least she had all of her action plans and feedback from Operation Fix-It to help guide the conversation with specific examples.

"I STILL DON'T GET it. Why can't our salespeople pitch ad inventory at the same price as customers self-serve on the auction?" Brian from Chicago was on fire. And had been for ten minutes straight.

"You probably understand our OPEX situation." Julia tried to explain without lecturing. "Fourteen out of every one hundred dollars of revenue goes to paying sellers' salaries, benefits, office space, etc." The looks on their faces said they didn't know that. She was glad she had set context.

"Sounds like a bargain to me," Jeff looked around the room for acknowledgement of his funny, funny joke.

Elbows in, Julia reminded herself. She continued her answer. "The prices are lower in the auction because it's fully automated and there's no personalized service or need for a seller. When you allocate the costs to maintain the technology team supporting it, that's about two dollars for every hundred dollars sold."

"Well then selling it in the auction is cheaper. We should all leverage it and give that price to the customers." Brian's tone was on the cusp of condescending.

Julia knew this was a key moment. Rather than rolling her eyes and saying "seriously??" to the group the way she wanted to, she tried again.

"Sellers are expected to negotiate higher prices than the auction because the difference between the auction price and the seller negotiated price is the margin we use to pay our sales team. When sellers sell at the auction price, LampLight doesn't have the money to pay their salaries, bonuses, and benefits."

"Then we're screwed." It was the first time Mario from the Latin American team had spoken.

Finally, an opportunity to turn this around onto positive ground, Julia thought.

"We aren't screwed, Mario. It's the opposite. Our biggest customers want white glove service and their choice of targeted inventory. This is a complex business with multiple audiences, reaches, targets, demographics, click through rates, and effective rates. Our customers need our sellers to guide them so they achieve their desired outcomes. And our sellers need to get paid to do it."

She could see a few lightbulbs of understanding flick on.

"That's why I've been investing in customer service level differentiation." Florence jumped in. "We do more for the clients who buy more and move our most price-sensitive customers to the auction. I don't allow my team to answer questions from accounts who are buying in the auction because they are, how do you say, double dipping."

Julia grabbed the olive branch. "That's a great approach, Florence. Think we could hear more about how you're doing that so we could leverage it other places?"

Julia had the pleasure of hearing Florence lead a great session about how to improve the capabilities of sellers rather than lowering prices. Julia was delighted have a leader on the team who understood the mechanics.

JEFF GRABBED Julia at the break. "I really don't appreciate you butting in on sales processes like that. I let you do your little tour, but you should just stick with pricing."

Julia was taken aback. She searched for how she had overstepped. She was being so damned careful around him. She thought through every word to figure out where she had messed up with him this time.

"I'm sorry, Jeff, I'm not sure what you mean."

"All that crap about how much salespeople cost and how they just need to be better sellers. I invited you to this meeting as a courtesy. Don't keep making me regret it. I'm the acting lead for this team and it won't be long until they give me the permanent gig. You need to get in line with my approach."

"Whoa." Julia put her hands up and took a step back. "I'm not trying to step on any toes. I just want to see our teams succeed together."

"Yeah, well I'll believe it when I see it." Jeff switched to all smiles as Matthew approached them. "Hey buddy, how's it hanging?" He clasped the other man on the shoulder. "Florence. Nice to see you."

Florence smiled at Julia with a look Julia read as sympathy. *Or had she just imagined that?* "I need to talk to Jeff for a moment." Julia took that opportunity to get some air before the meeting resumed.

She wondered if she should try Selah's dog park approach. When another dog didn't get the message that Selah didn't like getting humped, she would pin the other dog down and then roll it over.

Julia could alpha-roll Jeff and bite back.

But that would undo Operation Fix-It. She couldn't have him as an enemy.

Suck it up, Buttercup, she thought as she stood outside looking at the ocean.

Chapter 39

Julia made it to the office just in time for her 6:00 call. Her new global responsibilities expanded her hours to cover Europe and Asia. The early hour was good for her European team and not too bad for the Asia team. It was the most optimal time.

"You did all of that in the seven months you've been on the team? When did you sleep?" Martin's tone didn't sound as congratulatory as his words. He led the Europe, Middle East, and Africa team out of Paris.

"Yeah, but remember, we're still on hold with some of the new policy designs while I build support with Jeff's leadership team." Julia was presenting the policy changes she had created in the US to see if they were applicable to other markets. Local customs and business practices often meant different approaches for different countries.

"Glad the head of sales in Latin America likes me." Enrique laughed. "Mario lets me do what I want."

Julia was momentarily jealous that other managers gave their teams the support they should, but she turned it to the positive. "I walked you through all of that to show you where my head is on what we've had to do in the US to be more competitive. Anything in there particularly interesting to try in your regions, or changes that wouldn't work culturally? Other ideas you have to increase growth and efficiency?"

"Thanks for asking that, Julia." Sunil represented the Asia team. "So many HQ folks just assume every market is the same. We could never implement some of those policies in countries like Japan, but I'd love to brainstorm how we could do something that would get the same result." He started to sketch out an idea on the virtual white board.

THE PLAN for global growth was coming together, and her direct reports had gelled into a team over the past few weeks. Julia had used all her team-building tricks, exercises, and discussion topics to bring people together on common ground.

Problems were dealt with constructively and the siloed thinking that had been so prevalent before she pulled the team together into a cohesive group had stopped. The team was learning to appreciate each other, and even like each other in most cases.

THE GREEN BLOOMS of April appeared outside Julia's office window. She stared at the date in her Outlook calendar. April fifth. Today would have been her fifteenth anniversary if she and Cliff had lasted.

They had always made a point to mark their anniversary. She couldn't believe it had been a year since they'd sat at a Seattle jazz club celebrating with a performance from an amazing guitarist.

That morning, she got a mysterious text from Rob asking her to pack an overnight bag for a night away and to not worry about Selah. She wasn't sure what to make of it but was glad to have a distraction today.

Her bag was waiting for her at home. She was working later on this Friday afternoon than she had planned.

At two in the afternoon, she got another text from Rob.

Why are you still at work?

Good question. Got stuck with one final thing I had to do. ETD in 15 minutes, home in 45.

She raced home, not sure what to expect. Rob met her at the door with her bag and they headed right back out to the car with Selah.

"Where are we going?"

"You'll see. I want to celebrate your first unniversary."

"My what?"

"Didn't you say today is your wedding anniversary?"

"Yes."

"This is your first year not married, so it is your unniversary."

"Ohhh, I get it now." Julia laughed as comprehension bloomed.

They headed south for about a half hour. As he turned down a back road, Julia couldn't stand it anymore.

"I have no idea where we're going. I haven't spent much time in this neck of the woods, but I know the town is that way." She pointed to the right as he turned left.

"We aren't going to town." Rob grinned, and his eyes crinkled at the corners.

Julia was surprised when they pulled into the parking lot of a grungy rundown-looking diner. "We're grabbing an early dinner here? I'm not very hungry yet. Have you been here before?" She didn't like the look of the place and was worried for their health.

"Nope. We're here for what's behind the restaurant. Grab the dog and follow me. I'll get your bag and the other stuff."

Rob walked up the cement path to a small gate in a chain link fence. He tapped in a code and the door buzzed open.

Julia followed him along a path past gas pumps and a little white building. He headed across the asphalt down a narrow row of metal buildings. She saw a small plane pull up to the fuel pump.

"You bought an airplane?"

"Nope."

"You're showing me an airplane?"

"Nope." Rob kept on walking. "I like keeping you in suspense." He stopped in front of one of the buildings and turned a key in the lock. As he opened the door, Julia saw mounds and piles of equipment, toys, furniture, and various household goods. The hangar was absolutely crammed. Everything was stacked up around a tiny plane.

"Is this yours? I didn't know you had a plane."

"Nope. It's Paul's."

"Paul as in Gertie and Paul?"

"Yep. I obviously can't use my own plane, well, I mean, the one that's mine until my divorce is final, since Camille gets it. I don't have the money for another one right now. Bit of a sore subject. Paul lets me use his."

"Paul just lets you borrow his plane?"

"Yep. It's a mutually beneficial arrangement. As you know, engines and other parts go bad from disuse. Paul doesn't fly it as much as he wants to. He lets me take it when I need it, within reason. All I have to do is re-fill the gas tank based on what I use and write the hours in the logbook."

"What a good deal. I hope he doesn't mind dog hair."

"That's what vacuums are for." Rob went into the hangar and emerged with a tool that looked like a big hairpin. He inserted it into the nose gear and began pulling the airplane out of the hangar.

Julia was concerned there would be an avalanche of equipment raining down on them, but as the plane was removed, she saw there was a plane-shaped set of shelves holding everything in place. She pulled the door shut behind Rob and made sure it was locked.

Rob put Selah's bed on the backseat. As Julia stood there wondering how to get Selah into the plane, Rob called the dog from the other side of the plane with kissing noises, and she jumped right in. Rob put a harness on her and clipped her into a ring on the side of the backseat. She could sit up and lie down but would be safe if anything happened.

"Are you sure she'll be okay back there?"

"Oh yeah. I've flown a lot of dog rescue flights over the years. If she's like most dogs, she'll just go to sleep after take-off. We won't fly high enough to hurt her ears."

Dog rescue flights? Julia had to ask him more about that, but he looked like he was concentrating on his inspection, and Julia didn't want to distract him when safety was involved.

Rob finished his walk-around inspection of the plane before getting in. Selah was snuggled down in her bed ready for what came next.

Julia climbed in the right front seat and fastened her rather intricate seat belt.

"Here, put these on." Rob handed her a hefty set of

headphones. "They have noise cancellation, which you'll need when I power up."

Julia donned the headset. She was glad it was in place when Rob started up the very loud engine. He entered the taxiway and headed to an open area near the runway.

"I'm going to do what's called a run-up. It's a test of all the key equipment to make sure it's working before we're in the air."

"Do you have to go through this whole process every time you take off?"

"Yep. Every time, even if I just landed to get some gas. Every procedure has a checklist and always following it helps keep everyone safe."

Julia liked the sound of that. She leaned back in her seat as he tested the propeller, oil pressure, and all kinds of things she didn't understand. She had spent plenty of time working on antique cars with her dad as a child. She was mechanically inclined enough to follow some of it.

Rob made a few calls on the radio, and they were off down the runway. Julia didn't talk during takeoff. She figured it was like talking in someone's backswing in golf. "Engine instruments are all in the green. Let's go flying." The runway fell away as Rob took off to the north and executed a sweeping turn to the south.

"You okay over there?" he asked.

"You're surprising me with an overnight trip in a private plane and you think I have anything to say other than wow?"

"Mission accomplished. Told you she'd be a good flier." Julia looked back at Selah who was calmly looking out the window just like it was a car. Julia watched the trees go by down below. They were cruising along at about a hundred and forty knots according to the dial, and it wasn't too bumpy.

"Where are we going?" she asked.

"You'll see." He held up his index finger indicating she should hold that thought and answered a radio call. "Wilco, ten degrees right, oh three lima."

It sounded like a foreign language.

"Sorry about that. Air traffic control asked me to change headings to avoid another plane, and I was letting them know I'd comply."

"No apology necessary. Please do what you have to do!"

Rob made several more calls to air traffic control. It sounded like he was being handed off by section as they headed south.

She found his radio voice very attractive. It deepened and sounded confident and in control. It got her pretty churned up.

They flew south for about thirty-five minutes when Rob started their descent.

"Portland?"

"Portland. Actually, a little airport outside of Portland."

Julia kept a hand on Selah as they landed. She was a trooper. The three of them hopped out of the plane.

Julia followed him into an office building on the field where they were greeted by an energetic young woman with blue hair.

"I heard you coming in on the radio. Your rental car is all set, and we have your card on file." She handed Rob a set of keys. "What an adorable dog!" she exclaimed reaching over to pet Selah who happily jumped up and placed her front paws on the counter.

"Thank you. Selah, down." Rob gently pulled Selah off the counter and headed outside. Julia appreciated that he had thought of everything as he placed the dog seat cover in the rental car before asking Selah to load up.

"We're heading to the Spotted Owl which is a dog-friendly hotel. After we check in, we'll go down the street to a restaurant that allows dogs on their patio. I figured you'd want to keep Selah with you on such an emotional day."

Julia had forgotten it was her original wedding day as she had been delightfully distracted by the flight and Rob's pilot voice.

ONCE AT THE RESTAURANT, they munched on their salads while Selah enjoyed a dog biscuit they ordered for her from the doggie menu.

"What a great find," Julia said between mouthfuls.

"I was just thinking the same thing about you."

"Smooth, hot shot."

Julia reached for the bill when the server placed it on the table. "My weekend, my treat." Rob snatched it from her grip.

"Rob, you paid for the airplane gas and the rental car. Camille is taking the bulk of your paycheck for a while. Don't you think it's fair for me to pay for dinner and the hotel?"

Rob's face was unreadable. "I can cover this."

"That's great, and I appreciate it, but it's a hardship for you when you're strapped for cash. I'll just get it, and you can spend your money on something for yourself."

"Julia. I said I could get this."

"Don't be like that. You did all the planning for this trip, and we're both enjoying it. No worries."

She signed her name and turned back to gaze at Rob.

His face was steely, and he wouldn't look at her. She wondered what his problem was and decided not to poke.

Maybe it was a pilot thing.

Rob was quiet on the way back to the hotel. They stopped for ice cream on the walk back. "I am reminded of that gelato we had in Seattle. That was a fun night."

"Yeah, it sure was." Rob seemed to have put whatever was bothering him aside and joined in her good mood.

BACK AT THE HOTEL, Selah snuggled into her dog bed. "Want to watch a movie?" Julia asked.

"I would rather watch you."

"Watch me what."

"Enjoy yourself. Come over here." Rob pulled her to him.

Julia floated on the sensations of being loved and being in love. His tender kisses replaced the memories of past anniversaries with new images of happiness, belonging, and feeling desirable.

She sighed as she let her hands roam over Rob's body, encircling him and holding him close.

This was different. Warm instead of hot, loving instead of lustful, connected instead of just a physical act. There was a tenderness here she hadn't felt before with Rob or anyone else.

They moved together, sighing between the sheets as he entered her in one long stroke and held in place. Julia's breath filled her chest as Rob filled her.

She rolled him over so she could set the pace, basking in the power of erasing her past and building a new future. Slowly, she began to move, to take that upward climb to the peak.

She bent down to kiss him as they rode each other. She

stayed right where she was as the waves of pleasure subsided. She could feel the aftershocks of a great orgasm pulse through Rob.

She was safe, like the rest of the world was miles away.

She could get used to this – a world where only she and Rob existed, and their main goal was to love each other and be loved.

Wait a minute, she thought. She was in love, but was he?

She certainly thought so, but her official declaration and more casual statements remained unanswered.

That felt like great sex between two connected people who loved each other, but he hadn't actually said it.

"You okay?" Rob interrupted her thoughts. "You seem to have gone a million miles away."

"Yeah, I was having an annoying line of thought about where we're going instead of basking in what we just did together."

"I thought we were staying in for the rest of the night. Did you want to go back out?"

"No, I mean us. Where this relationship is going."

"Where do you want it to go?"

"I would be fine with it staying right here. Two people having exclusive fun together, enjoying each other's company."

"That's what we have. Why are you deconstructing it?"

Why indeed, Julia thought.

JULIA'S FACE hurt from smiling as they touched down after the short flight back to the airport the next day. They tucked the plane into its tiny spot amidst the clutter and Rob noted his miles in the logbook. "Thanks for the ride." She patted the plane on the nose cone.

"Thank YOU for the ride," Rob said to her with a two-eyed wink.

Julia reveled in her new reality on the drive home. Best unniversary ever.

Chapter 40

Julia added thyme to her lentil soup and replaced the lid. Work stress had driven her back into the kitchen.

Today was a bit sunnier than it had been all week, but the soggy Seattle spring weather put her in the mood for soup. And to see Rob. Whenever they were together, they laughed, they shared, they celebrated.

She fell deeper in love with him with every week that passed.

If he was going to turn into a jerk, she'd know by now.

Julia poured a glass of red wine and joined Selah on the floor for some pets, satisfied her soup was in good shape.

She left the front door unlocked in case Rob stopped by. She hoped he would. He often came over unannounced now and stayed over regularly.

Five minutes of cuddle time later, she heard Rob's car in the driveway.

He walked right into the house and slammed his computer bag onto the floor with a thud. He didn't even stop to greet Selah. Julia turned on a bright smile.

"Hi! Can I get you a drink? Something to eat? Oh, you look tired. Do you want to lie down?"

"I don't want anything," Rob snapped.

Julia didn't know what was wrong, but she backed off and gave him space. "I needed to cook. Soup's ready. Let me know when you want dinner. It's fine to simmer until then." She went back to the stove to give it a stir.

His phone rang before he could answer her. "Hey Calvin, now's not a great time, I only have a couple minutes." He paused to listen. "Didn't you get my voicemail from this morning? I need the ten percent discount we discussed. The bid came through without the discount. If we can't get that settled, I can't get it approved, and you won't get it by the end of the month. I hurried so you could hit your quota, but I'm stuck without that discount."

Julia tried not to eavesdrop, but it was kind of hard when he was yelling into the phone about four feet from her. Funny he was arguing about pricing.

"Everything okay?" she asked when he finished his call.

"No, damn it. I had a bitch of a day. License servers were blowing up, I had three open purchase orders I had to close but couldn't get the funding for them, and this jerk got me into trouble with a stupid comment about the status of a project."

"Why don't you take a couple deep breaths and relax?"

"I don't want to relax! I want the whole fucking world to just leave me alone. I wish I had a place of my own instead of being here or in Leenie's basement. This all just sucks."

Julia understood how he felt. She just wanted to scream about work most days. She channeled her frustration into cooking. She wondered what Rob did with his.

"Want to talk about it?"

"No."

"Is there anything that would make you happier?"

"Yes. A motorcycle. There's a break in the rain that I'd love to take advantage of with a long ride to clear my head."

"We could go get you a bike." Julia wanted to help. She didn't like seeing him unhappy.

"No 'we' can't, Julia." He made air quotes. "Camille is getting almost my entire paycheck. So not only can't I just go buy a motorcycle, I won't be able to buy anything for another ten months! I'll miss the entire summer riding season." He spoke through gritted teeth.

Julia thought there was an easy solution. She had been reviewing her finances that day, and since she had been so frugal since her separation from Cliff, she had a few thousand dollars to spare. She would prefer to save it given what was coming up, but she could use it to make him happy.

"I could spot you the money. And when you're flush again, you could pay me back. How does that sound?"

"Pretty damn awful actually! Why are you always trying to buy me things? You never let me pay for anything. It's Portland all over again!"

"I don't do that!" *Why was he yelling at her when she was trying to help?* Now she knew how he let out his frustration — at her! "You come in here all mopey because you don't have a toy, and I can get it for you. Problem solved, and then you attack me because your job sucks. All jobs suck. What the fuck?"

"Motorcycles are not toys." His voice was dead calm. "And that's not how it works. I'm not going to let you buy things for me. I have to be able to buy them for myself. And I have to deal with it until I can again."

She walked closer to him, her tone conciliatory. "I know, but that's a long way off, and you want a motorcycle now. If you can get along with a low-end one, I can help you."

"I don't want a low-end motorcycle. And I certainly don't want any motorcycle you would buy me."

"What's your problem? I'm trying to help you!"

"Offering to make my problems go away with your money is not helping me. I'm not Cliff!"

His comment hit her like a slap. "I'm very clear about that," Julia shot back. "I'm also very clear I don't need you screaming at me."

"You're right, you don't. I'll just go!" He grabbed his car keys and slammed out of the house.

Julia stood there looking at the door. She heard the sound of Rob pulling out.

She had never seen him like this. Sure, he got mad and frustrated once in a while, but this time he'd had fire burning in his eyes.

She wondered if he was going to come back or if he had left for good.

JULIA SAT on the sofa eating her soup while Selah eyed the bread on the plate next to her. Rob's words echoed in her head. She knew he wasn't Cliff. And she knew he was strapped for cash. Why shouldn't she help him out? He would do it for her if it were the other way around.

This was nothing like the Cliff situation. She liked to share what she had. She liked giving gifts. If she happened to give them to people she was in a relationship with, what was the harm in that?

He's overreacting, she thought as she bit into the bread. *Well, he can overreact all he wants.*

She didn't know where this relationship was going anyway. Yeah, the sex was great, but she could take what she'd learned and use it with someone else. She could increase that miserably low number of sexual partners to more than four.

Done. She didn't care if Rob wanted to look a gift horse in the mouth. She was just being helpful. Screw him.

But even as she thought it, she knew that wasn't how she felt. She loved him and hoped he would come back.

She steeled herself against the possibility it might be over.

He had never said he loved her.

"Thanks for sticking with me, puppy." *Funny, that's the same thing she used to say when she was with Cliff,* she mused.

Chapter 41

A big friendly-looking Newfoundland hound ambled over to say hello at the dog park on Saturday. Julia was pulled out of her thoughts of Rob as she let him sniff her outstretched hand.

"Hello big guy. Aren't you adorable." Julia scratched him behind the ears, and he leaned his huge frame in for more love.

"Sorry, he got away from me. Rufus, you should come when I call you."

Julia looked up from the dog into beautiful brown eyes in a kind face. "No problem. I have a soft spot for newfies."

"How about for their owners?" Julia was taken aback. "Sorry again. I flubbed that. I've seen you here a bunch of times and always wanted to say hello. You just have a great vibe about you and your dog is awesome."

He was flirting with her. Julia was not used to that, even after her experience with Rob, who she hadn't heard from in over a week.

"Thanks, I think. I like newfies because they're big and

fluffy and friendly like Rufus here. Does that describe you, too?"

He laughed. "Not too fluffy, but I can work on that. Maybe not shave for a few days." He stroked his clean-shaven face. "I'm Carlos."

"Julia."

"And who's this?" he asked, squatting down face-to-face with Selah who greeted him with kisses.

"That is my ferocious watch dog, Selah."

"Selah? Like the biblical term for a musical interlude in a psalm?"

"No, but major style points for being able to quote the Harvard Dictionary of Music." Julia's interest in this stranger grew. "Selah like the town near Yakima, Washington where the shelter picked her up."

"Oh, she's a rescue? Well, who saved whom?" Carlos scratched Selah's neck and made googly eyes at the dog. Then, he looked up. "What do you do for fun, Julia, other than come to the dog park twice a week?"

"Are you stalking me?" She laughed. She was still reveling in his use of "whom."

"No, just noticing. And I never see you here with anyone, and now I'm close enough to see you aren't sporting a wedding ring. Want to have coffee?"

If Julia was going to date again, she might as well take a lesson from Rufus and lean in.

"That sounds great, but–"

"Don't say but."

"Okay, *and* I have a get together with some friends this afternoon. Raincheck?"

"Here's my card. Call me if you want. I'd love to get to know you and your dog better."

A guy who looks like that, has a great dog, and knows musicology? Winner.

Rob who?

———

TWO WEEKS HAD PASSED since Rob had stormed out and she hadn't heard from him. She hadn't tried calling him, either. She'd been buried with work and, anyway, she was pretty sure she was the wronged party. All she'd done was try to be nice to him.

Julia looked up at the knock on her office door.

"Hey J-Money. Do you have a minute to talk about this Arc deal?"

"Sure Kate, come on in. I declined the last version of the quote because the pricing was all wrong, and I sent it back to the sales team with my notes. I'm sure they're freaking out, but it's bad business. Don't cave in to the pressure from them."

"About that. It just came through the contracting process as approved. And I doublechecked the prices — they're the lower prices you rejected."

Julia saw red but tried to keep it together and not have a tantrum in front of her team member. "Can I see?"

"Yeah, I'll forward you the email. Apparently, Jeff pushed it through."

"He can't do that!" Her grip on her inner monologue started to weaken. It was okay in front of Kate. "That's a flagrant violation of the policy."

"Is it?" Kate asked. "When he was your peer, yeah, but now he has Blane's authority level, so technically he can overrule you."

"Fuck."

"My sentiments exactly. Now what do we do?"

"As you said, Kate, he can do that. I'll have a chat with him about what happens when he overrules pricing decisions and gives lower prices out. Other agencies will hear about it because they all talk, and if they don't hear about it from each other, the salespeople will tell them."

"It's like a never-ending battle. Is this what it'll be like all the time when Jeff gets the permanent gig?" Kate's comment was accompanied by what Julia read as a look of horror. She tried not to mirror it.

"Not on my watch." Julia spoke with more confidence than she felt. She had to motivate her team, but she knew in her gut this was exactly how it would be when he got the job.

"Any news on that front? I mean, it's been weeks since Blane left and no word. Jeff just keeps acting like he's our real boss."

"No, not yet. I'm sure we'll know when there's an update."

"Rumor is it's him and the announcement is happening next week."

"Rumors can be wrong. Leave this with me, Kate, and thanks for alerting me about it."

She had never hoped more strongly that a rumor wasn't true.

Julia didn't need more drama. Mediation with Cliff was that afternoon. She didn't know how much more she could handle before succumbing to the anger and darkness. She was worried she'd find out.

———

IT WAS a rainy day in Seattle, typical for late April, and the weather matched her mood. It would get sunny in July. When this would all be over.

As she drove to the mediator's office, Julia tried to get some perspective and calm her nerves for what was sure to be a long afternoon.

She crossed the bridge into downtown thinking about the good times she and Cliff had when they first got together. The ski trips to Colorado and Maine, their first house, their first dog…

Then she remembered having to leave her beloved first house because Cliff got a job south of Boston and the commute was killing him, the lay-off, the anger…

But wait, she was supposed to be visualizing the happy times on her way into the meeting. If she showed up at their pre-trial mediation thinking the worst of him, they'd never reach an agreement.

What if it was like the movies, sitting across from each other at a long conference table while their lawyers negoti-ated in angry tones and wastebaskets were hurled at each other? She was concerned she wouldn't be able to behave herself. Her inner monologue was already in tough shape from her work drama.

JULIA STEPPED out of the elevator into the posh and sedate office of the mediator. She was early, not surpris-ingly, since she hated being late for anything. Her lawyer, Marty, joined her right at the stroke of one. But where was Cliff? Neither he nor his lawyer were anywhere to be found.

After hanging up her coat, an assistant led Julia to a conference room. "Cliff will be in a similar room down the hall, and Jerry – he's the mediator – will go back and forth between you. We call that shuttle diplomacy."

"I don't have to see him? Amazing. Thank you." Julia was relieved. Maybe this wouldn't be so bad after all.

Jerry came in as the assistant left. "Hello. I'm Jerry. I'm your mediator today."

Julia shook his hand. "Nice to meet you. Thanks for your time."

Jerry looked to be in his late sixties with a serious demeanor. Julia wasn't going to get any empathy from this guy, but that was okay with her. She just wanted a professional to get her through the process. "No sign of Cliff yet, so I'll start with you. Here are the rules." He relayed them in a no-nonsense tone. "Unless you specifically instruct me otherwise, anything you say to me can be disclosed to Cliff and vice versa."

"Understood." Julia nodded her agreement.

"As you know, this is non-binding and if you don't come to an agreement, you'll go to trial instead. Your trial date is set for August." August sounded like a long way away to Julia. "We can do this like an auction, or we can do it like you're buying a car."

"Let's do the car thing. I like a bottom-line approach." Julia nodded again.

"Good choice. That's my preference, too. What's the highest percentage you'll give him before you walk out?"

Julia knew she had to come up from her forty percent offer. She wanted to get this over with quickly. "As per Marty's guidance, I won't give him more than fifty percent." Marty nodded.

"Well, then, we have a problem here and we might as well just go home now."

Chapter 42

Jerry took off his wire-frame glasses. "The starting point is fifty/fifty. No court is going to let you out for less than fifty percent of everything, and Cliff's opening offer is seventy percent plus thirty thousand dollars in legal fees."

"Why isn't it fifty-fifty?" Julia asked. "I thought the whole system was based on equal division of assets. It's a no-fault divorce state. He hasn't contributed financially in ten years. I made that money."

"The laws were put in place to protect non-working housewives whose husbands were the primary breadwin-ners so they weren't left high and dry after a divorce. It seems outdated now and shouldn't apply to this situation, but it does. Like many things in life, this process isn't designed for fairness. You aren't getting out of here for fifty percent."

Marty made a dismissive sound from next to her.

Julia made the tough call. "I hear you. My offer is fifty."

Jerry left and would be back with the counteroffer, unless by some miracle, Cliff agreed to fifty percent.

"That's not my walk-out number," she said to Marty when they were alone, "but I didn't want Jerry to tell Cliff what it is. It's fifty-five."

"It won't be that much." Marty sounded confident. "Even fifty is generous. You got this."

The minutes ticked by. Fifteen became thirty. Thirty stretched to forty-five.

Julia used the time to do some math. She didn't have enough assets in cash to pay fifty-five percent of the equity in the house. That was over five hundred thousand dollars. She would if she sold it, but housing prices had gone up in Seattle. She wouldn't be able to replace it at a reasonable price. It would be more lucrative in the long run to keep building equity in the house and use other assets to pay him off. She could give him most of their retirement portfolio and only keep a tiny nest egg for herself. She had hoped to keep her 401k, but part of that was in play now, too. At least she would have a place to live.

"What the hell is taking so long?" Marty interrupted her thoughts.

"I have no earthly idea. He's usually pretty good at math."

"Maybe he hasn't shown up yet. I'll go find out."

Marty returned a few minutes later. "He's here. Jerry's assistant says they've been working on their offer this whole time."

Jerry arrived about twenty minutes later. "Sixty-five percent of everything including your next bonus and unvested stock, and he'll reduce the legal fees to ten thousand. He also wants the engagement ring."

Julia was still reeling from the lack of movement on the number when Jerry sat down with a spreadsheet and started filling in numbers that would give Cliff sixty-five percent of their assets.

Julia gasped as she saw him move their entire retirement account into Cliff's column on the spreadsheet.

"I know that's a bit of an irritant," Jerry said when he heard Julia's sharp intake of breath.

An irritant? *An irritant?* she thought. Adding over four hundred thousand dollars to Cliff's column on the asset/debt spreadsheet was more than just an irritant.

She wanted to scream. *It's not like Cliff had some debilitating disease that stripped him of his master's degree and ability to work. He chose to stay home and beat off!*

The angry words formed in her mind, but just in time, her inner monologue kicked in. It was not in her best interest to alienate the mediator. She stayed quiet.

Jerry slowly removed his glasses and looked at her with what she thought was a hint of sympathy even though he was not supposed to take sides. "You've clearly proven that you know how to make lots of money. Cliff has clearly proven that he cannot."

With a deep breath and a long sigh, Julia nodded as the mediator finished entering the amounts into Cliff's column.

Julia's eyes grew wide when she saw him add her upcoming bonus to the column of numbers for Cliff. "Why would he be entitled to my bonus? I don't get it until September which is nine months after our financial separation."

"Because you earned it while you were still in the same household."

"No, I earned *part* of it while we were in the same household. If we have to, we should only count six months not twelve since our date of financial separation was January third. That's only six months of LampLight's fiscal year."

"Great point." It was Marty's turn to jump in. "Come

on, Jerry, you've dealt with this with other LampLight execs before. You know the drill."

Julia's panic showed a bit. "And I might not even get a bonus this year. We won't know until it's awarded. It's not obligatory."

"I hear you." There was Jerry's calm tone again. "But you have six years of history at LampLight, and an increasing bonus each year. Your judge would have no reason to believe that it would be different this year."

She had reason to believe it would be different, but it didn't sound like her argument would be well-received.

"And the same goes for your next stock grant. He would get sixty-five percent of that, too. And that's in addition to sixty-five percent of your vested stock."

"I'm confused again," Julia said. "We have no idea what the future stock price will be. It'll take four years to know that due to the vesting schedule. I will not be financially tied to this man for the next four years."

"Cliff's lawyer has accounted for that and presented this model for calculating the future stock price."

"No," Marty said. "You know that's not how we do it. We take today's stock price and apply it to the future to get the estimated value of the unvested shares. If we agree on that, it doesn't matter if it goes up or down. The calculation is the calculation."

Julia was glad Marty was making his money today.

"Are you following all of this Julia?" The mediator's tone was neutral, but Julia still didn't like the implication that she couldn't do math.

"Yes. I take the risk that the stock will go down and I've overpaid, but I get a definite number today. He risks that the stock goes up but doesn't have to deal with me after today either. Since the stock hasn't moved much in the last six years, I'm willing to risk that."

The three of them did some math and pulled together an offer of fifty-five percent with the current stock price as the calculation point and her 2012 bonus as the baseline.

"It's great to work with decisive people who understand math." Jerry gave her a supportive grin and left the room.

Julia was livid. She tried to keep her cool, but she was angry. *So angry.* She stared past her lawyer as she thought about what was happening.

Julia had worked for the last eighteen years, maximizing her 401K contributions every year, paying extra on her mortgage so she could pay it off early and live better later in life. She skipped the trappings of success like extravagant vacations, fancy clothes, and expensive cars so she could retire early. She shared the money with her family instead of using it for herself. She had been taught that high moral ground was achieved through self denial.

It was all for nothing.

In a single movement of money across a simple spreadsheet, her dream was gone.

She should have just spent it all. That way, he wouldn't have had anything to take.

So much wasted sacrifice.

"WHAT'S TAKING SO LONG?" Marty asked, looking up from the file he was working on for another case. "We pulled that whole offer together in about fifteen minutes. It's already after three." At least Cliff was annoying more than just her, Julia thought.

"No idea. Maybe Jerry is trying to convince him that our offer is the best he'll get?"

She looked out the window at the bustling city. Cities always looked beautiful from thirty stories up, just as her relationship had seemed unblemished before she had examined it.

Another hour ticked by.

"I'm going to see what's taking so long. This is ridiculous. We should've been out of here an hour ago." Marty bustled out of the room.

It was four-forty in the afternoon. She had paid for the mediator until five. Time was ticking away, and she seemed no closer to an agreement. She didn't want to wait until August for resolution.

A few more minutes ticked by.

Jerry finally came back into the room looking frustrated. Marty was with him. "He wants sixty percent of everything plus the engagement ring, but he'll drop the legal fee request. No judge will make you give your engagement ring back. It's the one item that's yours and yours alone because it was a gift."

"I need a second." Julia knew that Cliff knew she hated that ring. But she knew his mother would have a conniption if he didn't get it back. It was her last bargaining chip, and she wanted him to pay for it.

At sixty percent, she was still almost a hundred thousand dollars short. She might be able to swing it at fifty-eight.

She did the math. He would get everything. Their entire retirement portfolio. All of her LampLight 401k. All of her vested LampLight stock. Fifty-eight percent of her future bonus and next stock grant. Even with all that, she would still owe him just under fifty grand. The ring had been appraised for eighteen thousand dollars. Deducting the value of the ring, she would owe him a check for thirty-two thousand dollars in September. Hopefully, she'd be able to pay that with her bonus. If not, she'd have to cash out the remaining forty-two percent of her September stock vest.

Even if she got a new job with a huge signing bonus, they weren't paid upfront. It would be a year before she would see that money. And it wouldn't be possible to save that much from her annual salary in just the few months she had before it was due. She would only get that potential bonus and stock vest if she stayed at LampLight. But she would owe him the money either way.

Every scenario had the same ending. Stuck at Lamp-Light and stuck working for Jeff.

Julia took a deep breath to steady herself. "Okay, Jerry, fifty-eight percent, the ring, and a check in September for thirty-two thousand. No legal fees."

Jerry took the offer back to Cliff at four forty-five.

After paying him off, she'd be house rich, but cash poor. Pretty much broke.

JERRY CAME BACK QUICKLY this time.

He sat down with a heavy sigh. "No deal."

Chapter 43

"He'll take fifty-eight percent plus the ring. And he's added the stipulation that you have to refinance the house to remove his name from the mortgage. If you don't agree, he'll push for alimony rather than a lump sum which could wind up being even more money."

After such a long day, Julia lost her cool. "Now Jerry, I am NOT going to throw away all of this money and then spend another eighty grand to refinance! He has a job now. Why would he get alimony?"

"Let me interrupt your energy on that," Jerry said, maintaining his calm. "He probably won't win the alimony, but why won't you re-finance?"

Julia felt her exterior shell crack even more. "I only have eight years left on my mortgage. No bank will give me an eight-year loan. That means additional interest and payments for me."

"I think he'll walk out if you push him on this." Jerry said.

"He doesn't have to, because I'm leaving." Julia looked at Marty. "Am I being irrational here, or do you agree?"

"You should've walked an hour ago." Marty shook his head with a look of disgust. "I don't think the court will make you give any more than fifty percent. It's worth the risk."

Julia began to gather her things for a quick exit.

Jerry body blocked her. "Please don't go – I'll get Cliff to agree. You want this to be over, right?"

"Yes."

"Keep in mind that if you're the one who walks and then the judge awards him the same deal that we just negotiated, you'll be stuck paying all of his legal fees." Jerry let that sink in. "I know the assigned judge in your case. He doesn't like women who make more money than men. I don't think he'll give you a fair deal."

"This just gets better and better." Sarcasm dripped from Julia's words. She took a deep breath and thought about the price she was willing to pay for getting out of this failed relationship. "Okay – I'll make a good faith effort and call three mortgage companies to see if I can refinance with the same terms. And I'll throw in the ring. If he doesn't agree to that, I walk, and we'll go to court."

Jerry nodded. "I'll emphasize the phrase 'same terms,' which means the same interest rate and period of the loan."

"But I won't be able to get an eight-year mortgage," Julia protested.

"Exactly. But if he signs something that says the 'same terms,' you're off the hook."

Julia smiled. Maybe Jerry wasn't so impartial after all.

JUST BEFORE THE stroke of five, Jerry came back in with the deal. Fifty-eight percent of everything plus the ring and a good faith try at a refinance with the same terms. The final payment of fifty grand could be made in September after her next bonus cleared.

He had called her bluff on the ring. She should keep it just to spite him. But she was a better person than that.

It was time to put up or shut up.

"Don't sign this." Marty was emphatic. "Try your luck in court."

"I want this to be over, Marty. I could wind up paying even more if I wait."

He considered. "I hate to say it because you're getting screwed and it pisses me off, but go ahead."

"I know the feeling." Julia signed her name to the paperwork with a steady hand.

Marty stood up. "You should make a quick exit. Your part is done. I'll block them if they try to leave so you don't have to see them."

"Thanks Marty. I'll be in touch." She headed back out to the elevator.

———

TRAFFIC WAS TERRIBLE.

She wanted to laugh. She wanted to cry. She was relieved. She was scared.

She didn't know how she would pay her bills in her reduced financial position. She was reeling from the bureaucracy she now had to go through.

She was drained, emotionally and economically.

But shining through the clouds was the feeling that she was done.

As she got through the worst of the traffic and was moving at highway speed, she called Lesley. "It's over. And he got most of my money."

"How does he live with himself?" she asked. "Do you need anything?"

"No, I'm fine, but think we could hang out tomorrow night?"

"I'll call the girls and set it up. Meet you at Raymond's at six tomorrow."

She wasn't alone. She had amazing friends. She'd be okay.

JULIA WOKE up the next morning feeling both elated and heartbroken. It was an odd mix that left her confused. She knew she had done the right thing getting Cliff out of her life, but the thought of all of that money slipping away made her physically ill.

She had pledged to love him and be with him forever. And now, they were nothing. Nothing but angry had-been best friends who would never have a regular friendship or anything other than basic human regard for each other, if that. It was surreal.

With a deep sigh, Julia folded back the covers and swung her feet onto the floor. She had to go to work. Yes, just yesterday, she had been steaming mad in a conference room at the mediator's office, but today, she had to go back to work as if nothing had changed.

JULIA MOVED from one meeting to the next all day, kind of on autopilot. One email in particular caused her to stop and take notice. It was from Cliff. She was surprised to see his name appear in her inbox.

The email said how sorry he was and he hoped they could be friends again now that the mediation process was over.

Without hesitation, Julia wrote him a short email that summarized exactly how she felt.

As I warned you when you went down the negative path, I would not have a relationship with you afterwards. So, while I wish you a happy life, it will happen without me in it.

He had continued down his warpath even after she warned him that this would be the outcome. And now he had to live with it. She felt only a small twinge of guilt as she hit send.

And then she went back to work.

AT 5:30, Julia heard a knock on her door and looked up to see Lesley's smiling face, partially blocked by a bottle of champagne and two flutes. "I thought you might need a drink."

Julia laughed out loud, which felt very good, and invited Lesley in. "Quick, close the door and close the blinds – you know LampLight has a no-alcohol-during-working-hours-policy."

"Yeah, well it's five-thirty, and I bet you got here before seven like usual, so you're done for the day."

Julia acknowledged the wisdom of Lesley's comment. "We're meeting in a half hour at the bar. I was just packing up to head over. I don't want to be in my office any longer today."

"Let's head out! I'll bring the champagne to the next steak and bourbon get together instead. See you in ten minutes."

· · ·

"CAN WE SIT IN THE BACK?" Julia asked when they got there. "That'll decrease the risk of seeing a lot of Lamp-Light people here. I'm not in the mood for anyone but my besties right now." Raymond's was close to campus and frequented by LampLight employees. But it was convenient, and drinks were cheap.

"You got it."

They were early, so even though the other ladies weren't there yet, they went ahead and ordered margaritas.

"Talk to me, Goose." Lesley leaned forward. Julia described the mediation process, hitting the high points. "I'm going to cut off his balls."

"You'd have to find them first," Julia joked. They laughed, which was just what Julia needed.

Once the giggles subsided, Lesley reached across the table and took Julia's hand. "Are you okay, really?"

Julia almost broke down – she'd been bottling up her emotions for weeks, but the middle of a busy bar surrounded by LampLight employees was not the place to lose it. Julia pulled it together and answered with honesty.

"I'm mostly okay. I'm happy to be done and have it settled. I can't help but feel bad about the way things ended and that we'll never be friends again. How can I go from 'I love you' to 'never speak to me again' in less than six months? But fuck that guy."

"Yeah. Fuck that guy, Julia. I've known you for five years. In that time, you've never been in love with Cliff. The day you decided it was over in December was not the beginning of the process. It was the end. It was the day you gave yourself permission to break out of the denial and admit to yourself that you didn't love him anymore." She looked at Julia cautiously for a response.

"Hell, Les, you nailed it. That's exactly what happened."

"Case closed." Lesley nodded with finality.

"Yeah. Maybe we can talk about something else now. How's the house renovation going?"

"You'd think that a new kitchen would be pretty straightforward, but man, this is difficult. If some material is not in stock another thing was measured incorrectly." Lesley shared her frustrations at her ongoing house project while Julia provided sympathetic support.

Movement near the table caught Julia's eye. She thought it was one of the girls.

She was wrong.

Chapter 44

"Rob, hey!" Lesley spoke before Julia. "How's it going? I was just heading to the restroom. Jules, you good?"

"Yeah, thanks Les. It's okay." Lesley knew they weren't together anymore, and Julia appreciated that she checked in before leaving her alone with him.

"Hi." Julia looked up at Rob's tall frame and into his beautiful blue eyes.

"Hello there." He looked as uncomfortable as she felt.

"It's nice to see you. It's been a while." She couldn't look away. Her heart pounded. She had given a lot of thought to what she would say if she saw him again, but she was so drained right now she couldn't think of any of it.

"Yeah. Well. Work has been a nightmare. I haven't had time to breathe much at all."

Julia laughed. It was such a thin excuse. Two could play that game. "Yeah, me too. I guess our thing had run its course." She was tired. She had lost her ability to fight for what she wanted. Everything seemed hopeless anyway.

Rob's face flushed. "If that's what you think, I guess." He sat down without being asked.

"Well, don't you think so? I was surprised when I didn't hear from you." Julia cringed when she said that. So much for playing it cool and being the strong executive she knew she was.

"You didn't reach out either."

"Fair point. But if our relationship was delicate enough that one argument could end it, then I guess there wasn't that much there to begin with." Julia fought unwanted tears. She wanted off the emotional rollercoaster.

"It wasn't just an argument," Rob snapped. "It was pretty fundamental to the foundation of our relationship." He leaned closer and lowered his voice. "I don't want a sugar mama."

Julia leaned back, affronted. "I was just offering to help you."

"No, you were offering to *buy* me. I'm not for sale."

Julia flinched. He might as well have stabbed her in the heart. "You know what, Rob? I don't want to have this conversation. Margaret, Melanie, and Gertie will be here any minute to join me and Lesley, and I'm here to have fun."

"Sorry to ruin your good time." His tone was cold.

Julia refused to watch him leave and stared at her margarita glass instead. She took a few deep breaths and remembered the hurt she felt at their argument.

Why did she have to waste so much time with nothing to show for it?

Her marriage ended in anger and divorce after she invested years trying to fix it.

She was broke after years of careful money management.

Her job was in the shitter even after she spent months

trying to fix it. Jeff would be her boss. Another asshole with power over her.

Good thing she hadn't fought to keep Rob. That would have been a disaster, too.

JULIA SAW MARGARET, Gertie, and Melanie come in the door and waved to them. Lesley came back from the bathroom, and they all converged at the booth.

Gertie threw a bag of candy on the table and handed Julia a rubber mallet. "What's this?" Julia picked up the brightly colored bag to inspect. They were little penises.

"My friend brought the candy to a bridal shower. The mallet was my idea. Dump 'em on the table and smash 'em with the hammer. Trust me, it'll help."

"Smash away, Jules!" Lesley opened the bag and dumped the hard candies on the table.

They laughed until they cried.

"Oh my gosh Gertie, that's hilarious!" Margaret heartily approved as she took her turn with the mallet.

"Ladies, Rob was just here." Lesley grabbed the mallet. "I'm not sure whose penis Julia is imagining on the table right now."

"Yeah, what happened with you two?" Margaret asked.

"We had a fight. He left. He never called me again. That was weeks ago."

"Dude, you know the phone works both ways." Gertie sounded just this side of judgy. She was his friend first, after all.

"I know, but I've just had so much to deal with," Julia said. "Work, money, mediation. I haven't really thought about him much." The lie stuck in her throat.

Four pairs of eyes just looked at her. "Okay, okay. I do

think about him. But I think Melanie was right all those months ago. I should've waited. I jumped in too soon and there are plenty of other guys out there. Rob helped me get through a tough spot. I'll get back there once I've paid Cliff off and things are settled at work. I wouldn't be a good partner right now anyway."

"I'll let it slide this time because you had a rough week, Jules, but I'm going to keep pushing." Lesley smashed another candy penis.

Their server approached the table, surveying the crushed candy. "Looks like a good party."

"We better clean this up before we get kicked out," Melanie said with an apologetic look at the server.

"No worries. Who wants another drink?"

They all held up their empty glasses.

Chapter 45

"Revenue is up, but profitability is in the toilet. Randall and the higher-ups are breathing down my neck." Jeff was in rare form during their sales forecast meeting.

The US and Global heads of sales joined via videoconference, but Julia, Stu from Finance, Lola from legal, and Abe from human resources were in the conference room with Jeff. Julia saw everyone back away from their screens even though Jeff couldn't actually hurt them. "What's going on and who's going to fix it?"

Stu spoke up first. "It looks like some mega deals were signed with terms well below our average weighted prices. As those deals are fulfilled, our profit is tanking. Julia, you and your team fell down on the job here."

Julia's heart raced as she felt the spurt of adrenaline from being called out. "Are you referring to the Arc, Sweet, and UHY deals by any chance?" she asked.

"Yep, those appear to be the deals dragging down profitability."

A surge of protective energy coursed through her from

the barb Stu aimed at her team. She remembered her former colleague Scott's advice, again. *If it feels good to say it, you probably shouldn't say it.*

Scott's voice in her head telling her to keep quiet lost as the need to protect her team from attack won.

"Our rejection of those deals was overruled. They went through anyway. My team did nothing wrong." She stared daggers at Jeff, sure she was conveying her anger through her eyes.

It felt good to say that. Even though Scott was right, and it would probably cost her. She didn't care at this point.

The room was silent. Julia wondered if people could hear her heart beating. This was the moment. She didn't break eye contact with Jeff.

"Overruled by whom?" Florence asked.

"Jeff." She still hadn't blinked.

Red blotches appeared on Jeff's cheeks. "Your team wouldn't play ball. I did what had to be done to close the deals. That's within my jurisdiction as the lead for the team." His hand slapped the conference room table to punctuate his point. "Maybe next time you could actually help instead of blocking the deals. You're on probation."

What the hell did he mean by probation, she thought. Julia's cool tone belied the fire she was feeling. "I'm the pricing lead. My team and I gave fair prices that protected margin while granting discounts in line with the customers' volume commitments. I'd be happy to share the recommendations we made with everyone so they can check for themselves and reach their own conclusions about the health of those deals."

"My team, my call. End of story." Jeff stood to make his point.

The staring match continued.

Julia couldn't stop the dismissive shake of her head.

No one came to her defense – they just left her hanging.

"Okay everyone, can we all calm down here?" Dave interjected through the conference room speaker from Los Angeles. "Let's move to next month's forecast."

"Fine." Jeff looked disgusted and took his seat. "But Julia, this isn't over. I want to see you in my office right after this meeting."

THAT WAS IT. Julia finally admitted the light at the end of the tunnel was an oncoming train. Jeff had thrown down the gauntlet by calling it *his* team. No one had disagreed with him.

The team's lawyer and their human resources partner were in the meeting and neither said anything. He wouldn't be this arrogant unless he knew he was definitely getting the job as Blane's successor.

And he had attacked her team. It was one thing to treat her badly, but when he brought the integrity of her team into question, *game over*.

Julia couldn't continue in this job. She had to quit.

She would let her team down, she would let herself down, and she would walk away from a job that could have made a huge and positive impact for the company.

No promo.

No money.

Just failure.

She tried to cool her jets during the rest of the meeting. With the fifty thousand dollars she still owed Cliff hanging over her, she had to keep this job. *Damn*, she wished Scott's advice had kicked in.

When the meeting ended, Julia dutifully followed Jeff to his office even though every fiber in her being urged her to walk out the door instead.

Chapter 46

"What's your problem?" Jeff turned to her, anger evident on his blotchy face. "You can't call out your supervisor in the middle of a meeting like that. I thought things were better now that you went through your 'little process' with my team." Julia was sure the air quotes around *little process* were meant to diminish her and her work.

She dug deep to remain calm. "I'm just trying to help the company get paid for its value proposition."

"You're not a team player. I like team players on my team."

"Team players who cover your ass, you mean?" Sorry again, Scott. Another comment to put in the bucket of things she shouldn't have said but felt so good.

"This team is going to be mine officially as of next week, Julia. And I'll have full authority to do whatever I want with people who don't play ball."

Julia let the silence reign for a few seconds. Then she looked directly at him with a smug smile designed to infuriate. "Anything else, or can I go now?"

It looked like it worked.

"Get out of my office."

———

THE LADIES GATHERED around the taco bar Julia had created in her living room. It was steak and bourbon night. "We aren't going to have steak and bourbon every time?" Gertie asked with a fake pout.

"I'll put it back into the rotation."

"Oooh, I met the perfect guy for you, Jules. I didn't want to mention him while you were seeing Rob." Margaret sounded excited.

Julia shuddered at the mention of Rob's name. "I don't think I'm in the right head space for that right now at all." In fact, she still had Carlos' card sitting on her jewelry box waiting for her to take action. She hadn't because she hadn't been in a good mindset to start something new. She still thought about Rob too much to make room for someone else.

Melanie leaned in. "Oh, come on, it would be fun."

"It's just not the right time for me."

"Because of Rob?" Melanie's question hit home.

"I've been so busy at work."

"You can't bullshit us, Jules. What gives?"

Julia looked at her dear friends. If she couldn't share with her besties, who could she share with?

"There's part of the story I didn't share, I guess because it makes me feel bad." Her friends leaned in. Julia took a deep breath and continued. "I started to repeat the Cliff pattern. I apparently don't know how to nurture without making it about money."

"Whoa. That's not true. You're a loving and caring friend. You provide amazing emotional support for everyone around you. What're you talking about?" Julia basked in Melanie's support.

"I've been too embarrassed to tell you this, but here goes. The night of our fight, Rob came over enraged about a bad day at work. He said he wanted to go on a motorcycle ride but he didn't have a motorcycle."

"I remember that part," Lesley said. "Then you had a fight because he was in a bad mood and he left."

"Not exactly. The part I left out of the story was that I offered to buy him one."

"You didn't." Lesley fell back against her chair.

"Oh Jules," Melanie added.

"And I said it multiple times, like 'what's the big deal, I'll just buy you one.' Talk about repeating the mistakes of the past."

Lesley sighed, long and hard. "Julia. I love you and I mean this in the nicest possible way. You have to find other ways to show your love to your partners."

"Or you could forget that guy and adopt me." Gertie did an effective job of sounding serious.

After laughing at Gertie's joke, Julia continued. "Yeah, I know, but it's like my job. If I had bailed on my job when things first went badly with Jeff, I could have saved a lot of drama. If I start something new with someone who doesn't have the Cliff history, I could be someone else. Start fresh. I met a guy at the dog park who seems interesting."

Even as she said it, the words sounded hollow.

"Do you have a picture?" Gertie asked.

Lesley laughed and then turned back to Julia. "What you had with Rob was good. Give him a call. You bruised his delicate male ego. I saw him at that bar. He's heartbroken. He's not going to call you first."

"I'll think about it. It's all so hard. He might not want to get back together anyway."

"The divorce is behind you." Gertie slapped the table. "Work always sucks. That's not new. Stop hiding and start living."

"Yeah Jules, your birthday's coming up." Lesley's tone sounded supportive and like a lecture at the same time. "Make forty the best year of your life and the beginning of a new path. New year, new life, great sex. Remember?"

JULIA PONDERED Gertie's statement as the conversation moved on from Julia to topics she preferred. *Stop hiding and start living.* She'd had a taste of that while she and Rob were dating. That did feel like life. Fresh and invigorating as she'd discovered her inner sex goddess and explored new parts of herself.

She couldn't use her divorce as an excuse for not fully embracing life. She would go forward without looking back. This is what forty would look like!

If Rob didn't want to be with her, she would find someone else. She didn't need him to be whole.

She realized now that while she thought she wanted sex, what she wanted was an equal partner.

She would get to the bottom of how Rob felt about her. The ball was in her court after their altercation at the bar. And if he didn't love her, she still hadn't called the yummy Carlos for that coffee. There were more guys like Rob out there, she just needed to look more closely.

She created a good life for herself and would get through her work drama with the same energy and attitude as her divorce. She would get a new job. She would pay Cliff off and make more money.

Yes, she was J-Money, but her recent treatment by the leadership team and Jeff taught her that she didn't just want the money.

She wanted respect. She wanted to be valued.

She settled for the money because she wasn't getting credit in other ways. Money was just a placebo, masking her true desire for impact and respect.

She understood that now.

One thing she knew deep in her heart - she wouldn't settle, wouldn't compromise again.

She would keep fighting until she had everything she wanted.

Chapter 47

She called Rob after work the next day. She hadn't had much time to think about the actual words she would use, but she decided to turn over a new leaf and just go with the flow.

He answered on the second ring. "Hi." He sounded tentative. "I'm glad you called."

Good start. Julia's heartbeat quickened. "Can we talk?"

"We are talking," he said sounding more like himself.

"I mean in person."

"That'd be nice."

"Meet me at the Cantina?"

"How about somewhere quieter? I'd love to see Selah, too. Can I come over?"

"Sure. When is good for you?"

"Now? Is now good? I really miss her."

Julia was happy to let Rob pretend it was about Selah. "Sure, now would be great. She'll be delighted to see you."

. . .

SELAH WENT crazy when she heard Rob's long hellooooo on the other side of the door. He didn't just walk in this time. Julia noted the symbolism.

Letting Rob and Selah play and cuddle gave Julia a chance to collect her thoughts. He looked amazing and his cologne shot right through her, just as it had before. Funny how his cologne was enticing while cologne on salespeople made her gag.

"Thanks for calling." He looked up at her from his position petting Selah. "I wasn't sure you ever would."

"I bet. Thanks for coming over. We have to talk."

"Do we have to?" Rob asked faking a sheepish tone.

"Yes, I'm afraid we do. I have some apologizing to do."

"You?"

"Yes, me," Julia admitted. "You're right. I try to fix things with money. It's a well-engrained habit, one I want to break. I don't want to repeat my enablement and gift-giving pattern with Cliff. I do want to make you, I mean, people I care about, feel loved and appreciated. I just have to learn to do it with words, attention, and affection rather than money."

"Why did you amend that statement? Aren't I one of the people you care about?"

Julia chose honesty over denial. "I don't just care about you, Rob. I love you."

Rob shrugged his shoulders and held up his hands. "I'm out of my depth here. I was prepared with a whole speech about how I messed up and how you were just trying to help, and I lost my shit because I'm broke right now."

"Join the club. Sounds like we're both sorry. I want to do more than just be sorry. I want to work on this. I thought about starting fresh with someone new and telling myself you were just a rebound, but that's not how I feel. I want to try again with you."

Rob's blue eyes glistened with unshed tears. "I'm so glad to hear you say that. I've been a mess." Julia saw him take a deep breath. "I wanted to call every day but also wanted to respect your space. And I was angry. When I saw you at Raymond's Bar laughing and talking with Lesley, and then the rest of your girls, you looked happy. It was great to see you happy. I also saw you don't need me to be happy. It hurt to know you had moved on so easily."

She flashed back to crushing candy penises on the table at Raymond's. "It's easy to be happy when I'm surrounded by people I love. I'd like to see how much happier I could be with you in my life every day. As my equal partner."

"Now I'm the happy one." Rob's face filled with joy, his eyes crinkling at the corners from his smile.

It felt good to say it out loud. She wanted an equal partner. A smart, capable man who could keep up with her mentally and physically. She thought it was too much to ask for, but here he was. She didn't have to settle for less. This was what forty would look like.

On cue, Julia's stomach grumbled.

"Did you skip lunch again?"

"Yeah. Mind if we head to the Cantina now?"

"That'd be great, but there's something I have to say first." He reached for her hand. "I love you. I love you so much." He looked into her eyes with intensity, telepathing his love. She had waited so long to hear that.

"Looks like I'll get what I want for my fortieth birthday after all."

"Not the response I was expecting," he laughed.

"Try it again, then."

He took her other hand, too. "I love you. I have for a long time."

"And I love you, Rob. I have some work to do to break out of bad habits. Will you be part of that?"

"Yes. As long as I pay my own way." He drew her into a tight hug.

Rob gently pulled away and looked into her eyes. "That probably won't be our last fight about money, but I hope they all end with us hugging and being in love."

As equals, Julia added silently.

MAKE-UP SEX. Another new experience for Julia. She had heard about how great it could be to come together after a fight. The luxurious, slumberous, gooey feeling of snuggling in bed with Rob after a magical night almost made the fight and weeks apart worth it. Almost.

Rob had taken his time to reacquaint himself with all parts of Julia's anatomy after dinner, reminding her how much she had learned in the bedroom. The great sex part of her mantra was reactivated, and she was going to keep it that way.

He had stayed over since today was her fortieth birthday. They were going out to dinner that night and neither of them wanted the evening to end.

Chapter 48

At work on her birthday, Julia sat at her computer staring at the spreadsheet that controlled her life. It was a bit dramatic for her to think of this spreadsheet that way, but it held the formulas, assumptions, and calculations that measured the months until she was done paying Cliff.

She would've thought over four hundred thousand dollars a year would go a little farther, but paying Cliff had wiped out her cushion. Planning for daily expenditures was not something Julia had experienced for the last ten years.

She didn't like it.

The whole spreadsheet counted down to September fifteenth which was the day bonuses were paid. She also thought of it as Pay-Off Cliff Day, or POC Day. She had to endure the pressure for four more months. Then, if she got the bonus she and her lawyer had projected, she could afford the final payment and be free. Done with him emotionally and finally, financially.

But if Jeff screwed her, which she thought was very likely at this point, she would have to renegotiate with Cliff.

Either way, she could also walk out of LampLight once and for all.

She'd been thinking deep thoughts about what she could do instead. She loved building teams and mentoring people. She had looked into becoming an executive coach and had a stack of information about the various certification programs. She just needed the money to take them. She hoped her bonus would be enough.

JEFF STORMED into Julia's office, pulling her attention from the spreadsheet. "I can't believe you're doing it again, even after our talk."

"Doing what, exactly?" Julia tried to keep the daggers out of her voice. She was already in a pretty bad mood from her monetary situation.

"Messing with my deals. What's your problem? Do you like stealing money from my seller's pockets? Do you enjoy stopping them from making a living wage?"

Again with this shit, she thought. The fantasies of telling him to shove it started swirling in Julia's head.

It was go time. She was done.

She would find another way to get that last fifty thousand dollars.

All the work she'd done on Operation Fix-It, only to get no credit.

The global team she'd taken on for no extra money.

And then to have to deal with the fact that the incompetent Jeff was about to be named as Blane's successor. She didn't have to stick around and deal with petulant children masquerading as executives.

It might cost her that bonus she needed or even her job, but she couldn't take it anymore.

She *wouldn't* take it anymore.

"You know Jeff, this routine is getting a little old. I refuse to be intimidated by your bullying." Julia stood up from her desk to look him in the eye. "My job is to make sound business decisions in line with corporate strategy." She pointed her finger at him and felt the delight of righteous indignation fuel her. "That strategy is set above you." Condescension dripped from her words. "Take it up with the big boss if you have a problem with that." She looked at him with defiance, daring him to come at her again.

"Don't worry, sweetheart, I will." He stomped out of her office with even more anger than when he'd entered.

Julia couldn't sit. She paced her office letting some of the energy out.

Man, that felt good.

That lasted about ten seconds before her cooler mind started talking.

Fuck, she thought. She had just sealed her fate. The minute Jeff got the big job, she'd get fired. Even a pay raise on a new job wouldn't get her the fifty thousand she needed to pay Cliff off on time.

She would have to go back and ask for an extension for the final payment. *Deep breath*, she thought. *It'll be okay. Channel your inner Rob.*

She had to get out of there.

She walked over to her computer to check her calendar for her next appointment to see if she could cancel it.

A new meeting had just been scheduled titled "Organizational Update" from Randall, Jeff's boss. It had the ominous phrase "please prioritize" in the meeting invitation. All of Blane's former direct reports were on the invitation.

This was it. The big reveal. *Jeff certainly works fast*, she thought. She pictured him storming out of her office and directly into Randall's telling him how awful she was. And she hadn't even been there to defend herself.

She had fifteen minutes to get her shit together. Her brain was in high gear, envisioning scenarios of throwing her own tantrum in the meeting.

She could say, "I won't work for that asshole. I quit!" and storm out. That would be fun.

She could bring a list of his semi-illegal, non-compliant actions and toss the stack of paperwork onto the conference room table with a flourish before announcing she was lodging a formal legal complaint.

She could just resign, yell "good luck bitches" and slam the door behind her.

No, she wouldn't do any of that.

The heavy feeling of dread filled Julia as she dragged herself to the conference room. The high from her confrontation was over, the wind knocked out of her sails by the realization she had to suck it up and keep her head down until she could get another job.

If you didn't have to work for it, it wasn't worth having.

She paused with her hand on the conference room door handle. *Elbows in,* she thought and put on a happy face.

MOST OF THE leadership team was already there or on the video call. Jeff looked up from his conversation with Dave and smirked at Julia.

She gave him her biggest smile before sitting down, like he hadn't just screamed at her. She took a seat next to Florence from Europe.

"Hey, Florence! So good to see you. I didn't know you were in town."

"Oui! I am here, learning that the famous constant

spring rain of Seattle is no joke." She laughed her throaty laugh. "I would love to talk to you right after this meeting if you have time."

"I would love that." *If I'm still employed,* Julia thought.

Randall entered the room. A hush fell over the crowd.

"Thanks for joining on such short notice." He smiled at everyone. "I'm delighted to share that we've made our decision on the new leader for the team. Jeff, thank you for leading the team for the last few months while we conducted our search." Randall led a round of applause. Julia joined in half-heartedly. Jeff beamed at the group.

Randall continued. "I'm also happy to share that even after an extended external search, we've decided to appoint one of our very own internal leaders to this senior role."

Internal hire, here it comes, Julia thought. Her nightmare scenario was coming true.

"This person embodies seasoned sales leadership and business acumen, and has grown our business steadily over time, bringing a fierce competitive angle to every deal."

The fact Randall viewed Jeff as a strategic leader made Julia physically sick. She felt the roil of stomach acid deep in her core. She looked at the table.

Randall kept going. "Please join me in congratulating Florence Paillard as our new Senior Vice President of Global Sales, Marketing, and Operations for the advertising division."

Julia's mouth dropped open as her head snapped up. Relief washed through her, and she enthusiastically joined in the applause and calls of congratulations.

Don't gloat. Don't gloat. Don't gloat, Julia repeated to herself as she caught Jeff's eye. He looked stunned. She almost felt bad for him. *Almost.*

Florence stood up to address the team. "Thank you all. I'm honored and humbled to lead this great team and will be scheduling one on ones with each of you to get to know you better and dive right in."

Julia was elated. A strong female manager. Someone who got the business. A real leader.

Her new boss continued her comments. "There's lots to do to close this quarter strong. Let's get to it." The meeting broke up and people headed back to their offices to process the news.

"Felicitations, Florence." Julia congratulated Florence in her best French accent. "I'm thrilled for you, and for us!"

"Merci, Julia. Follow me to my new office, please."

JULIA FELT the snap of nerves. What had Jeff told Florence about her? Did Florence know Julia's head was on the chopping block?

Only one way to find out. Julia steeled herself as she followed Florence down the hall to Blane's old office.

Julia was shocked at what she saw. The drab furniture was gone, replaced with a flowered sofa and bright pillows. Live plants graced the corners, and the big corporate desk had been replaced with a modern glass-topped conference room table. The look said class and style in a feminine, powerful way.

"Julia, please take a seat. I have a lot to say to you."

Julia sat and conservatively crossed her hands on the table in front of her. She looked directly at Florence, waiting for her to start.

"First, I want to commend you on your leadership of the team. From our first meeting together, I was impressed with how you managed the, how do you say, 'male energy' of the sales team." Florence made air quotes.

"Thank you, Florence."

"I also want you to know Randall and I have seen how Jeff treats you, and it's not okay. He's unprofessional, sexist, and a poor leader."

Florence saw the truth.

Julia didn't know where this was going, but she started to feel hope she wasn't about to be fired.

"I'm telling you this because I trust you'll keep it to yourself. Jeff is in Randall's office right now being let go. Of course, we'll say something like 'he is focusing on family' or some crap like that, but I wanted you to know the truth."

"My lips are sealed. Thank you for telling me. It's been a tough few months." Julia was embarrassed that emotion welled up in her eyes.

"Yes, I know. You handled it brilliantly. I wanted to leap to your defense so many times, but I had to work the politics. I couldn't be viewed as playing favorites during the interview process."

"Thank you. I get it." Julia wished she didn't understand, but she knew first-hand how tricky office politics were, requiring careful calculation and strategy.

"But now I can share the plan Randall and I have set out for you."

Julia took a deep breath, letting Florence's words sink in. Her advocacy felt like oxygen in her veins. "Sounds good."

"You've already made such an impact in your short time as the global monetization lead, and I saw you took that on with no complaints even though you got neither money nor a promotion."

"I was happy to have the opportunity to have bigger impact." Julia smiled as she wondered what was coming next. This was certainly not the direction she'd expected this meeting to go. She felt energized and seen.

"We'd like to give you that well-deserved promotion, and a cash bonus for what I will call your can-do attitude in the face of adversity."

Julia was floored. She waited for the catch. "When will that be?"

"Oh, I do like you so much. Way to advocate for yourself by asking that question. Both are effective immediately."

Florence handed Julia a piece of paper. She read it to herself.

Due to the highly positive impact you have made on the business and the increase in morale of your team, you will receive:
- Promotion to Vice President
- 10% salary increase
- $200,000 special stock award
- $100,000 cash bonus

Julia's mouth dropped open. "You're kidding me."

"I never kid about money," Florence said and winked at Julia.

Somehow, it was okay when Florence did the winking.

—————————————

Chapter 49

—————————————

Julia was nearly bursting with excitement as she drove home through the dark and rain. Respect and rewards for her positive impact. "Rob, you won't believe it." She yelled into the phone.

"I believe a lot of crazy things." His tone was jokey, as usual.

"Ha ha, I know." She appreciated his light-hearted humor. "Get this. Jeff didn't get the job."

"Wait, what? But he acted like it was already his."

"I know, but they fired him today." New joy filled her at the outcome and saying it out loud.

"Did he screw an employee or something?"

"Maybe that too, but they saw the way he treated me and lots of others, and they bounced him. And there's more good news. Florence landed the exec role instead of Jeff." She loved saying that out loud, too.

"Florence? From Europe? You like her. That's good, right?"

"Yes, it's amazing. But it gets better." Julia enjoyed

stringing this story out instead of jumping to the bottom line like she usually did. "They promoted me."

"Finally! That's great sweetie! Good thing we're already planning to celebrate your birthday tonight!"

"We'll celebrate in style because the promotion came with a big raise, some stock, and a bonus that was awarded on the spot." Not wanting to flaunt her money based on their fight and resulting agreement, Julia did not share the amount. She was learning. "The bonus is enough for me to pay off Cliff. POC Day can be today! No more stress about making sure my bonus is big enough to cover my last payment to him. And I'll start rebuilding my assets."

"That's amazing! I'm so happy for you. It's all over then. No more Jeff, no more Cliff, just a promotion in a role you love and the money you deserve with a boss who sees your impact and values you."

"That's a great summary," she said beaming.

"It's going to be a wonderful evening celebrating you."

<hr>

"TO THE NEW Vice President of Advertising Monetization."

Julia clinked her glass of champagne to Rob's Lemon Drop Martini. "It feels good."

"I bet. All your hard work. And then the justice in the end, knowing your positive impact was known."

"I can't wait to tell the team. This is their success, too."

"But mostly yours, Jules," he said. "Can you just take a moment, please, and reflect on your accomplishments?"

Julia sat back on her bar stool. She looked out the window of the French restaurant at the Olympic Mountains and Puget Sound. A ferry chugged out of the terminal on its way to one of the islands. Tears stung her eyes as she felt her burdens fall away.

No more Cliff.

No more Jeff.

No more money worries.

No more wondering what she was doing and whether she was on the right track.

A rewarding, high impact job.

A man she loved who loved her back.

Amazing friends.

"Okay, I've basked in my own greatness. What's next?"

Rob laughed. "Not quite sure that was long enough to truly celebrate it."

"It was. You know I'm quick. I'm ready for what's next."

"Like what?" Rob put his elbows on the bar and propped his head on his hands to give her his full attention.

"I'm looking forward to living without all of the negativity I've been carrying around with me. I've let it hold me down. No more. Florence has my back at work which will help me succeed."

Rob nodded. "Finally. Any more thoughts about the coaching thing? I know you'd be great at that. You could be your own boss and never have to deal with this crap again."

"I do love that idea." Plans started swirling in Julia's ever-busy brain. "And I love being all in with you. That means blazing new trails of partnership as equals."

"Let's test that." Rob's eyes turned mischievous. "I'd like to buy dinner."

"But I just got…" Julia stopped herself. "Yes, Rob, that would be lovely." She couldn't keep her mouth from forming a thin line as she held the next comment in.

"Was that so hard?" he asked.

"Actually, yes. And I already feel bad about having a second glass of expensive champagne. But I did it. And I'll keep doing it."

"Progress!" Rob raised his glass again for Julia to clink. "You said you're ready for what's next." Rob wink-blinked at her. "Look behind you."

Julia spun around and saw Lesley, Melanie, Margaret, and Gertie walking toward her. She couldn't contain her squeal of happiness. "Happy birthday!" they yelled, drawing the attention of the entire restaurant.

She hugged each of them in turn as Rob poured champagne. Julia loved them all so much. Her support system. Her board of directors. "Thanks for coming ladies. I couldn't have gotten through this without you." She included Rob in her circle.

He lifted his glass. "To my talented, brilliant, and powerful partner. I love you."

Melanie jumped in. "To having a boss who values you."

Margaret picked up the theme. "And who rewards your high impact."

"To getting boned!" Gertie yelled. "I mean…to love!" They all laughed.

Lesley looked Julia right in the eye. "To Julia. New year, new life, great sex."

They cheered as glasses clinked. Julia soaked it all in.

She had done it. Julia was unleashed.

- The End -

About the Author

Laura Preslan worked in the technology industry for thirty years leading teams, delivering successful projects, and coaching colleagues through tough situations.

She found many of the same political and people-based issues at every company she worked at as a consultant, advisor, or employee from start-ups to Fortune 100 companies.

This experience influenced her goal to create a new genre of women's fiction written by and about powerful female executives and the unique challenges women overcome at work and at home.

When asked why this vision is important to her, Laura said, "So many of us have compelling stories to tell about terrible toxicity we have conquered at work and how we found balance at home. None of us are going through this alone. With courage, creativity, and self-awareness, we will succeed in work, life, and love. I encourage all of us to write our stories (fictionalized, of course). The more we talk about it, the better things will be for those who come after us."

Find out more about Laura at www.laurapreslan.com.